I0710645

THE FATHER
OF HIS PEOPLE

NICHOLAS SNOW

Translated by Vicky Politis
Cover design by George Christakos

Copyright © 2024 by Nicholas Snow

Paperback: 978-1-963883-91-6
eBook: 978-1-963883-92-3
Library of Congress Control Number: 2024911059

All rights reserved. No part of this publication may be reproduced, distributed, or transmitted in any form or by any electronic or mechanical means, without the prior written permission of the publisher, except in the case of brief quotations embodied in critical reviews and certain other noncommercial uses permitted by copyright law.

This Book is a work of fiction. Names, characters, places, and incidents either are the product of the author's imagination or are used fictitiously. Any resemblance to actual persons, living or dead, events, or locales is entirely coincidental.

Ordering Information:

Prime Seven Media
518 Landmann St.
Tomah City, WI 54660

Printed in the United States of America

BY THE SAME AUTHOR

The Andrew Bond World War II spy stories:

"H2S Home Sweet Home" P7M, 2023 (Bombing campaign against Germany and electronic warfare, December 1943-March 1944)

"Malayan Enigma" AuthorHouse 2016 (Japanese invasion of Malaya and Singapore, December 1941-February 1942)

Also,

"Assassins" AuthorHouse 2007 with Guy Feaux de la Croix

"Last love" AuthorHouse 2014

"The Shield" AuthorHouse 2005

*In memory of my mother who
taught me to fight the good fight*

TABLE OF CONTENTS

PROLOGUE

The importance that Churchill gave to Greek affairs is apparent by the fact that he came to Athens on Christmas Eve, 24 December 1944, at a time when the German offensive in the Ardennes was at its peak.

He met with Archbishop Damaskinos (a former wrestler!) who he had not at first trusted, considering him to be pro-communist and a presumptive dictator. But after their meeting, Damaskinos earned his trust. Churchill pressed the Greek parties to accept him as their regent.

The Good Father recounts recent Greek history in terms of the idea that Churchill knew about Stalin's past as an informer and agent of OKHRANA and blackmailed him regarding Greece. It records a historical event and interweaves it with a fictional narrative which is set against an actual political environment.

"Instigator" of this book is my old friend, ambassador Dr Agis Christopoulos who knew the story of my uncle, Dimitris Nikolopoulos. He suggested that I carry out research at the archives of the Ministry of Foreign Affairs and write his story. When an article was first published in the Greek newspaper, *To Vima*, it created quite a stir, and was followed by dozens of phone calls, emails, comments. It was re-published on blogs and sites by friends, acquaintances and many anonymous people in Greece and abroad.

This was followed by Mr Dionysus Mousmoutis asking me to write a more detailed account, which appeared in the Greek magazine *Istoria* in April 2018.

However, many authors and friends such as Ms Eleni Kekropoulou and Mr Phaidon Tamvakakis, insisted that, on its own, the story provided material for a novel. So, I accepted the challenge and wrote *The Good Father*.

Wolf, the dog in the book, is based on my own dog and faithful friend with the same name.

PART I

Prelude to Death

CHAPTER 1

Soviet Union, January 1938

Tbilisi, January 1938

Valentin Sergeyevich Slusar brought his gloved hands to his mouth and blew in a vain attempt to warm them. His warm breath created a small cloud in the frigid air.

It was diabolically cold and his fingers, despite the gloves, were frozen, making it difficult to turn the scattered pages of the voluminous files of OKHRANA, the Secret Service of tsarist Russia. Pages, some half chewed by mice and insects, some yellowed, some half torn, some typed, others handwritten, and some so poorly written, he could barely make out the words. There were also photographs, some well preserved, others as faded as the faces depicted on them, faces that seemed to be trying to escape from the paper, to disappear in anonymity.

The brazier that burned in a corner of the small office was not enough to heat the room. But they had to economise on the use of wood. The state services and even the GPU[1] had to limit heating according to the requirements and provisions of the five-year plan. Limitations on consumption. Notices everywhere. An emphasis on heavy industry and the armed forces. The Soviet Union was alone, or nearly alone, against a hostile capitalist world. The country had to be strong, very strong, to avert any attack against it or, if attacked, to fight back and emerge victorious.

Of course, as an agent in Tbilisi, not far from the Soviet dictatorship of Azerbaijan, he knew that the Soviet Union was not entirely isolated. It exported foodstuffs, wheat, butter, eggs, raw material and oil to the west, in order to have foreign exchange to import whatever it lacked, such as machinery and advanced technology. A large part of its oil production from Maykop and Baku was destined for Germany …

But these were matters of high politics and it was better not to know about them and if you did, to pretend that you did not know and above all, for your own safety, not to discuss them.

His job was different and it was important.

The five-year plans were not going well and had fallen behind the objectives, in terms of numbers as well as quality.

However, Comrade General Secretary Stalin and the executive office of the party had discovered the reasons. There were reactionary elements, enemies of the people, saboteurs everywhere. Using thousands of cunning ways, they prevented the realisation of the plans. However, the most treacherous aspect was that these elements could be found within the ranks of the party itself, the state machinery, the armed forces. The directive that Lavrentiy Beria, head of the GPU, had received was precise. Find them! Arrest them! Send them to court! They will be executed! Only in this way can the Soviet Union progress, and its historic objectives be

---

[1]   The secret service of the Soviet Union, later known as the NKVD.

realised. Only in this way can the real, historic nature of socialism and then communism be established.

Slusar's assignment and that of hundreds of others in the GPU, was to uncover those enemies, those miasmas and saboteurs. One way was to search the archives of OKHRANA. Here they would find useful evidence regarding the agents of the tsar, those that had betrayed him and among whom some had penetrated the party, the army, the state services.

Slusar placed the files of suspects into a separate stack, which he would study meticulously later, comparing them with the names of state officers in the region and officers from Georgia.

He removed his glasses and cleaned the clouded lenses. He put them back on. He glanced out the window which had fogged up from the difference in temperature.

There was snow everywhere, on the roofs, the windows. The roads and sidewalks had vanished under a white blanket. Icicles hung from the eaves of the roofs. Drops fell slowly wherever the air was warmer, melting and falling from windows or chimneys.

Slusar turned to his files. Taking the next one, he opened it.

At first, he didn't understand.

He looked more carefully.

He confirmed what he had seen.

His lips began to tremble.

Was it possible?

Were his eyes deceiving him?

He looked once again at the photograph in the file. He took his magnifying glass and looked again.

It was an early photograph, taken some 25 years ago.

But there was no doubt. He did not have to search for a recent photograph. His photograph was everywhere now.

Slusar tried to control his agitation.

He closed the file, placed it inside another one and hid it under the stack of files and papers.

Fortunately, he was alone in the office and no one else had access to his files. He would forward the files that he had selected to send to his superiors in stages. This way he would have time to think and decide what to do.

Slusar left the office. He needed to get some air, even though it was freezing outside, just to take a few steps in the snow so that his heart, which was pounding so loudly that he was certain it could be heard, could stop racing.

* * * * *

Moscow, Greek Embassy, January 1938

My dear sister,

Although somewhat irregular, you will receive this letter through the diplomatic pouch. This way, I will not fear that it will be opened at the post office and I can write freely.

As you know, I arrived here a few days ago to serve as ambassador of Greece to the Soviet Union. Promotion or exile? Promotion *and* exile?

Nevertheless, Moscow and Russia (I still find it difficult to think of the country with its new name, Soviet Union, and I suppose for us Greeks, it will always be Russia) cannot be compared to my previous posts, gay Paris, beautiful Rome, exotic Addis Ababa.

I arrived in the dead of winter and the cold is truly bitter. It can't be compared to the cold of Greece or western Europe, even when it's snowing. You go out only when necessary, wrapped in a scarf and coat, preferably of fur, with boots and two pairs of woollen socks, gloves, a hat (also of fur) which make you look like an animal, almost like a bear! But even so, the cold is penetrating. It is so intense that the uncovered parts of your face feel as if they are on fire. And when it is warmed again, it hurts, as if it is still on fire. If I had a moustache, small icicles would be hanging from it and would break if I touched them!

Even in the embassy, which is reasonably well-heated, the cold is still dreadful.

It's no wonder that the Russians drink so much vodka. How else can they warm themselves? The houses and offices, with only a few exceptions, do not have central heating. The rooms are heated with braziers and fireplaces, but coal and wood are hard to come by and are rationed.

Therefore, vodka is the only solution. The people drink large quantities, with the blessing of the country, which has increased its production and its taxation. Revenue from the taxation of vodka is very important, so much so that it constitutes a large percentage of the total revenue of the budget. Do you know what I've learnt? The previous budgets are called 'drunken'! Unofficially of course. However, a serious problem with alcoholism is emerging and the authorities are considering ways of dealing with it.

My first sense of this country is the cold, not only outside, but also in the souls of the people. Gloom. Fear. Frozen hearts. Desolation. And queues. Queues everywhere. For a little bread (rationed), a little food (rationed), for shoes, clothes, badly sewn and coarse (all rationed). Nothing like Paris!

But what's more, there is great insecurity and fear. People live from day to day, not knowing what tomorrow will bring … will there be food? Medicine? Will there be clothes? Will there be hope? (I don't know. They don't know). Will there be life?

It seems obvious to us that there will be. But not to them. Life is very cheap, without value. Millions died in the Great War and during the civil war. I've heard it whispered, unofficially of course because the regime conceals the facts and there are no statistics, that in Ukraine but also elsewhere, millions died of hunger a few years ago. Can you imagine it? Millions died of hunger, as if it were an underdeveloped African or Asian country. This, in a European country, in a country where the regime claims that it is interested in its people. It is thought that the regime not only did nothing to deal with the problem, but allowed it to happen on purpose, to restrain the opposition and dampen the morale of the Ukrainians who resisted the collectivisation of agriculture.

Collectivism, a word which is probably unknown to you. It means, simply, that there is no private ownership of land, farms belong to the state now and are exploited by state organizations called *kolkhoz* and *sovkhoz* … more new words.

However, it seems that they're not proving to be effective. It is rumoured that production has fallen and is much smaller than it was before the war. But again, there are no officially published records.

The greatest problem is the lack of information. The country provides very little information, only what it wants, and foreign diplomats consider it to be unreliable. But it's difficult to gather trustworthy data. Our movements are limited. Even as diplomats, we require a special pass to venture outside Moscow and only if it is approved. Therefore, we rely on unofficial sources, whatever they might be, not knowing if they are dependable …

These are my first impressions. I will write again soon.

I hope you're all well, your children, my nieces and nephews, Achilleas and Kostakis. Achilleas is now a university student … his first year!

Kisses to all of you.

With love,
Dimitris,[2]

* * * * *

---

[2] Dimitris Nikolopoulos had served previously as Consul in Addis Ababa and at the Embassy of Greece in Paris, among other posts. Inspired by Ethiopia,

Report from the   To: The Ministry of Foreign Affairs
Embassy of Greece in Moscow   Athens, Greece

As you know, I undertook my responsibilities as Ambassador on 3 January 1938. My predecessors have already informed you of the difficulty in obtaining information regarding the situation here. The official sources, newspapers and information from the Ministry of Foreign Affairs, are one-sided and entirely unreliable. All the western diplomats here consider them to be propaganda. There is a mutual, even if latent, suspicion that neither they nor we (the western diplomats) express ourselves openly. They pretend that they are informing us and we pretend to believe them.

The persistent problem is obtaining accurate and trustworthy information. All the western embassies, with great discretion and extreme caution, have developed 'private' information networks from different sources, official (state officials) and unofficial (private citizens), whom they pay and provide favours. Payment is made in western money, foreign notes or gold sovereigns, which have a much higher value on the black market than the official rate. American dollars, British pounds, French francs, German marks, Swedish kroner, even Greek drachmae, are in great demand. Payment is even accepted in items such as silk stockings and French perfumes for the wives or mistresses of the party members. Despite the austerity of the regime and the vigilance of the dreaded secret service, the GPU, the black market is flourishing. Here you can find anything, or almost anything. I suspect that the black market network includes the GPU itself, which tolerates it and closes its

---

he published in French *Contes d'Ethiopie* and *Lettres de la fleur nouvelle*. The term 'drunken budget' was coined by Trotsky (see Musial 2010, p.153). Achilleas Kyriazis was born in 1919, Kostas (father of the author) in 1920, the son of Despoina (Despo) Kyriazis, née Nikolopoulos, sister of Ambassador Dimitris Nikolopoulos.

eyes to what is going on and the fact that some of its members, from the lowest to the highest echelons, benefit from it. Everything can be sold here and everything can be bought. The problem is that, since it is an unofficial market, one can never be sure of the quality of what one buys. Where objects are concerned, if you have some expertise, you can avoid forgeries and imitations. You can determine whether a piece of jewellery, which once supposedly belonged to an aristocratic family of the tsarist era, is authentic or fake.

However, where information is concerned, it is much more difficult. You cannot tell if it is true or not. All you can do is to cross check it as far as it is possible, or to evaluate it rationally.

We have just received information that the Soviet Union is planning to send an unspecified number of the new edition of the Polikarpov I-16 fighter aircraft to the Republican forces in Spain. It concerns the type 17 aircraft. It has a reinforced armament, two 7.62mm ShKAS machine guns mounted on the outboard side of the main gear and two 20mm ShVAK cannons on the wings. It will have an air-cooled, 750hp M-25V engine providing a maximum speed of almost 300 mph on the surface of the sea and 270 mph at 15,000 feet.[3] The Soviets estimate that it is superior in every way, except perhaps for its manoeuvrability, to the Italian biplane Fiat CR-36 of the phalangists. The I-16 is also exported to the Chinese forces that are fighting against the Japanese. Unofficially, the Soviet authorities have left it to be believed that they would agree to the sale of this type to our air force.[4]

---

[3] The Soviet Union gave a total of 475 Polikarpovs of various types to the Spanish government. The pilots nicknamed it the *Mosca* (Fly) and their opponents, the Spaniards of Franco's air force, the Italians and Germans, called it the *Rata* (Rat).

[4] Ultimately, in 1938, Greece chose to purchase the Polish PZL-24 and G which was the main fighter aircraft used at the Albanian front.

An evaluation of the Soviet economy and political situation follows below.

The goals of the five-year plan and the collectivisation of agriculture do not appear to have been achieved. Collectivisation during the 1932-1933 period brought a terrible famine, especially in Ukraine. The government, of course, does not release any information; it conceals and denies the facts. However, information that has reached the western embassies describes deaths due to starvation of unprecedented dimensions, possibly seven million deaths, of which five million in Ukraine, where we have heard even of many instances of cannibalism.

The regime has unleashed an unparalleled wave of terrorism, with arrests, executions following mock trials, and sometimes without trials. Rumours claim that up to the end of 1937 approximately 1.5 million people have died in prisons, concentration camps and exile. Information received by the British Embassy from its source within the GPU/NKVD is that, of 1,565,410 people arrested during the period 1 October 1936 to 1 November 1938, some 668,305 have been executed.

A total estimate of the victims during the period of terror, from 1929 to 1938, comes to over 12 million. If this is true, it is truly horrifying. Twelve million, one and a half times the total population of Greece![5]

The five-year plans emphasise heavy industry and armaments. It is a major undertaking. The Soviet army and air force are the largest in the world and are constantly being strengthened. It is estimated that the armed forces in all the corps come to 3.8 million, with a total of about 18,000 tanks of all types and over 7,000 aircraft.

---

[5]   The population of Greece at the time was approximately seven million.

Even if the estimations are not entirely accurate, there is no doubt that the Soviet Union is preparing for war. The question is with whom? For defence against invasion? From Japan? Their relationship at the border with Manchuria is strained. Invasion? Against whom? Poland? Their relationship has always been tense and it seems that the Soviets have neither forgotten nor forgiven their defeat near Warsaw by the Poles and Jozef Piłsudski in 1920.

On the other hand, they enjoy a good and mutually beneficial relationship with Hitler's Germany. Perhaps the Soviet leaders haven't forgotten the assistance of Imperial Germany in sending Lenin from his exile to Leningrad in 1917. It is rumoured that the relationship continued in secret and quietly during the Weimar era. Germany sent its pilots to the Soviet Union for training since it had been forbidden to have an air force. In exchange, it provided technical assistance to the Soviet Union for the development of its industry with a particular emphasis on defence.

The relationship with the new regime in Germany is on-going and intensifying. The Soviet Union is exporting more and more products such as raw materials and agricultural goods, oil from the Caucasus, Maykop and Baku in ever increasing quantities to Germany, which is almost entirely dependent on them. In exchange, Germany exports to the Soviet Union high technology products, and especially machinery, which it needs for its industrialisation.[6]

However, the overly ambitious five-year plans are not progressing without unexpected difficulties. Leaks of information, as always unofficial and which, unfortunately, cannot be confirmed, state that the true outcomes deviate dangerously from the goals in terms of quantity, but even more so, in terms of quality.

---

[6] The amicable cooperation between the two dictators resulted in the notorious Molotov–Ribbentrop Pact of 1939 and the partition of Poland after it was invaded by Germany and the Soviet Union at the beginning of World War II.

For this, the leadership of the Communist Party of the Soviet Union blames conspiracies, sabotage, subversive elements, enemy agents (without mentioning them by name).

Essentially, they are looking for scapegoats and this time within the upper echelons of the army and the party.

From my predecessor's reports and the Soviet and international press, you are aware already of the events of 1937, the arrest of Marshal Mikhail Tukhachevsky and his supposed collaborators, the mock trial of last June, that they were condemned and executed. What is significant is that this was only the beginning.

What followed and has not stopped is an unprecedented wave of arrests and terror which is spreading everywhere. No one feels safe. Everyone is prepared to denounce someone else in order, as they hope, to save themselves. This is the situation today.

However, I'm worried that the persecutions will spread to include minorities that live in the Soviet Union. Stalin and his people don't trust them and view them with suspicion. In any case, suspicion is the main feature of the leadership and the present situation.

I fear and worry that these events might extend to our expatriates, the Pontic Greeks, who live mainly in Georgia.

I want to do whatever is possible to keep these people safe. I consider it an obligation of Greece, as a country with laws and my personal obligation, as its representative in the Soviet Union.

I request your support, approval and assistance in this attempt.

Minister Plenipotentiary of Greece to the Embassy in Moscow
Dimitris Nikolopoulos[7]

* * * * *

---

[7] See the bibliography for sources. The author conducted research at the archives of the Ministry of Foreign Affairs in July 2017. There was no

Tbilisi, January 1938

After many misgivings as to what to do, Slusar made a major decision, the decision of his life. He knew that what he planned to do was dangerous, deadly dangerous if he were to fail. But it could be incredibly profitable if he succeeded. Security for the future, for a different future.

Slusar had no illusions.

Only idiots had illusions in the Soviet Union in 1937 and at the beginning of 1938.

No one was safe. From the ordinary citizen to the highest echelons of the Party and the leadership of the army. There was suspicion that touched on paranoia. The revolution was eating, devouring its children, with an incredible and unrelenting bulimia, unsatiated no matter how many victims it consumed.

He had no illusions that he was safe even though he was an agent of the GPU, no matter how loyal he was to the Party or how good he was at his job. To survive was, at times, only a matter of luck.

Given that Trotsky, the victorious leader of the revolution had fallen out of favour and was obliged to go into self-exile in Mexico in order to save himself, who was safe?[8]

Given that the Commander of the Red Army and victor of the civil war, Field Marshal Mihail Tukhachevsky, had been executed, who was safe?

---

reference to these events or to the persecution of the Pontic Greeks that followed. The existing documents concerned only insignificant routine matters, visas, etc. However, every embassy submitted annual (and, often, more frequent) reports. But there were no such reports in the archives for 1938. They have either been lost or removed on purpose, unknown when, why and by whom.

[8] Trotsky was assassinated in Mexico in 1940 by GPU agents.

Given that the former head of the GPU, Nicolai Yezhov, had fallen out of favour and was executed, who was safe?

Certainly not an ordinary agent such as himself.

What he had discovered, what fate had handed to him, was a guarantee of safety. It was worth a lot, he didn't know how much but … he would find this out during the negotiations. Nevertheless, it would be enough for him to change his life, to escape from the immense prison that his country had become, to escape to a country of the west or, better yet, to Latin America (like Comrade Trotsky), to change his identity and live a quiet and different life.

He was amazed at his audacious thoughts and dreams. Fortunately, a method for reading his innermost thoughts had not been discovered! It was unimaginable that he, as an agent of the GPU, could be dreaming of a life in an enemy capitalist country. Nevertheless, the Soviet Union had excellent relations with some of them, such as the Germany of Mr Hitler …

Having made his decision, he laid out his plan of action.

He stayed late at the office, with the excuse that he had a lot of work …

After everyone had left, and after making sure that he was alone, he locked the inner door, took a camera that belonged to the office, closed tightly the shutters of the office, spread open the document on his desk and photographed it. Then he folded it and hid it among the other papers.

He then descended to the basement where there was a small darkroom (fortunately, the GPU had one). He took out the film, developed it and cut the two relevant negatives which he then placed in the enlarger and projected onto a sheet of photographic paper which he then hung to dry.

He waited with bated breath.

Luck was on his side. No one had bothered him.

He returned the camera to its place.

He placed the two photographs in an envelope which he put in the inner pocket of his jacket.

The first step had been accomplished successfully.

Now, for the second.

He had to find a suitable accomplice and he already had someone in mind.

He had to approach him carefully and discreetly.

* * * * *

Greek Embassy, Moscow, January 1938

My dear brother,

Your report created a small stir. Well, not such a small one, quite a big one in fact.

How did I find out?

There is nothing new under the sun, especially for a good journalist and owner of a newspaper, such as I. I'm boasting, but what can I do, I have to pat myself on the back and I know that you won't misunderstand me. We have our sources …

The first commotion, albeit small, was at the Air Force and the Ministry. A commotion because they had not thought about how they would be able to procure a 'communist' (as some termed it) fighter aircraft. However, some others do not appear to dismiss the idea. Having noted the performance of the previous versions of the type used in the Spanish Civil War, they consider it to be a reliable aircraft, superior to the British Gladiator[9] which is a contender,

---

[9] The Gloster Gladiator was the last biplane fighter of the RAF, the first having been put into service with squadrons 3 and 72 in January 1937. Two squadrons, 80 and 112, took part in the Greco-Italian War in Albania in November 1940. Two Gladiators were given as a gift to the Greek Air Force. The first Hawker Hurricanes MK 1 were put into service with Squadron 111

and approximately equal in power to the Polish PZL, even though the first choice is the new Hurricane which is now being developed by the British if, of course, they would be willing to sell it to us in time.

But this is the least.

The situation in the Soviet Union, as you are experiencing it, and as we learn from various sources, is dreadful, outrageous. I wonder to what lengths man can go, what he can do, and I mean this in the negative sense. What kind of age are we living in? ... Totalitarianism is emerging everywhere, dictatorships everywhere, in Italy, Germany, a civil war in Spain, Portugal, Brazil, even the milder versions in Greece and Turkey, communism in the Soviet Union. What has happened to democracy? Does it have a future? If I'm right, there are less than 20 democracies in the entire world ... Democracy, for which we have fought and believed in and served with the newspaper in support of our former Prime Minister, Eleftherios Venizelos.

If everything that we hear about the Soviet Union is correct, we're witnessing the greatest crime in world history ... I cannot understand how enlightened and progressive people anywhere can praise communism and the Soviet Union, even now ...

Can't they see that the Russian Revolution, which overthrew a corrupt and obscurant regime, has degenerated into something even worse?[10]

But I am deviating.

---

in December 1931. The Greek Air Force received the Hurricanes as a part of the RAF in September 1942 and used them in the Battle of El Alamein.

[10] On the basis of human victims, Stalin holds second place in history in terms of conducting mass murders, first place being held by Mao Zedong during the Cultural Revolution (possibly 15 million victims) and third place held by Hitler (six million Jews and tens of thousands of gypsies, homosexuals, communists, etc.).

Your report has caused quite a turmoil.

As you know, there are two political poles in Greece which collaborate harmoniously on a superficial level, but under the surface, are antagonistic.

Prime Minister Metaxas and King George.

Metaxas is inspired by Mussolini and Hitler, at least insofar as the internal organisation of the country, his anti-communist stance, the youth, etc. are concerned. But he is not pro-Italy and less pro-Germany than he was during the First World War. He is aware of Mussolini's expansionary tactics and is worried. He can't forget the events that occurred in Corfu.[11] At the same time, he's trying to remain on good terms with Hitler so that Hitler can keep Mussolini in check.

King George, as opposed to his father, Constantine, who is openly pro-German, is fanatically pro-British, out of self-interest, of course, as he realises that the future of the dynasty is supported by Britain. Therefore, he occasionally comes into conflict with Metaxas even though it was the latter who brought him back to the throne after the coup of 4 August 1936 and the notorious referendum that followed. But of course, you know all this. We have discussed these events at length.

You're well aware that, as former supporters of Venizelos, we are also pro-British. Simply because we believe that we have common interests.

We would be naïve to think that the British government is pro-Greek because of a belief in ideals, of partiality, of what it owes

---

[11] In 1923 Italian officers, who had laid out the Greco-Albanian border with Albania when it became an independent country after World War I, were assassinated by unknown perpetrators (possibly Albanians). Mussolini, who became dictator in 1922 and became known as Il Duce, accused Greece and demanded compensation, etc., sending ships from his fleet to fire on Corfu in order to impose his terms.

to ancient Greek culture. Not that there are no Britons, especially those that are cultured, who truly love Greece ... but I fear that the era of Lord Byron has passed ...[12]

But, fortunately, we still share common interests.

Britain has always needed allies and a stand-in in the Mediterranean against its other great opponents, tsarist Russia in the past and fascist Italy now. Mussolini is becoming a threat with his rhetoric and desire for the revival of the Roman Empire and his *Mare Nostrum*. And he is unsatiated. Italy already occupies Libya,[13] which borders with the British protectorate of Egypt and the important canal, which is Britain's path to Iraq, its other protectorate, and to its oil as well as to India. Mussolini has captured Somalia, Eritrea and Abyssinia, which border on the British colonies of Kenya and Uganda.

Britain needs a counterbalance in the Mediterranean and who better than us, also a naval nation and, in general, a friendly country. This explains Britain's support of King George.

But what has troubled the government the most is your concern and worry regarding the Pontic Greeks. I can tell you, in confidence, that the news reached the Palace, where I have some sources.

Maniadakis and others, especially Metaxas, don't look upon this favourably, because they consider the Pontic Greeks to be communists or, at least, pro-communist. Communists here are being persecuted and sent into exile to the islands or to prisons such as the one in Nauplion. The government doesn't feel that it should assist possible supporters of the Pontic Greeks.

The Palace, fortunately, has taken a different position: The King wants to show that he is king and protector of all the Greeks

---

[12] This was said to Kostas Kyriazis by his friend and publisher of the *Daily Mirror*, Hugh Cudlipp, during the years of the junta in Greece.

[13] Italy had occupied Libya since 1911, after a war with the Ottomans.

in the world (an ecumenical King, somewhat like the ecumenical Patriarch, doesn't that sound good?). Therefore, he is not opposed to helping the Pontic Greeks.

The government, also, cannot officially refuse to accept persecuted fellow countrymen that are in danger. Mavroudis is well-disposed to repatriate the Pontic Greeks and is supportive of the idea. Therefore, I don't think that you will receive clear orders. They will leave it to your discretion. We will, of course, support you with every means possible and through the newspaper, despite the censorship, with all the power that we have at our disposal, with whatever connections we have.

Fortunately, there are still some people who take us into consideration. Recent Greek history has been so fluid and there have been so many changes, that some wiser (or more calculating) people in the government believe that there will be more changes in the future and that it's best for them to side with certain people, such as us, who might, in future, be powerful again.

It's a confusing situation, but, then when has it not been so in Greece?

Therefore, proceed with caution and may God be with you (as we are, wholeheartedly).

I embrace you,
Spiros[14]

* * * * *

---

[14] Spiros Nikolopoulos founded the newspaper *Ethnos* in 1913. See the bibliography for information regarding Dimitris Nikolopoulos and the matter concerning the Pontic Greeks. Nikolaos Mavroudis was Deputy Secretary of the Ministry of Foreign Affairs. Prime Minister Ioannis Metaxas had retained the office of Minister of Foreign Affairs.

Tbilisi, January 1938

Slusar looked at the man standing nervously in front of him.

'How are you Comrade Agouridis?' he asked.

'I'm fine Comrade Slusar, fine,' the man replied hastily to the formal question which, nevertheless, was not a common one. Usually, party members did not waste time with cordiality and unnecessary pleasantries.

'Comrade, let's take a walk outside. I'm stiff from sitting at my desk for so many hours … it's bad for the circulation.'

Without waiting for a reply, Slusar rose and left his office and the building. Baffled, Agouridis followed him. This was entirely unexpected and unusual! To take a walk together! But he could do nothing other than obey.

The weather, for January in Tbilisi, was nice today. Very cold, which was to be expected, and snow, but the sky was blue and the sun, although weak, gave an impression of warmth by its very presence.

They took a few steps in silence, taking care not to slip, their shoes making occasional crunching sounds on the frozen snow.

'Comrade Agouridis, you have a married sister in Moscow, am I right?' Slusar asked, breaking their silence.

'Yes, Comrade Slusar,' Agouridis replied, astonished. What did his sister have to do with his application for Party membership? But, of course, Slusar, would have done his research. Anyway, there was nothing reprehensible. His sister and her husband, a Russian, were good Soviet citizens, they had never been in trouble. But the way things were now, it was not necessary to have given a reason in order to be accused of something. A careless word or a personal jealousy was enough for an anonymous accusation and then, it was impossible to prove that there had been no wrongdoing and to try to save yourself …

'Is there a problem with my sister?' Agouridis dared to ask, apprehensively.

'No, relax. I found out about her when I was looking at your file when you applied to become a Party member. Honestly, why do you want to join?'

'Well, it's written in my application, comrade; I believe in the ideals of communism, the revolution, in Comrade Stalin. I want to participate actively as much as possible.'

Of course, that's what everyone said. But for Slusar, there was something else on his mind.

'Your application is being considered favourably,' he replied. 'But there is another matter, somewhat delicate.'

Slusar hesitated and looked directly in his eyes, before taking his next step.

'Can I trust you? There is a matter that can change both our lives … for the better.'

Slusar was taking a calculated risk, even after having examined all the alternatives. There was the danger that the other man would betray him, but what would he gain? Slusar was the more powerful of the two. If he said anything to the authorities, Slusar would say that they were lies, the malicious and treacherous lies of a foreign agent (Agouridis was a Pontic Greek, and this was the reason he had chosen him) who wanted to slander a Party member and the GPU, because his application for Party membership had been rejected. Why would Agouridis risk this? In order to win someone's dubious favour? On the other hand, the gain for both of them would be great and tangible.

Agouridis remained silent.

'Although you're a Soviet citizen you're of Greek origin,' Slusar observed. 'Your family escaped to tsarist Russia in 1917, having left Trebizond to escape the Ottoman persecutions. You must have been seven or eight years old at the time.'

All this information was in his file.

'Your parents have died,' he continued. 'You're not married, you have an older, married sister in Moscow. How long has it been since you last saw her?'

'Two years, comrade.'

'Two years. Good. Would you like to see her?'

Agouridis was increasingly curious about the turn that the conversation was taking.

'I would like to see her, but travel is not easy, comrade.'

'That can be arranged. I can issue a special pass for you,' Slusar replied.

'Are you surprised?' he added, sensing the other man's confusion.

"The real reason you will go to Moscow will be to take a message to the Greek Embassy. Because you're of Greek origin, you can do this …'

Slusar explained what the message would be and what they would gain. If Agouridis accepted to go, they would discuss the details later.

Slusar had chosen Agouridis and the Greek Embassy out of necessity. The information that was for sale would be of interest to all the foreign embassies. The problem was that he was from Tbilisi and had no way of going to Moscow. Of course, in Tbilisi there were no people of British or French origin, but there were Pontic Greeks. Therefore, his choice was limited, basically only one. If the Greek Embassy refused the transaction, then he would have to think of alternatives, which would be more complex and more difficult.

He hoped Agouridis would agree.

In any case, any intelligent person would understand the value of the information that he held. Its value, literally, in gold.

* * * * *

Embassy of Greece, Moscow, January 1938

My dear sister,

I was very happy to receive your news.

As I wrote to you, I'm beginning to acclimatise, to get used to the cold and gloomy atmosphere. The Russian winter is terrible, but it has its joys. If you can survive a Russian winter, you can survive anywhere! I'm joking, of course.

I've begun to familiarise myself with my surroundings, the official and the unofficial. Among the latter is the black market. I discovered and bought a beautiful 19ᵗʰ century bronze and blue porcelain lamp for my collection. You'll like it!

You amuse me with your concern, your wish to see me married. You know that I enjoy my freedom, but you might be right perhaps, I'm "mature" (as you write) now and should think of marriage. You want to introduce me to some suitable women when I come for the Easter holidays. You write that they were enthused by the portrait that my friend Gounaropoulos painted of me. Of course, as it was painted by a friend, it flatters me!

Nevertheless, I will submit to your commands. Can I do otherwise?

I have a lot of work. We are bombarded with applications for repatriation by Pontic Greeks who are afraid of the situation here and want to return to Greece. We work long hours issuing visas, trying to get them approved by our Ministry of Foreign Affairs as well as by the corresponding Soviet services. Spiro must have told you about the difficulties that we face. We have received now the first approvals. I'll continue doing this.[15]

I embrace you,
Dimitris

---

[15] For the very brief time that he was ambassador in Moscow, Nikolopoulos succeeded in repatriating as many as 150 Pontic Greek families.

CHAPTER 2

Soviet Union, February 1938

Without making use of his diplomatic status, Dimitris Nikolopoulos stood patiently in the queue like an ordinary citizen waiting to visit Lenin's Mausoleum in Red Square. This was what the anonymous stranger had requested in the note that he had left under the front entrance to the embassy. The guard had found and delivered it to him.

It was a brief, handwritten message in Greek, without a name or signature.

Meet me tomorrow between 12.00 and 13.00 in the queue at Lenin's Mausoleum. It regards information of utmost importance that will be of interest to you.

Nikolopoulos didn't know what to make of it. The way the stranger had chosen to communicate with him was certainly unusual. But the Soviet Union was an unusual place, full of fear, suspicion and secrecy. He asked himself what kind of information the anonymous author of the note had that was of "utmost importance" … like a cloak and dagger novel of Dumas … Should he attach any importance to it? Was it serious? But who would attempt such a joke in a country like the Soviet Union in 1938? And what did he have to lose if he did what the note requested of him? A few hours away from the office. At least, it would satisfy his curiosity … *Information of utmost importance that will be of interest to you.*

The queue advanced slowly, disappearing inside the mausoleum and exiting from the other side as people paid their respects to the deceased and hurried off on their errands.

Step by step, he approached the entrance to the mausoleum … and still no one had come up to him. A few metres more … should he continue or not? What did he have to lose? In any event, he had never visited the mausoleum.

He entered the sombre, depressing interior, passed in front of Lenin's sarcophagus and proceeded to the exit.

As he was leaving, someone in a hurry brushed by him, murmured an apology in Russian and distanced himself.

The ambassador clenched in his hand the small piece of paper that the stranger had slipped to him.

He resisted the temptation to open it till he returned to his office and shut himself in his office. He opened it and read it. It was in Greek.

I have in my possession documents that bring to light important information about a very highly placed individual of the Central Committee of the Communist Party of the Soviet Union. They will be extremely important to you. If you are interested, meet me tomorrow afternoon, 18.00 to 19.00 at Red Square. I will find you.

No signature.

The ambassador re-read the note, folded it and put it in his wallet. He had not decided what to do with the note.

Or, whether he should go to the appointment. However, his interest had been aroused. A very "highly placed individual" … revealing documents. Who could they be referring to? What kind of documents? Real or false? Maybe it was a hoax? If it were a hoax, for what purpose?

He decided to go. He had nothing to lose … and at the very least, he would satisfy his curiosity … He had confronted other strange situations at his other embassy postings but this one promised to surpass them all … if it was real.

Wrapped in his coat, scarf, fur hat, gloves and boots, the ambassador made his way to Red Square. Night had fallen, it was the hour when the state services in the surrounding buildings closed for the day, and the square was full of people. Perhaps this was why the stranger had chosen this hour. The darkness of night and the crowds provided an excellent cover.

He glanced around him. He was beginning to feel that he was taking part in a spy novel. Of course, in the dark and because of the crowds, it was impossible to know if someone had been following him. But he didn't think that anyone from the embassy had followed him. This was a small advantage in being with an embassy of a small country. If he were an American, a Briton, a Frenchman, a German or from another embassy, he was certain that GPU agents would not have left him out of their sight …

He began to walk slowly, pretending nonchalance, just someone going home after work, a part of the crowd. A shadow, among so many others.

He cast a hurried glance at his watch: It was 18.20. What had become of his contact? But it was still within the time frame. However, the cold was bitter and he didn't know if he could last till 19.00.

'Do you, by any chance, have a match?' he heard a voice behind him ask in Greek.

Surprised, he turned around abruptly.

The man, a shadow in the dark like himself, was holding a cigarette.

The ambassador searched his pockets, found matches and offered them to the man.

'Mr Ambassador, I am the person who contacted you. For the time being, my name is not important. I am a Pontic Greek.'

He lit his cigarette and the flame of the match lit his face momentarily. He was a man of about 30.

'I'm sorry I made you wait but I had to be certain that no one was following you.'

He returned the matchbox, together with a folded piece of paper.

'I have written some information in this note about documents that I have in my possession and who they concern. If you are interested, we will meet here again tomorrow, at the same time. I will show you the documents. Good evening, Mr Ambassador.'

'Good evening,' the ambassador replied as the man vanished into the darkness and the crowd.

He quickly returned to the embassy, closed the door to his office and opened the small note.

He read the few handwritten lines.

He paled. His hands trembled briefly, till he calmed himself.

What he read was incredible. Monstrous. Could it be true? And what if it was?

There was no turning back now. It was so incredible that not even the wildest imagination could have thought this up, if it weren't true.

Nikolopoulos waited impatiently for the next meeting.

Dressed warmly as before, he walked to Red Square, making sure that he was not being followed.

As he arrived, he walked slowly and waited.

A little later he heard the familiar voice.

'Follow me discreetly.'

The man walked ahead and the ambassador followed him.

The man stopped under one of the few lampposts on the square. The ambassador approached him.

'Do you have a cigarette?' he asked.

The ambassador took a packet of cigarettes from his coat pocket and gave it to him. The man took it and at the same time put a folded piece of paper in the ambassador's hand.

'Take a look,' he said. 'This is the document.'

The ambassador unfolded it and cast a glance under the faint light of the lamppost.

There was no doubt. The name on the document was clear, the letters, the number 3316 written on the photographs. There were three photographs, two of them were small and showed a man frontally and in profile, and one photograph showed him in a coat and hat. The man in the photographs was much younger, perhaps from 35 years earlier,[16] but it was definitely him. Somewhat thinner, a black mustache, the same large nose, the same hard look.

The man stretched out his hand and took back the document. He folded it and put it back in his coat pocket.

'Is it authentic?' the ambassador asked, somewhat concerned. 'How did it come into your possession?'

'From a friend, a GPU agent, who found it in Tbilisi. It is authentic, Mr Ambassador. What I've shown you is a copy of the original,' the man replied.

'And what do you want in payment?' Nikolopoulos asked.

'The man who found it wants to be paid. For myself, only two visas for my repatriation to Greece.'

'And how much does he want?'

The man told him an amount and added, 'In dollars, British pounds and, better yet, gold sovereigns, or a combination of these.'

---

[16] In 1911, to be exact.

The amount was considerable, but reasonable, considering the significance of the information.

'I will need some time to collect the funds,' the ambassador replied. 'As you can understand, we do not have so much money readily available.'

'So, you're interested?'

The ambassador nodded.

Of course, he was interested! It was a significant document for whoever had it.

'However, I would like to have the originals,' the ambassador said.

'You will have them when the transaction has been concluded. How much time do you need?'

'For the money? I will need a week, maybe ten days. Is this alright?'

'Fine.'

'How will I contact you?'

'I will contact you. When you're ready, give me a sign in your office at the embassy. Position a chair near the French window so that it can be seen from the outside and put your coat on it, the one you are wearing now. It will be a signal for me to meet you that same night, here, at the same hour.'

'Fine. For the visa you'll have to make an application at our Consulate at the embassy. Are you familiar with the procedure?'

'I'll do it as soon as we have completed the first step. Now I must go. Good evening Mr Ambassador.'

'Good evening, Mr ..., Mr...'

'For the time being, my first name, Yiannis, is enough,' the man replied before disappearing.

The ambassador thought about the next step. He did not intend to ask the Ministry for approval of the transaction, or for the transfer of funds. If he did, there was the risk of some kind of bureaucratic complication, or a delay at the very least. He would act unconventionally.

He would get the money from his own resources. Fortunately, he was still a bachelor, without family obligations, and well-off. He had to see how much money he had in Moscow. Then he would ask his siblings for the difference, which could be sent through the diplomatic pouch. Completely irregular and unconventional. However, the trophy was worth this detour around the official route and many more if necessary.

Back in his office, he took note of his available funds, then wrote a letter to his brother asking for the balance that he needed, explaining that it was for a very important matter. He did not say what it was, that could wait until the matter was concluded. In case the Ministry opened the envelope, it was better for them not to know why the money was needed and to believe it was for his own use. Fortunately, they knew that he was an avid art collector.

He put the letter in an envelope and sealed it, wrote the address and marked it "personal". It would leave with the next diplomatic pouch.

He then sent a telegram to his brother telling him to expect his letter. They had agreed beforehand that this was how he would alert him that a letter was arriving with the diplomatic pouch. Spiros had contacts in the Ministry who would give it to him.

A few evenings later, he went to a cocktail party at one of the embassies. Feeling as though they were marooned in a hostile and unfriendly environment had created a bond between them. The cocktail party, aside from providing an opportunity to socialise, with only a few Soviet officials present, was also a way of exchanging information.

After greeting his hosts and exchanging a few words with other diplomats, Nikolopoulos approached the British ambassador,

Aretas Akers-Douglas,[17] who he knew from having served at the same time at a post in another country. There was a certain familiarity between them.

After exchanging a few formalities, they began discussing current events.

'Do you believe any of these senseless reports that are coming to light from the trials? If they are even slightly true, the country appears to be overrun with traitors, saboteurs, enemies of the people, foreign agents and I don't know what else,' the Briton observed.

'I agree with you. But there is something else,' Nikolopoulos said, giving expression to certain doubts which had not abated.

'What do you mean?'

'Would you believe that one of the highest placed officers of the Party had once been an agent of OKHRANA and had informed on his comrades during the tsarist regime?'

'Is this a theoretical question?' the Briton asked, before continuing. 'In this country nothing surprises me. But tell me, between us, have you learnt something?'

Nikolopoulos nodded.

'Yes, I have. However, I'm not sure that the information is entirely reliable, although it appears to be.'

'Do you think that the information might be false? Let's say, to be used by the GPU as evidence to incriminate someone?'

'I thought of that,' Nikolopoulos replied. 'However, the individual is very powerful, and so highly placed that probably no one would even dream of forging documents to implicate him.'

---

[17] Aretas Akers-Douglas, 2nd Viscount of Chilston, was the ambassador to the Soviet Union from 1933 to 1938. The name Aretas is the Hellenistic form of the unusual "Harith", the name of kings of Nabatea, a wealthy Arab country primarily involved in the spice trade. Its capital was Petra, in today's Jordan.

'My dear friend, you've aroused my curiosity,' the Briton replied.

'I can't say anything more until I know more and am convinced.'

'Will you let me know when you are certain about the matter?'

'I will, I promise. Unofficially, of course, because of the interests that our two countries have in common. Then, you can ask your Foreign Office and your government for a formal confirmation from my government. But this will have to wait. We will meet again when the time comes ...'

The days passed with a full workload, granting repatriation visas and with the procedures necessary for arranging travel to Greece for the fortunate ones.

The funds arrived.

Time for the final step.

* * * * *

Greek Embassy, Moscow, 5-8 March 1938

The ambassador placed the chair in his office close to the French window so that it could be seen from the outside and threw his coat over it, as they had agreed.

He waited impatiently for the appointed hour. He arrived a little early and strolled around the square a few times. Fortunately, not long after, Yiannis arrived at five minutes past six, perhaps equally impatient.

'Everything is fine,' Nikolopoulos said. 'How do we proceed?'

'Tomorrow, at the same time, same place. You'll give me the money and I'll give you the copies of the documents, which you have seen already. You will receive the originals as soon as the visas have been issued and travel arrangements have been made for our return to Greece.'

'Who is the second person? Your wife?'

'My fiancée, who is also Greek,' Yiannis replied.

'Until I receive the originals, I cannot give you the money. I hope you understand. My government would not approve,' the ambassador said.

He had not told him that the money was his, not the government's. There was no reason for him to know.

'I understand, Mr Ambassador. How much will you give me tomorrow?'

'Half?'

'Accepted. In any case, it's only a matter of a few days. Tomorrow I'll apply for the visas. With your intervention, I hope they'll be issued quickly. This is to our mutual benefit, so that the transaction can be completed quickly.'

'That's right. If you submit your applications tomorrow, I'll see to it that the visas and all other arrangements are finalised on the 9th of March. In four days. The final exchange will take place in the embassy.'

'Agreed. So, until tomorrow.'

They bid each other farewell.

They met the next night. Without exchanging any words, Yiannis gave the ambassador an envelope and took the one that was handed to him. Nikolopoulos opened the envelope, confirmed that it was the right one and closed it.

'I'll wait for you at the embassy,' he told him. 'Thank you, Yiannis.'

'And thank you, Mr Ambassador. A new life is being offered to us in our homeland … I hope the documents will be useful to Greece,' Yiannis replied.

They shook hands.

Back at the embassy, alone in his office, the ambassador looked calmly at the document.

Shocking, for sure. Valuable, although he could not think how it would be useful to his country.

Now he had to write a report as to how the document came into his possession. Carefully, without naming his contact or mentioning the source of the money used for the payment. This information would be divulged "in due time", according to the formal diplomatic language.

With the originals in hand, the experts at the Ministry wold have time to examine and confirm their authenticity.

He opened the top drawer of his desk, where he kept his personal papers, placed the documents inside, closed and locked it.

On the 10th of March, his report with the originals would travel to Athens in the diplomatic pouch.

In the meantime, the guard at the embassy had grown curious regarding the strange habit of the new ambassador who went out into the cold night for a lonely stroll. Of course, it was well known that he was unconventional. An aristocrat, a bachelor, a fanatic collector, an author … However, were these characteristics enough to justify the peculiarity of his evening strolls? Or was there something else?

The guard was one of the informers of the GPU that were at every embassy, their eyes and ears open for anything that might be deemed suspicious. He decided that he should inform his superiors. Let them decide. It's possible that these evening strolls were innocent and nothing else. But if they were not, then no one would be able to accuse him of neglecting his duties.

His superiors took note of the information that was given to them. Agents followed the ambassador discreetly. They noticed his brief meetings, possibly innocent, with an unknown person. They were unable to identify the other individual.

They ordered the guard to search the ambassador's office.

When the ambassador left for the night, the guard went up to his office. He made sure that the staff had left the embassy, took out his passkey (he had made a wax replica of the lock before the current ambassador had arrived) and unlocked the door.

He did not turn on the light but used his torch to illuminate his way to the desk, which he searched carefully with his gloved hands.

He found nothing suspicious.

Then he tried the drawers. One was locked, the others were not. There was nothing interesting in the unlocked drawers. He had a passkey for the locked drawer which he opened and cast the beam of his torch inside.

What he found made him freeze. Terrible.

He did not touch the document but closed the drawer and locked it. He left hurriedly, locking the office door behind him. He had to inform the GPU.

By habit, Nikolopoulos was always the last to leave his office after waiting for the rest of the staff to leave. A few days later, before leaving, he looked over the matters of the day. That night the main matter was his report regarding the document. He read it one last time. He was satisfied. If they asked him for more information, he would either prepare a supplementary report, or he would give an oral report when he went to Athens for the Easter holidays.

Tomorrow he would receive the originals which he would send immediately to Athens in the diplomatic pouch.

This would be the most important achievement of his career. A truly significant contribution to his country and not only … How would he use it? What would he reveal to his family, his siblings?

Absorbed by his thoughts, he did not notice the French window opening slowly. The guard had left it closed but unlocked.

Without entering the office, the GPU agent separated the curtains quietly, raised his hand that held a pistol with a silencer, aimed and fired.

The bullet entered Nikolopoulos' temple. Death was instantaneous. The ambassador fell forward, onto his desk.

The agent replaced the gun in its holster and entered the office. He took the document and the ambassador's report. He then took a pistol from his coat, placed it in the ambassador's palm. He had already fired it once, so that a bullet would be missing and the barrel would have a mark.

With his fingers he spread a small amount of gun powder around the wound which was bleeding. This way it would appear that the ambassador had committed suicide.

Of course, a proper forensic examination would have shown evidence of the staged suicide if, for example, a ballistic study was made of the bullet. But there was no risk of such an investigation being conducted.

When the event was formally announced, the GPU would send its own forensic doctor, who would sign a report that had been prepared for him in advance.[18]

The next day, Agouridis, full of expectation, arrived early at the embassy to deliver the documents and pick up the visas.

Turning into the street where the embassy was located, he froze.

The entrance was blocked by police cars and policemen were standing about, preventing anyone from entering or exiting the embassy.

What had happened? What should he do?

He was not sure what to do, feeling an icy invisible hand wringing his innards. But he had to find out …

He walked slowly toward the policemen.

He approached one of them, greeted him and asked: 'What has happened, comrade?'

'What do you want, comrade?' the other asked, scowling. 'Why do you ask?'

'I've come to pick up my visa,' Agouridis said truthfully.

---

[18] The assassination took place on 8 March 1938 and was officially declared a "suicide".

'The embassy is closed. The ambassador was found dead last night,' the policeman replied.

Agouridis felt a knot tightening in his stomach.

'But, how?' he stammered.

'That's enough, comrade,' the policeman said, frowning. "I don't know anything more. Go, you're in the way.'

'When will the embassy open?'

'Comrade, how should I know? I'm only a policeman!'

Agouridis said goodbye and left quickly.

* * * * *

To: The Foreign Office
From: the British Embassy, Moscow
Subject: Death of the Greek ambassador

I have been informed of the sudden death of the Greek ambassador, Mr Dimitris Nikolopoulos in the building of the Greek Embassy.

According to the official forensic report it was suicide. The ambassador was found dead, seated at his desk holding a pistol from which a bullet was missing, with a gunshot wound in his temple.

I have my reservations regarding the official report of the Soviet authorities. What was the reason for his suicide? Why didn't he leave a note explaining his reasons for taking his life, as most suicides do?

The ambassador was a particularly dynamic man, with many interests. I had met him personally at a previous post where we had served in our respective embassies. Under no circumstances did he appear to me to be a man with suicidal tendencies.

A relatively recent conversation that I had with him makes me question the idea that he took his own life. He asked me at the time if I could believe that a highly placed official of the party could have been an informer within the ranks of OKHRANA. He assured me that the question was not theoretical, but that it concerned a real person, whose name he could not reveal. He promised to share further information with me once he was able to confirm the matter.

I'm assuming that the GPU was informed of the matter and murdered him. They staged the suicide so that the information would not be leaked.

I will try to look further into the matter although I doubt that I will be successful, given the situation here.

Signed: AAD

* * * * *

Tbilisi, Georgia, March 1938

'You did well to return quickly,' Slusar said. 'I hadn't heard the news. There are well-kept secrets within the GPU as well. The question is what really happened and what are we going to do now? I'll try to find out more and learn how he died. However, I don't think it was of natural causes. It's too much of a coincidence for the death to have happened on the day when the transaction was to be concluded. In my job, we are suspicious. We always believe the worse. There must have been a leak, somehow the GPU found out about the document and closed his mouth ...'

'A leak? How? Only we knew ... no one else.'

'The GPU has ears and eyes everywhere. It's possible that someone saw you when you met. Or, there was an informant within the embassy. Anyway, the most important thing now is that the transaction has failed and we must be alert to the fact that the GPU knows about the document or even has it in its hands. This is the situation we are now faced with.' Slusar talked and thought at the same time.

'Which means that we aren't safe,' he added.

'The GPU will certainly try to find where the document came from. The GPU may be slow, but it is methodical. It will search the archives of OKHRANA, whatever has been stored in Leningrad, Moscow and other large and small towns, perhaps even here.'

Agouridis paled as he listened to Slusar, even though the latter appeared to be calm.

'However, we have a small advantage, that of timing. We know what has happened and therefore, we can be the first to act. We also have the money of the down payment. That's important.'

'So, what are we going to do?'

'Two steps,' Slusar decided. 'First, I'll make the document disappear. If they search, they won't find anything here. So, they won't be able to point the finger at me. Second, you will disappear. That way, no one can connect us.'

'How will I disappear?' Agouridis asked.

'You will change location and identity.'

'Location and identity? How can that be done?'

'Everything can be done with money and connections. Fortunately, we have both. From one point of view, the general situation here helps us. People disappear all the time. As well as documents. You're an engineer. I'll create a new identity and new documents for you. I'll find a job for you in a factory somewhere else. With the help of friends who'll be paid. It's the only solution. With some luck, we'll succeed. You'll 'disappear' in a new job, a new environment. The same with me. We'll both 'disappear' but we'll always be in contact … The life of each of us is in the hands of the other. Do you agree?'

Agouridis agreed. What else could he do? It was the only hope for salvation.

Now he had to take the final and more difficult step.

Andromache was a schoolteacher.

He was waiting for her when the school closed for the day. When she saw him, she hesitated momentarily because he had not told her that he would be waiting for her. Then she quickened her steps and ran into his arms.

'When did you arrive? Are you well?'

He embraced her tightly, silently.

'Let's go for tea,' he said, taking her by the arm.

The weather was milder, the first signs of spring had appeared. It was no longer bitterly cold, with winter's ice and snow.

They walked toward one of the few cafés that were open in the city

'What's wrong?' she asked, seeing his troubled look.

This was not the man she was used to, optimistic, happy, sentimental when he was with her.

'What's wrong?' she asked again. 'Did you get the visas?'

'No,' he replied. 'The ambassador died suddenly, and the visas had not been signed.'

They entered the smoke-filled café, found an isolated table, sat down and ordered tea.

'So, what will happen now?' Andromache asked, looking at him with her large, vivacious eyes, those eyes that had enchanted him, those eyes that could look straight into the depths of his soul.

What would happen now that their dream to go to Greece had evaporated, that Agouridis knew could evolve into a nightmare … something she did not know and for her peace of mind should never learn.

'But how?' she asked.

'I don't know. I only found out on the day that I went to pick up the visas. And I came back here. A new ambassador has to be appointed. But … but,' he hesitated, 'there is something more important.'

'More important? What? You're making me worry.'

He took her hands in his, held them tightly, looking into her eyes.

'Do you love me? Do you trust me?' he asked with intensity, as if his life depended on her reply.

'I love you. Always. But you frighten me … What's going on?'

'I must leave, change jobs and city. It is imperative. For us both. I can't tell you much more now, for your own safety. There has been a misunderstanding which might be dangerous under the current circumstances.'

'Are you being investigated? Has someone accused you of something? Have the police called for you?'

Andromache paled. In today's environment, anonymous accusations were commonplace, "traitors" were everywhere …. A careless word to the wrong person could lead to an investigation, an arrest, a trial and worse…

'Relax. No, I haven't been called by the police, nor am I being investigated. But I have certain suspicions and it's best that I take precautionary measures. For both of us, until the danger has passed and the situation calms down. Do you trust me?' he asked again.

She did not reply.

What were her eyes telling him? How was she dealing with the crumbling of their dreams?

'Don't lose hope, my love. We're alive. We have each other. We'll manage. We'll achieve our dream; we'll make it a reality. We haven't been defeated. It's only a postponement. We haven't been defeated. Be patient.'

'Patient,' she murmured. 'Hope in this gloom? In this country which has become a vast open prison? What hope? What kind of future?'

Her eyes filled with tears.

He took her in his arms, caressing her hair. What could he say to her? What hopes did they have now for a different, better life?

The future suddenly seemed uncertain and ominous. But they were both young. Agouridis would not lose his courage nor his hopes. The future could bring something new, something better.

If he couldn't believe in this, then he had no reason to live.

CHAPTER 3

War, Soviet Union, Southern Front, August 1941

It came as a total surprise.

At dawn on 22 June 1941, without the blare of sirens, without a declaration of war, the Luftwaffe began Operation Barbarossa, putting an end to the hypocritical friendship of the two dictators and putting an end to the Molotov-Ribbentrop Pact that the two Ministers of Foreign Affairs had signed two years earlier, with warm handshakes and smiles for the journalists of the world.

Hundreds of German aircraft of every type dropped bombs, and the fighter aircraft Messerschnitt 109, flying low, fired on Soviet airfields close to the frontiers.

Only one day before, the Soviet Air Force had been the largest in the world. By the next night it had almost ceased to exist, at least at the front lines. Thousands of aircraft had been transformed into shapeless masses of aluminium, iron, wood, fabric, and burning rubber. Huge columns of black smoke rose above the airfields.

The few fighter aircraft and bombers that had survived, such as the biplane and monoplane fighters Polikarpov I-15 and I-16 flew in an attempt to slow down the German ground attack and the Katyusha rocket launchers. The experienced German pilots, with their better fighter aircraft, caused an extensive loss of human lives. The skies belonged to the Luftwaffe, the Stukas and medium bombers.

Undisturbed, the Stuka dive bombers, their sirens sounding a shrill wailing noise as they descended, began to bomb the known locations of the Soviet defence and artillery. The medium bombers attacked behind the front lines, the supply lines, roads, railway stations, bridges.[19]

After the first aerial strikes, the Germans launched artillery attacks in preparation for the invasion on land.

Then it was the turn of the Panzers and the infantry for a new 'blitzkrieg'. Millions of men, from Finland to the Black Sea, started out for the greatest invasion in history. It was as if all of central and western Europe were attacking the East. Germans (together with the Austrians who were now a part of the Reich), Italians, Hungarians, Rumanians, Bulgarians, Finns, but also volunteer Spaniards, Scandinavians, Frenchmen, Belgian-Dutch, Croatians,[20] advanced eastward, some on top of Panzers, armoured

---

[19] During the first week of the war, the Soviet Air Force lost 6,000-7,000 airplanes, most of them on the ground, a number which surprised even the Germans when they surveyed the extent of the catastrophe that they had caused, the airfields that they now controlled. In the air battles the German pilots succeeded in an incredible, for that time, extent of destruction. First among them was the ace Werner Mölders, whose record numbered over 100 bombings and over 100 aerial victories.

[20] Aside from the German allies, there were also units of fascist volunteers from the occupied countries, such as the Viking battalion made up of Scandinavians or the Charlemagne regiment consisting of French-Belgians, etc.

vehicles, cars, others on foot with carts, on horses and mules. The scene was reminiscent of the previous war.

There was chaos on the Soviet side.

Lines of communication had collapsed, there was no central plan and central leadership was impossible. Each local governor had to assess the situation and act according to his judgement. The officers corps of the Soviet army had been hit hard with the purges of 1938 and there were now few experienced officers. Furthermore, the climate of terror had eliminated any desire for taking initiatives. Everyone waited for orders, but orders were not forthcoming, or if they came, they were either no longer valid or they were contradictory.

Ordinary soldiers, non-commissioned officers, lower echelon officers and occasionally the commanders of larger units fought, often with bravery and self-sacrifice. The ordinary soldier did not lack courage.

But it was as if amateurs were fighting against professionals in an arena that benefited the professionals. The summer, with its clear skies and dry, even ground lacking in natural obstacles, aside from rivers, benefited the tactics of the blitzkrieg. Airplanes. Panzers. Motorised vehicles. A rapid, in-depth advance. A disorganised enemy. Pincers that closed in immense circular movements, a net that was cast in stages by the slower infantry battalions that followed the motorised vehicles.

The front was splintered everywhere, with the Axis forces advancing to Belarus and Ukraine while the Rumanians moved toward Odessa. Soviet units put up resistance wherever they could. Others tried to retreat. Others came from behind the frontlines as reinforcements, intensifying the chaos at the frontlines and the congestion on the roads. They proved to be an excellent target for the Luftwaffe. Clouds of dust and smoke everywhere. Cut off, the Soviet units were surrounded. Without supplies, petrol, bullets, food, and medicine, they were obliged to surrender.

At the main front, where the German pincers encircled an immense pocket of men, 600,000 prisoners were captured. There were countless dead.

When the invasion began and the Stavka was informed, the commanders of the army met with a terrified Stalin at his dacha[21] outside of Moscow. General Georgy Zhoukov was among them. Had they wanted, had they dared, they could have arrested Stalin and unseated him, accusing him of the catastrophe that was emerging.

They did not do it.

They discussed the situation and came to a decision.

And Stalin survived.

A scorched earth policy was put into effect. Like Mikhail Kutuzov and Napoleon in 1812. As the Russian Army retreated, and until it could regroup, until reinforcements could arrive from Siberia, until new reinforcements could be mobilised, the Germans were not to find anything useful. Factories were to be emptied out and relocated behind the Urals, together with as many civilians as possible, with engineers and skilled workers having priority. Whatever could not be moved had to be destroyed. The crops. The animals. The invaders were not to eat Soviet barley and wheat.

Because the Soviets expected the Germans to continue their unrestrained advance toward Moscow, they concentrated their forces to its defence. However, to their shock, the German advance suddenly and unexpectedly changed its focus. Hitler was not about to repeat Napoleon's mistake of aiming for Moscow. It was not a priority. He instructed his generals to direct a major effort toward economic targets: the wealth of Ukraine. Its infinite plains. This was the land vital to the Reich. And later, a second, essential phase, the Caucasus and the oil of the Caspian Sea. Without that

---

[21] Stavka was the High Command of the Armed Forces.

oil, the German army and industry would not be able to survive a lengthy war. To achieve that, from a tactical point of view, as Carl von Clausewitz, a 19th century Prussian general and military theorist had said, the enemy army had to be destroyed. A large part of it had been destroyed on the Centre front. But an even greater encirclement could be achieved in the south, around Kiev. They were not expected there. Moscow would then fall like a ripe fruit.

On 30 July, the German 6th Army reached the outskirts of Kiev and launched its first attack against the outer defence lines.

Kiev had 850,000 residents. Nikita Khrushchev, the local commissar, mobilised 160,000 people to build 65 kilometres of defensive works, trenches, 750 fortified bunkers, 32 kilometres of antitank ditches. All available older men, those who were not serving already in the armed forces, were mobilised and organised in five militias, reinforcing the four infantry divisions of the 26th Army under Lieutenant General Kostenko. The first German attack was repelled. Kiev prevailed, a fortress protected by the Dnieper River which met, a little farther north, the tributary Desna.

The summer brought increasingly high temperatures. Most of the roads were dirt roads and dust covered the parched ground. Swirls rose above the tracks of tanks, wheels, animals' hooves, the soldiers' heavy combat boots.

Clouds of dust and smoke rose from the fires that had been set to destroy the dry grass and the remains of the harvest, the wooden farmhouses and storerooms of the *kolhoz*, entire villages, as well as smashed cars and tanks, together with buildings in the city that had been struck by the first bombardments of the Luftwaffe.

The Soviets reinforced the city with as many forces as they could muster, trying to maintain a single front with its centre in central Russia, outside of Moscow.

The German forces of General Heinz Guderian in the north was to cross the Desna River and then turn south, to the east of Kiev. The southern pincer, led by General Paul Ludwig Ewald von Kleist, was to disrupt the Russian front, cross the Dnieper at Kremenchuk, 150 kilometres southeast of the city, and advance north to meet Guderian's forces, cutting off the two railway tracks to the city and closing the pocket in an immense encirclement.

The Germans kept pressure focused on the city's defences frontally in order to draw attention away from the encircling manoeuvres. The exchange of fire was so intense that it was reminiscent of the great battles on the western front during World War I.

The unit of T-34/76 tanks led by Ivan Tolmides arrived by train at Kiev's central station. From the specially-built wagons, the tanks descended to the ground on ramps, started their engines and traversed the city, stopping at the outskirts, in the countryside, behind the line of defence.

One battalion with three squadrons, one with the new T-34/76[22] tank, and the other two with the older and lighter BT-5 and T-70 tanks.

Commissar Slusar, together with the commander, gathered the men and delivered a speech, complete with patriotic slogans, asking the men to fight bravely, to defend the country, the holy Russian land and communism, against the Nazis and the monstrous Hitler. The hour is difficult, but comrades, he told them, our country has survived many difficulties in the past as well. We have been attacked by the Mongols, Tatars, Teutonic knights, Poles, French, Germans, Turks and in the end, we have endured, we have been

---

[22] The T-34/76 tank with a 76.2mm tank gun and two 7.62mm machine guns was introduced in 1941 and was a shock to the Germans who did not know of its existence. With a frontal sloping hull (a world first), a weight of 26 tonnes, 60mm frontal armour, a crew of four men, a 500hp engine with an uppermost speed of 55 km, in 1941 it was the best tank in the world.

victorious. Remember Alexander Nevsky, Tsars Ivan III and IV, Peter the Great, Alexander Suvorov and Mihail Kutuzov![23]

Slusar was not convinced that his words had any effect on the men. How could he? It would be proved later, at the battle. But in any case, words of encouragement could only help.

Later, in a more relaxed atmosphere, while they were eating, he spoke individually to some of the men, trying to get to know them better. He did not pay any attention to Ivan Tolmides, nor did he give any sign of knowing him. No favouritism. Later, he hoped they would have a chance to talk in private. Three and a half years had gone by …

The crews climbed onto their tanks. The support unit of the infantry clambered on them, piling over the engine, behind the tank turret and caught hold of the handlebars.[24]

The engines groaned, leaving behind a trail of exhaust fumes of blue-black smoke.

They departed, traversing the antitank ditch over small bridges made of tree trunks and moved toward the German positions. The counterattack tactic was to push back the enemy that had approached dangerously close to the Soviet lines of defence.

Alerted, the German artillery began to fire. Black clouds of smoke rose, together with dirt and stones, wherever the shells fell and burst. The Russian infantry jumped from the exposed tanks, concealed themselves behind them and ran next to them toward the enemy trenches.

Explosions, flashes of light. Shrapnel, stones, dirt rattled on the hull of Tolmides' tank, blending with the howl of the engine.

---

[23] With the German invasion, Soviet propaganda began to make references to the glorious days of tsarist and earlier Russian history.

[24] This was a tactic that the Russians followed throughout the war. They did not transport their infantry in armoured vehicles, like the Germans and the allies, but atop tanks.

He peered through the periscope at the limited field of vision in front of him … the German positions ahead …

The tank shuddered, struck by an anti-tank round just below the machine gun on the hull. The bullet did not penetrate … where was that anti-tank weapon? The T-34 lurched over the rough terrain, its wide wheel tracks spewing dirt and dust behind it … The machine gunner at the hull fires at the German positions … where was that damned invisible anti-tank?

Glong! Like a pounding blow from an invisible supernatural hammer, another bullet struck, this time hitting the tank's turret, again without penetrating it.

Tolmides looked through the periscope, turning it … to survey what lay ahead, as the tank ploughed forward, lurching toward the German positions.

He could see the German trenches … There, a little toward the right, camouflaged by tree branches, approximately 200 metres away … the German 37mm anti-tank.[25]

'Stop!' Tolmides called out.

The tank stopped with a jolt, as if it had struck an obstacle.

Tolmides turned the turret to bring the cannon into position, peering through the periscope. Coming to a halt, the immobile tank was now in a stable position for firing. He stopped the turret and lowered the cannon slightly. A shot! The tank shuddered slightly as the round flew from the gun. The gunner opened the breech and the empty shell fell in the interior with a metallic sound. Smoke filled the interior, before escaping through the fume extractor.

The shell burst two metres in front of the anti-tank, sending shrapnel and dirt flying toward its protective shield. Slightly

---

[25] The main anti-tank of the German infantry, incapable of piercing the frontal armour of the T-34 tank.

adjusting his aim, Tolmides fired once again. The shell burst exactly behind the cannon, the shrapnel decimating the crew.

'Forward!' Tolmides shouted. 'Mihail, on it, level it!'

The driver stepped on the petrol pedal. The T-34 sprung forward again, closing the distance filled with smoke, dust and dirt as dozens of rounds from machine guns and guns struck the armour, in a cacophonous symphony.

The lower section of the hull encountered the shield of the anti-tank, crushing and passing over it and, with its tracks, grinding the already dead operator into pulp.

It forged forward, machine guns firing blanketing the ground behind them with empty shells. The German trench!

The T-34 did not stop. For a few seconds, the tracks were suspended in the air, before grasping by its rear side.[26]

'Stop,' Tolmides shouted and the tank stopped over the trench, with its outer front and back wheels over the tracks resting on either side of the trench, the others up in the air.

Tolmides turned the turret, bringing it diagonally vis-à-vis the hull. He lowered the gun as far as possible and shot one more explosive round into the trench. The Soviet infantry arrived behind them and jumped into the trench.

'Back out, Mihail,' Tolmides shouted to the driver. Mihail reversed the tracks and the T-34 turned back, leaving the trench.

Tolmides opened the hatch of the turret, carefully raising his head so that he could see better.

The commander's tank had raised a small flag, indicating a return to base for reformation and re-supplying.

* * * * *

---

[26] It was capable of passing over an obstacle (a trench) of 2.95 metres width. Unlike the German Panzers, they did not have a wireless.

The sirens sounded in Kiev, alerting the residents to proceed to shelters under buildings, and to the parks and streets where temporary pits had been dug out. The Luftwaffe was approaching.

Andromache called out to the children in her class, 'Children outside! To the shelter!'

As if it were a game, they had rehearsed many times for this moment. However, this time, it was not a game.

Andromache lifted her two-year old daughter Katerina. She had her always with her. After all, where could she leave her? The times were not normal; all the teachers who had children brought them to the school.

Led by their teachers, the children from all the classes ran to the courtyard and scrambled into the pits that had been dug there, two metres deep. The dirt that had been removed had been used to reinforce the sides, together with old furniture and bags filled with soil.

Andromache looked up to the sky. Katerina was quiet in her arms, silent.

All eyes were turned to the sky.

Hearts beat loudly. Children and teachers held each other tightly, as if trying to draw courage from one another …

Thunderous sounds. Anti-aircraft batteries opened fire, filling the sky with small puffs of black smoke from the explosions …

High above them they could discern small specks, the formations of fighter aircraft flying straight ahead, ignoring the barrage. They were flying overhead, but the bombs were intended for the railway stations and the bridges that spanned the river.

They could hear the faraway explosions.

The anti-aircraft fire grew fainter until it ceased.

The sirens were heard again, marking the end of the alarm.

Standing up, the teachers led the children out of the pits.

Andromache also rose.

Her breathing and her pounding heart returned to normal. She wiped the perspiration from her brow … Her mouth felt dry … She went to the water faucet in the courtyard and turned it on. Luckily, there was water. She gathered some in her hand, drank, and gave some to Katerina.

The other children and teachers drank as well.

'Comrade Director,' Andromache said to the director of the school, 'I think we should be careful. We have running water right now. But what if it is disrupted? If something happens to the network?'

'You're right,' he responded. 'Let's take our precautions and fill whatever we can - tubs, sinks, pails, bottles. Right now, all together.'

The director gathered the teachers and explained what had to be done.

Together with the children, they set to following his orders.

I wonder where Yiannis is. Is he safe? Alive?

'Dear Virgin Mary, keep him safe,' Andromache murmured to herself.

Sucking her thumb, Katerina looked up at her.

* * * * *

Slusar's unit headed northeast. German forces were advancing south toward the Desna River to Novgorod-Seversky and Shostka. They had to be prevented from crossing the river, the only large natural obstacle, before reaching the outskirts of Kiev.

The tanks ascended the ramps on the special train cars. They started toward Konotop, crossing the bridge over the Seym River, a tributary of the Desna. Fortunately, it was still untouched, and they arrived at Shostka. Nothing unexpected has occurred. The Luftwaffe and the Stukas were busy elsewhere. The expansiveness of Russia was an advantage as far as defence was concerned. The Luftwaffe could not be everywhere.

However, the German Panzers and motorised vehicles were fast and experienced. They were the first to arrive at Novgorod, surprising the Soviets and occupying the bridge over the river on the 24th of August. They were on the southern bank of the river.

The Soviets had to check their advance, to hold them back.

Slusar's unit descended from the train and began to travel northward, toward the river. The immense plain, almost flat, opened before them.

They positioned themselves inside and around the dwellings of a *kolhoz*, on a dirt road that led toward the south. Taking advantage of every cover, keeping close to the walls of the dwellings and barns, taking cover in shallow depressions in the ground and some small copses.

With the hatch open, the tank commanders searched the horizon, some with field glasses, waiting for the enemy.

Perspiration dripped from their foreheads, moistening their clothes. The heat was unbearable, almost tropical. The parched earth had cracked open, the harvested wheat had dried out.

On the horizon, the dust from the vehicles climbed upwards, like smoke.

They're coming!

Tolmides and the other commanders looked at the approaching dust …

In a short while they discerned the low silhouettes of the Panzers, dark grey masses which, covered in dust, had acquired shades of ochre …

They grew larger. They hadn't been seen yet.

Closer … closer.

He rotated the turret and aimed at one of the German Panzers, a Type 3, which he recognised from photographs.[27]

A little closer … a little closer.

The Soviet tanks opened fire. Black clouds rose from the Panzers. One stopped and began to burn, adding thick black smoke to the dust.

Tolmides fired.

A well-aimed shot. The Panzer stopped. The gunner opened the breech, the shell dropped. He placed a boring bullet, closed the breech block, and cried out 'ready' loudly so that he could be heard over the noise of the engine.

Tolmides fired again. The immobilised Panzer caught on fire.

The others stopped, searching for the concealed Soviet tanks. Unable to see the enemy, they fired without aiming. Bullets burst on walls and enclosures, piercing roofs, knocking down trees and branches. A barn full of straw caught fire, the flames spiralling upwards and the smoke mingling with the smoke of the explosions and the Panzers that were on fire.

The Panzers threw smoke bombs to conceal their retreat. Smoke and dust created a thick cover, making it more difficult to aim and to distinguish between friend and foe.

The commander of the unit called out an order: 'Forward! Pursue!'

The Soviet tanks left their hiding places and advanced forward in the smoke-filled atmosphere. The engines groaned and the smoke from the exhaust blended with the other smoke.

---

[27] The Panzer III, versions J and H, was the main German tank in 1941. It had a crew of five, weighed 23 tonnes, had a 50mm gun, a 300hp engine, and a maximum speed of 40 km/h on the road. It was inferior to the T-34. The German unit was the 3rd Panzer Division and had a standing bear as its emblem.

Tolmides tried to distinguish between friend and foe in the smoke-filled atmosphere. Uncontrolled, the tank bumped along over small obstacles, depressions in the ground and stones.

A Panzer, 300 metres ahead, slightly to the right, retreated in reverse, with its turret facing the Soviets.

Tolmides turned his turret, bringing it to a firing position. The German tank did the same, it had seen him …

Now!

The two cannons fired approximately simultaneously and both missed. Aiming at a moving target was difficult as the tanks lurched along on the uneven ground.[28]

The gunner fed a new round into the gun. 'Ready,' he yelled. Tolmides turned the turret, trying to keep the Panzer in his sights. The Panzer's cannon fired … the shell struck the tank frontally and ricocheted. Tolmides heard the clanging sound despite his ear plugs and the protective cover on his head.

He fired.

The shell struck and pierced the hull. The German tank proceeded to move, wavering, as if drunk … its cannon turned upward toward the sky.

The distance between them closed … less than 200 metres … the gun was ready … a firing shot. The Panzer stopped. Its black-clad crew abandoned it, falling to the ground, just before the tank began to burn.

The T-34 passed it.

Tolmides looked around him.

Smoke and dust.

---

[28] Unlike contemporary tanks, during World War II tanks did not have automatic stabilizing systems for aiming and shooting. Therefore, whenever it was possible, they preferred to use the cannons while in a stationary position.

The tanks in the plain were mingled in a disorderly way, the Soviet tanks advancing while the German tanks were retreating, then facing each other and exchanging fire, the Soviet tanks passing the Germans, the German tanks turning around and chasing the Soviets from the rear, amidst smoke and dust, leaving behind them damaged tanks, broken tracks, smoke …

Tolmides identified the commander's tank from the small flag that flew from the antenna of the wireless, the only tank that had a wireless. They advanced farther but the driver gave a warning signal that the fuel was running out! Consumption was greater on the uneven ground and when manoeuvring during the battle.

However, the commander gave no sign of retreating. Did he want to reach the river? Did he want to recapture the bridge? To destroy it?

The lead Soviet tank was struck by a German 88mm cannon. The Germans defending the bridge had 88mm cannons, still not in view, which were capable of piercing the armour of the T-34 from a distance of one kilometre. The Soviet tank stopped, beginning to smoke. Where were the cannons? A missile exploded next to Tolmides' tank, spewing dirt and dust. Tolmides felt a strange taste on his lips. Dirt. He spat.

He attempted to distinguish between friend and foe in the smoke and dust … Where were the cannons? He passed by a T-34 that was on fire, thick smoke spiralling upward … A little farther away, a Panzer, a shell without a turret. An internal explosion of artillery had hurled its turret far away and it lay upside down.

Tolmides saw the commander turning around. He was right. An attack against the unseen 88mm was sheer suicide.

Tolmides' tank turned around, returning to its original position. The Germans did not follow. They also needed a respite and to regroup.

The tanks reached their original positions. They turned off their engines to economise on fuel. When would new supplies arrive?

Would they arrive? What were the orders? Would reinforcements arrive? The infantry?

The commander of each tank reported to the commander of the unit: the situation with petrol, artillery … a calculation of their losses. There were only a few for the T-34s, some of which returned with damages, which the crews tried to repair as best they could. The lighter T-70 and BT-5 tanks suffered greater damage. But the Germans were held back … for the time being …

The crews had a chance to rest, to breathe clean air, drink some water from their canteens, to eat some tinned food. There was no hot food.

The commander attempted to communicate with headquarters to receive orders. Should he hold on to their positions as long as possible? Supplies were on their way. And an infantry to occupy the area and take over from them.

* * * * *

Afternoon.

The supplies had arrived. Two tankers with fuel, vehicles with cannons and provisions. And a unit of infantry, which began to dig trenches. The crews refuelled the tanks and loaded provisions and ammunition on them.

Specks appeared on the horizon.

A distant sound of engines that began to get louder.

Faces turned up toward the sky. Eyes peered through binoculars.

Judging from where they were coming, they must be German. Stukas!

The commander shouted out an order:

'Spread out! Find cover wherever you can! Stop refuelling!'

Tanks and vehicles scattered about, finding cover wherever they could, in depressions in the ground, buildings, clusters of trees. But the plain did not offer much suitable cover.

The Stukas arrived, circling around to reconnoitre, then began to dive, their sirens wailing. They aimed at their targets, dropping bombs. Rising from the dives, with open airbrakes, they regrouped a few hundred metres above the ground before beginning to ascend again.

Explosions, smoke, flashes of light. A bomb burst next to Tolmides' tank. The shock wave, together with stones and dirt, shook the tank like a whirlwind, but the armour was strong enough to endure the attack.

The Stukas flew away.

Tolmides opened the hatch of the turret, lifted his head and looked around. A storeroom at the *kolhoz* had caught fire, throwing a thick, spreading smoke that burned his eyes. A T-34 had overturned, struck by a bomb that had exploded almost next to it, creating a deep crater. One of the tankers was on fire, adding more smoke, and a repulsive smell from burning fuel and rubber … Two other lorries were destroyed, shapeless masses of steel flung around … Craters made by bombs that filled the air with more smoke.

The commander gave an order for the refuelling to continue from the tankers that had survived. Quickly! The Stukas might return. There were only two hours of daylight left. Quickly!

An explosion!

An artillery round.

The Germans had advanced their cannons, safely out of sight many kilometres away and had begun to fire.

The commander reported the situation over the wireless and received orders.

The unit was to advance a few kilometres, to a suitable spot chosen by the commander and to prepare for an attack. The infantry would hold the forward position.

The Germans were momentarily intercepted here, but then they advanced to other areas in the south … The situation was in total confusion … the 3rd and 4th Panzer units, the 10th and 29th motorised units detoured around Shostka, advanced toward Konotop and its railway hub.

* * * * *

Rumours ran wild in Kiev. The newspapers and radio gave their own, official information, but who believed them? The defence of their city would withstand. But what was going on elsewhere? Have you heard the news? The Germans are approaching Moscow! Stalin and the Party leadership, the government have abandoned the city and have fled behind the Urals! Nonsense! Comrade Stalin, Stavka, the government have remained in their places. They would never abandon Moscow!

The Germans and Finns were besieging Leningrad. The city had been blockaded, except for the supply line through Lake Ladoga. The Rumanians had laid siege to Odessa … The Germans had advanced farther behind Kiev, had reached Poltava, Dnipropetrovsk on the Dnieper River and were advancing toward Zaporizhia …

Nonsense, fake news, defeatism, spread by the enemy, their spies, the fifth column, to destroy our morale! We must gather our forces for the great counter offensive that will destroy the fascists! Don't believe the false rumours, denounce the enemies that spread them!

Andromache didn't know what to believe, not that it mattered. What mattered was survival, Katerina's, hers, the children from the school in her charge. What mattered was the everyday routine … The bombardment was still far away, but some bombs that missed their mark fell close by … A building had been struck and had collapsed to the ground not far from the school … The tram functioned only sporadically … Some roads close to the station were filled with craters, fallen bricks, plaster, wood, broken glass …

Like all the other teachers, Andromache had brought with her a few things from her room to town, to the school. She slept in one of the corridors of the school … Fortunately it was summer and hot … Many children had done the same … Circulation in the city was difficult and sometimes dangerous … You didn't know when bombs might miss their mark, when a building might collapse, when shrapnel or anti-aircraft shells might fall … death was falling from the skies.

Water would be turned off, then on again, they turned off … Fortunately, they had enough water. They wouldn't be thirsty … But insofar as cleanliness was concerned … this was a word they had forgotten. Impossible to wash oneself, wash clothes … there was not enough water for such luxuries. There was almost no soap. There was no privacy in order to bathe. Only a bit of soap and water for hands and face … Clothing stuck to bodies from perspiration and dirt. One could get used to the lack of cleanliness … What mattered was staying alive. She wondered if Yiannis was alive. Where was he? Would she ever see him again? Would he return? Would he take his daughter in his arms, would he dance her on his leg again?

The shops were almost empty … And to buy even the smallest thing, if you found it, if you were lucky, you had to wait for hours in a queue … Almost everything was rationed … Fortunately, at the school, they were assured of meals. Not enough to feel satisfied, but enough to survive, even if you were losing weight. There were rumours that the city was being evacuated. The few trains that came from the east, bringing supplies, went back filled with people and those of the wounded that could be moved. Priority was given to workers, together with machinery from factories that were being moved to the east, children, if there was space, those unable to fight, who, nevertheless, were extra mouths to feed in the city …

The director of the school informed them that he had received orders to evacuate the school. First, the children whose parents were not in the city and then the rest. The smaller children with their mothers, accompanied by their teachers, as well as Andromache. They could take with them only what was necessary, there was not enough space on the trains. The evacuation would take place in stages, from day to day, and they would be informed when it was their turn.

* * * * *

Tolmides' unit received the order to attack. The Germans were threatening Shostka from the east and had cut off the railway connection with Konotop.

The Soviet tanks started off, the hatches of the turrets open, the commanders' heads looking out.

Smoke and dust swirled upward as far as the eye could see. Only a dull sound of the engine was audible … but where was the central point of the German attack? They were following the railway track toward Konotop … abandoned villages, *kolhoz*, a few burned to the ground, but others still blazing … Emptiness. People had fled in any way they could and with whatever means available. Further to the east, the roads were full of people fleeing, with carts, mules, oxen, whatever herds have survived, plodding along on foot, their belongings piled onto carts, mattresses, clothes, pots and pans, small children, cages with chickens, leaving behind the debris of their march, broken wheels, carts, the carcasses of animals and bodies of people who had been unable to survive the heat or the hardship and who had no relatives to bury them.

Clouds of dust drifted upward, nearby. They were approaching! German Panzers! The commanders of the tanks closed and sealed the hatches, peering from the driver's periscopes.

They stopped, searching for cover. A level plain, good for distant battles, benefited the Soviets because the guns of the T-34 could penetrate the German armoured tanks before the German guns could pierce theirs … As long as they had not brought with them any 88mm cannons. And as long as the cursed Stukas did not arrive first!

The cloud of dust approached like a whirlwind.

Tolmides could see the German Panzers. He rotated the turret … aimed at a tank … a distance of 700 metres … But he wanted to let it come closer, to be sure … Had the Germans seen them? If not, they would see them very soon, even though the tanks were stationary and not raising any dust …

Tolmides' mouth was dry, he felt his tongue as being so swollen that it filled his mouth, perspiration was flowing from his brow.

500 metres.

He fired. A smell of cordite as the gunner opened the breech, allowing the shell to fall, placed a new bullet, closed the breech, and cried out 'Ready!'

The German Panzer had not stopped … the turret turned … aimed … smoke from the barrel, the shell struck the turret, to the right of the cannon. The armour was not damaged.

Tolmides made a slight correction … 400 metres! Fire!

He could see clearly the explosion at the centre of the Panzer's hull, between the seat of the driver and that of the gunner.

The Panzer shook and stopped.

The gunner reloaded the gun. Tolmides fired a second shot and hit his mark again. The Panzer caught fire, its crew jumped out, ran and fell to the ground and into a ditch.

The Panzers fanned out to flank the Soviets, to reach them sideways and strike the tanks on their sides, which were thinly armoured, and to strike from a shorter distance.

The battle became widespread, losing its cohesion. Every tank, German or Soviet, battled alone in the chaos of the battle, the smoke, dust, explosions, the limited view, the ruckus from the explosion, the noise of the engines, the screech of the tracks …

The atmosphere was suffocating … smoke from the cordite, fumes from the exhaust of the engines because the insulation and ventilation were faulty when the engines had to operate at full speed and the tank was closed. Perspiration, unbearable heat since the relentless summer sun burned the armour … The crew coughed; their throats were dry but there was no time for even a sip of water from their canteens.

Tolmides' eyes were glued to the driver's periscope. Where was the enemy? He tried to seek out their location through the smoke and dust … Where were the rest of the division's tanks? He could see nothing.

He ordered the driver to start off slowly toward the centre … He rotated the turret. A Panzer 300 metres away, straight ahead 30° to the right … It had stopped. It was on fire. The hatches were open and a thick black smoke was rising …

When he passed by it, the smoke thinned out somewhat. Another mass, another tank, green, half-burnt. A Soviet T-70 tank.

Where were the Germans?

A Panzer, approximately 800 metres to the left. Very far away. Tolmides turned the turret and cried out to the driver to change course. The tank hurtled over the terrain; he was unable keep the enemy in sight.

'Stop!' he called out to the driver.

The T-34 jolted to a stop.

Tolmides turned the turret. Suddenly it was struck on its side, nearly over the built-in periscope, by another, unseen, Panzer. The bullet did not go through, but the blow detached a few small fragments of steel from the armour of the turret which were flung into the interior. One of them hit the gunner in the arm, covering him in blood. The gunner screamed; his arm useless.

'Back!' Tolmides cried out.

With the two levers, Mihail reversed the tracks and the tank made a U-turn. Then, it turned toward the rear. What had happened to the German? He had lost him, like the other one that he had hit. With his heart beating loudly, he expected another shot … but it didn't come … The tank distanced itself at great speed. Tolmides took out a bandage, placed it on the gunner's wound and pressed on it to staunch the flow of blood. The gunner grimaced in pain.

Tolmides decided to open the hatch. It was almost impossible to see properly through the periscope.

Opening the hatch, he carefully lifted his head and looked around.

There was smoke and dust everywhere; however, there was no Panzer nearby. What happened to the Germans? Had they stopped? Had they passed them?

He ordered the driver to slow down. They had to economise on fuel. They had to return to the meeting point, the buildings of an abandoned *kolhoz* … If it was still in their hands … if there was anyone that they might come across.

They advanced slowly, carefully.

The *kolhoz* was in their hands. The tanks that had survived, some damaged, had arrived or were on their way. The crews emerged for a breath of air.

Tolmides jumped from the turret and checked the damage from the enemy shell. A dent almost the size of his fist. Nevertheless, the tank was still in fighting condition, the armour had not been pierced.

Slusar approached him.

'Has it been hit?'

Tolmides nodded.

'My gunner has been wounded, he's out.'

The commander gathered the crews. New orders. The Germans had passed them and were advancing toward Konotop.

Retreat toward there and engage with the German units, wherever they encountered them. Konotop was about 50 kilometres away … our men were still holding onto the banks of the Seym River. New supplies. Quickly. Whatever was left over, and could not be taken, had to be destroyed …

'Sergeant Tolmides, you will take over the command of the 3rd Squad. Its commander has been killed … for the time being you are promoted to sub-lieutenant.'

Orders? What orders? 'You will follow me toward Konotop. If we are separated, each tank and vehicle will meet at Konotop. Forward. Let's go.'

Slusar approached Tolmides.

'Since you no longer have a gunner, I'll replace him. In any case, now I have nothing else to do.'

Tolmides shrugged. He certainly needed a gunner … he climbed onto the turret and put out his hand to help Slusar climb up.

They entered the turret.

The tanks and vehicles accompanying them took the road southwards, returning to where they had come from.

War, Soviet Union, Southern Front, September 1941

The tanks of Tolmides' unit started off. Behind them, the buildings of the *kolhoz* and the tanks and vehicles that had been damaged and could not be repaired, were on fire, scuttled by their crews.

Tolmides and Slusar, like the crews of the other tanks, had raised their heads out of the turret for a clearer view, the hatch open in front of them forming a protective shield.

Smoke swirled around them.

They passed by the debris of battle, the burnt and destroyed tanks, Russian and German vehicles, the abandoned carts of civilians. Scattered around were people's belongings, open suitcases, clothes, mattresses, pots and pans, dead mules with their legs pointing to the sky, dead soldiers in various poses, on their stomachs, on their backs, some with their limbs shot off, others with no visible wounds, lying as if asleep … Clouds of flies swarmed around, sitting on wounds, contented flies that were getting fat from the war.

They passed a burnt-out BT-5. One crew member was hanging half in and half out of the turret. A charred corpse. Two others were lying on the ground …

Tolmides took a fleeting look … He was used to it, insofar as anyone can get used to such images … they no longer affected him very much … One got used to the harshness, the horror, the stench, one got used to slowly losing one's humanity and being transformed into something else. To what? An animal? A monster? Something sub-human? A person who shed the thin cover of civilisation and became primitive, a hunter, persecutor … What was it that they called humanity? Did it ever exist? Who was I before the war, just a few weeks ago? Who have I become? What am I capable of doing, not doing? Who is the person next to me, Slusar, the commissar? Why did he become an agent of the GPU? Is there any love left in me? Yes, there is … even though, in the battle, he had not thought of Andromache or Katerina for even a minute … Were they alright? Were they alive? Yes, they had to be alive, my God, they have to be alive! Anyway, Kiev had not fallen … Where could they be now?

'Have you learnt anything about the citizens of Kiev? Will they be evacuated?' he asked Slusar.

'Yes,' he replied. 'That's the information I received the last time I communicated with headquarters in Kiev. Is that where your wife and daughter are?' A question and ascertainment at the same time.

'Yes, Comrade Commissar. My wife teaches at the school.'

'I know … let's forget about calling me Comrade Commissar … I'm a member of your crew now. Valentin, call me Valentin.'

'As you wish … are you married, Valentin?'

'No Ivan … I'm married to the service,' he said with a half-smile.

'But marriage is not forbidden, isn't that so?' Tolmides smiled.

'Of course not! We might be devoted to the Party and to the Service but we're not monks!'

'So, you don't exclude marriage?'

'No. If there's an opportunity … Perhaps after the war. I think that things will change after the war … when we win …'

'Do you believe that? That we'll win?'

'I believe it, Ivan. Truly! Not as a commissar, but as a Russian. Else, what are we fighting for? We were attacked. We're fighting for our homeland above all, as we have always fought when we have been attacked, as Russians … not just for the Party, for communism. I am telling you this as a commissar, and I believe it.'

'How did you become a member of the GPU?'

'Oh, my parents were revolutionaries. Party members … they both fought in the revolution in the Red Army. My father died in 1936. My mother is still alive, she's in Moscow … I became a party member at an early age … a member of the Komsomol … Frunze Military Academy … but instead of becoming a career officer, I was chosen for the GPU … we went through difficult hours, days … you know all about it. But we survived. That's what counts. We survived.'

'And we will survive now?'

'Isn't that what every good soldier must do? To survive and fight again, until the last battle? A dead hero is good, but victory is gained by the living, heroes or not.'

'Strange words for a commissar,' Tolmides said with a smile.

'For a strange, unconventional commissar, I know,' Slusar replied in the same tone.

'I know. We have gone through a lot together. You helped me … you helped us. I will never forget it.'

'It's mutual, Ivan. We have a different relationship … certain invisible bonds that connect us … I won't forget this.'

'Nor I.'

Tolmides noticed an aircraft coming toward them, flying relatively low. He pointed it out to Slusar.

They hadn't seen any Soviet airplanes for days … the Luftwaffe ruled the skies. It must be German. But since there was only one, it must be reconnoitring.

He watched it growing larger as it approached them and gained height. He recognised it by its wide wings that were fixed to the pilot's window, high, and the stable, thin landing system. It was a "Stork".[29]

The Stork circled over them. It would alert the Germans. Then it took off.

The Soviet convoy advanced carefully. The Germans might be waiting for them, but where? In some depression in the ground? In that empty village? Under a small cluster of trees? Along the banks of a small stream? From where would the deathly strike come, unseen - from a Panzer or from an anti-tank?

They heard an explosion behind them. A shot from an anti-tank that had missed … More explosions. A T-70 was wrapped in flames. Where were the Germans? Tolmides looked ahead of him, searching … explosions around them … A blow on the hull to the right of the machine gun. A loud clanging sound, but the shot did not penetrate … Where was the anti-tank that shot at them? Unseen, but there, about 500 metres away, a small grove with low vegetation.

'An explosive!' he shouted to Slusar who had descended into the interior of the turret.

He placed the round, closed the breech.

'Ready,' he shouted.

Tolmides descended and turned the turret.

Fire!

---

[29] The Fieseler Fi-156 Storch, a single engine, two-seater reconnaissance and liaison aircraft that could land and take off in a very small and uneven area.

The shell burst among the branches, spreading debris, leaves and wood … the anti-tank fired again but missed … the shell only scraped the turret and was lost.

'Ready,' Slusar shouted.

Tolmides fired once again. The round exploded low among the vegetation.

The anti-tank responded. Would it succeed or miss? It struck the left track, damaging it. The tank's momentum forced the track at the rear of the tank to unwind, leaving the rear toothed wheel spinning. The tank ground to a halt.

Tolmides had seen the smoke from the round from the anti-tank. He rotated the turret, the engine working normally, feeding the electrical system of the turret. He aimed and fired.

The round exploded on a tree trunk behind the anti-tank, tossing leaves, branches and debris around. Two men fell, the other two tried to run away.

Yuri, the gunner, fired a burst with the machine gun. The two fleeing Germans fell to the ground.

German Panzers appeared suddenly from their cover, their guns firing and the Soviets responded. The battle spread, the dust from the tracks mixing with the smoke from the fumes, the smoke bombs which the Panzers threw to conceal themselves, and the smoke from the explosions.

Tolmides ordered the crew to abandon the tank. Immobile, it was now an easy target.

They jumped down, running and coughing from the fumes. They fell into a small gulley where some small, bushes were growing.

They tried to blend with the earth, their hands covering their ears protectively. The sounds of the battle were deafening.

A Panzer passed by about 20 metres from their hiding place, but the crew, preoccupied with the Soviet tanks, did not spot them.

The cloud of dust settled ... the sun approached the earth. Tolmides raised his head cautiously above the gully, behind a bush, and looked around.

He could see destroyed and immobile tanks and vehicles, some of which were still burning, enveloped in a thick smoke that rose high and then spread low over the battlefield caught by the breeze. Some tanks were smoking thinly, fires almost out or burning slowly. No sign of life ... only the debris of the battle.

Tolmides got to his feet and ran to inspect his tank. Aside from the broken track, it was untouched. The track could be repaired.

Tolmides called out to the crew and they started to work, taking out tool boxes and cylinders from those fixed to the back of the tank.

They raised the tank with the jack, gathered up the track, placed a connector from the spare track at the spot where the round had hit it, connected it and attached it to the cog wheel and tightened it. It was tiring work and the men were bathed in perspiration. They lowered the tank with the jack, released it and tightened the track a little more.

Mihail took his place, turned on the engine, tried the two levers for the tracks. The T-34 moved. Mihail stopped and the other three climbed aboard.

A brief rest, some water from their canteens, a bite of food.

Night was falling.

They had a meeting. What should they do?

They decided to follow the original orders and continue toward Konotop ... the tanks of the unit, those that had survived, must be heading in that direction, breaking through the German lines. Only there would they find provisions, if the town was still in Russian hands. There was no alternative. More German units were, without a doubt, coming from the north, tightening the encirclement.

What if Konotop had fallen … what if the bridges over the Seym had been destroyed or were in German hands … they preferred not to think about this.

It began to darken. The night provided them with cover. They moved slowly, without lights that would betray their location. With the help of a compass … south … the city was not more than 30 kilometres away. It was a clear night and the moon shed some light on the ground. Scattered across the horizon, they could see flames, some close by, others farther away, some faint, some strong. Villages and farms on fire, dry grass, copses, carts and vehicles that had been hit … They passed by the debris of a bombed-out Katyusha, an amorphous mass of aluminium and steel. What had happened to the crew? Had it survived or was it entombed in the debris?

They advanced slowly in the dark, as if they were touching the ground lightly. Tolmides and Slusar were seated on the upper section of the turret, looking around them, trying to seek out in the dark, some obstacle, a movement, danger. Tolmides glanced at his compass every now and then, giving directions to Mihail.

South.

The silhouettes of damaged tanks and vehicles looked strange in the dark. Dark, silent shapes, darker than the earth, as dark as some large bushes whose branches stirred softly in the air as if alive. A few dark and isolated trees as well as a cluster of trees, where danger may be lurking.

They reached a dirt road leading southward. The wooden power poles at either side of the road had been cut down. They took the road whose even surface made it easier for the tank, lessening fuel consumption. They were careful because others could be using the road. Germans or Russians. It was difficult to distinguish foe from friend or even to be recognised in the dark.

Slusar glanced occasionally toward the north.

'Ivan,' he said, 'look behind us.'

Tolmides turned his head.

About one kilometre away, maybe more, as it was difficult to judge the distance in the dark, he could see flashes of light. Covered lights of vehicles. Many. A convoy. To be coming from the north, with lights on, they must be Germans.

He looked around. He told Mihail to accelerate. The sound of the engine became louder, it could be heard clearly in the silence. But the Germans wouldn't be able to hear it because it was covered by the sounds of their own engines!

There!

About 50 metres away to the left of the road, Tolmides noticed a dark cluster of trees. A perfect hiding place in the dark.

'Mihail,' he said to the driver, 'leave the road and go under those trees.'

The tank turned off the road, reached the trees and took a position facing the road. Mihail put the tank in neutral without turning off the engine. It would need to feed the turret with electricity.

As the convoy approached them, they could see the lights and the vehicles. In front was a half-track 251 pulling an anti-tank.[30] About a dozen vehicles followed, among them a tanker, and another half-track at the end.

'What should we do?' Slusar whispered.

'We'll strike them,' Tolmides decided. 'We'll surprise them. Anyway, they don't have any tanks and they won't be able to position the anti-tanks in time.'

---

[30] The Sonderkraftfahrzeug 251 was the most widely used half-track, an armoured fighting vehicle. At the front were two regular wheels for steering. Behind, under the seats of the crew, were tracks. Lightly armoured, with an open top, it could transport ten soldiers, or supplies. It could also be equipped with various weapons, usually one machine gun, a short-barrelled 75mm cannon, a 50mm anti-tank, etc.

Slusar nodded. Tolmides was the tank's commander and had to make the decision. Despite his superior rank, Slusar quietly agreed. He was a soldier and it was his duty to fight.

Tolmides turned the turret slowly, bringing the half-track into focus and within aim.

'Explosive,' he said to Slusar.

For the light armour of the half-track he didn't need to use a piercing bullet.

One hundred metres. Tolmides fired.

The shot hit the motor and the two front wheels of the half-track. A flash of light blinded them for a few seconds. A thunderous roar. The half-track stopped, wrapped in flames. Soldiers jumped off from the back, ran and fell to the ground for cover. The vehicle in back couldn't stop in time and crashed into the flaming half-track. The driver backed up, stepped on the fuel pedal, and disengaged from it but crashed into the vehicle behind him which also stopped.

Yuri ran off a volley from the machine gun of the hull, strafing the convoy which was now lit by the flames of the half-track. Bullets ploughed into the first cars, motorcycles, and lorries. Germans jumped from lorries, some of them falling to the ground, wounded.

'Ready!' Slusar shouted, having loaded the cannon.

Tolmides turned the turret slightly, aimed and fired.

The round fell on the tanker with a tremendous flash of light. The fuel burst into flames, roaring like a dragon breathing fire. The darkness was lit by the flames. The remaining vehicles tried to leave the road in all directions, in an attempt to escape their unseen enemy. One came straight towards them, thinking that the trees would offer protection.

Yuri fired at it with the machine gun and the engine caught fire, the window shattering into pieces. The driver was killed and fell onto his steering wheel. The truck hit a large protruding rock and overturned with a loud crashing sound, hurling out crates filled with provisions. The fuel that had spilled caught on fire, further illuminating the night sky.

The surviving German vehicles switched off their lights and left, disappearing into the night. Only the half-track, the tanker and the first two lorries remained, burning brightly on the road.

Yuri stopped firing.

The night was illuminated by the flames. The men could smell the smoke of the burning fuel, rubber wheels and the stench of burning human flesh. Slusar grimaced. The crackling of the fire concealed the sound of the engine.

'Let's go,' ordered Tolmides. 'Let's move on.'

It was time to go. The flames could be seen from afar and other German units, suspicious now, might arrive to see what had happened. The survivors would certainly inform them of the ambush.

They were getting closer to Konotop.

The night was quiet. There were no sounds of battle. But in the dark they couldn't see if there were any Germans ahead of them. And even if they could, they would not be able to tell if they were friends and defenders of the city, or even if the city was still in the hands of the Soviets.

Tolmides gave an order to stop.

The city, dark of course, had to be about five or six kilometres away. The defenders' positions, on the outskirts of the city, were even closer.

Tolmides peered into the night through his binoculars. They needed some cover until daylight. Only then would he be able to assess the situation and decide what to do.

He noticed a depression in the ground with some vegetation around it. A good place to hide.

The tank moved slowly, descended into the hollow and stopped. Only the edge of the turret was visible, almost imperceptible in the dark.

They drank some water and had something to eat. Three hours to sunrise.

'Try to sleep,' Tolmides said to the crew. 'I'll keep watch.'

'No, I'll keep watch,' Slusar answered. 'As commander, you should be as rested as possible in the morning.'

Tolmides agreed, unwrapped his blanket and lay down on the ground next to the tank. He closed his eyes. The night was sweet, and the heat of the day had subsided. He looked at the night sky, the stars and the galaxy, so immense, so peaceful, so distant. Where were Andromache and Katerina? Perhaps under the same firmament but … so close … so far away …

Tiredness overcame him and he fell asleep.

He felt a hand touch him. He opened his eyes.

'The sun is rising,' Slusar told him.

Tolmides rose, rubbed his eyes, splashed some water from his canteen on his face …

Slusar offered him a cup of hot tea … How had he accomplished this small miracle? Where had he found firewood for a small fire? Mihail and Yuri also awakened and Slusar gave them some tea.

Tolmides raised his head cautiously over the hollow and looked around.

He could see temporary, isolated positions of German infantry. And …

Only 300 metres in front and toward the right, under a tree, an 88mm cannon. Its crew was preparing to fire. Fortunately, they were facing the city and the Germans had their backs turned to them.

Tolmides lowered his head and spoke quietly.

'In front of us there is an 88mm aimed at the city. This means that Konotop is still in our hands. Let's go. We'll take out the cannon before they notice us. Right afterwards, Mihail, we have to head toward the city at top speed.'

They climbed into the tank. Mihail turned on the engine. Now the Germans would hear them. But they wouldn't be able to turn their cannon around in time to strike.

The T-34 jumped out of the hollow like an unseen hunter from its hiding place, its engine groaning, its tracks hurling out dirt and dust from the rear. As it left the hollow, the front part looked up to the sky for few seconds like a submarine emerging from the sea, before climbing onto the bank of the hollow and falling to the ground with a thud. Mihail accelerated and the tank dashed toward the cannon.

Tolmides saw the crew turning their heads in surprise. They gestured and screamed. He could see their open mouths but couldn't hear their voices over the roar of the engine and the screech of the tracks.

He turned the turret, aimed and fired. From such a close distance, even though they were moving, he couldn't miss. The explosive round fell into the rear side of the cannon, in front of the breech. Fragments and debris flew around. Some of the crew fell, wounded. Yuri aimed in their direction and fired with the machine gun. Then they passed it by.

Mihail changed gears and accelerated. The tank lurched forward like a bolting horse, jumping over the uneven ground and leaving behind a thick cloud of smoke that escaped from the two exhaust pipes. The crew inside held onto whatever they could to steady themselves. The T-34 was extremely strong but its suspension was basic and when it moved over uneven ground, it was like riding a galloping horse.

German machine guns opened fire. Flashes of light and clouds of smoke swirled around the tank. Mihail manoeuvred ... from the driver's periscope he could see the Russian trenches at the outskirts of the town. A shell burst 10 metres to the left, tossing dirt and small stones on the tank, sounding like hailstones hitting the armour …

They reached the Soviet positions … they passed over a trench, moved forward and reached the first houses of the city. Some had been destroyed by the German shelling. Mihail reduced speed and took the tank behind a half-ruined house to seek cover from the Germans. He stopped.

Tolmides sighed heavily, as did Slusar. Their eyes met. They didn't have to speak. Their eyes expressed clearly what they were thinking. 'We made it. We escaped.'

The crew opened the hatch. Fresh air. They took deep breaths.

Two Soviet officers approached them.

'Where did you spring from?' the first one, a major, asked in a surprised voice.

'Valentin Slusar, commissar of the 33rd Tank Battalion … and this is Ivan Tolmides, commander of the 3rd Squad. Has information arrived regarding the unit?'

The major nodded and gave them orders as to where they would meet up with it.[31]

* * * * *

Andromache carried Katerina, supporting her on right arm and in her left hand she carried a small suitcase with some necessities. Katerina had her hands wrapped around her mother's neck. Andromache led the children from her class to the railway station. When they started out, they had taken the tram, which moved screeching and slowly on the rails. So many bombs had fallen around the railway station that the road was filled with

---

[31] The Germans eventually crossed the Seym River near Konotop on 7 September 1941.

craters and it was covered with so much debris from the destroyed buildings that neither the tram nor cars were able to pass through.

They could reach the station only on foot.

Andromache led the children who were holding hands and walking in a double file. They detoured around the craters and the ruins over which, at times, they had to climb.

Over there, the façade of a tall building that had collapsed, but the various floors remained untouched, revealing the flats … a small kitchen … a dining room … a few bedrooms with beds and chairs.

Farther away, a pile of bricks, stones, plaster, beams, glass. An overturned table, with three legs pointing to the sky. The fourth leg could be seen five metres away.

'Children, watch out for glass,' Andromache warned them from the top of the pile of debris, supervising the children as they clambered up and then climbed down the other side.

Farther on, two old women were bent over the debris, searching for something … What was it? Had they been they living in the building that had collapsed? Were they trying to salvage some of their belongings? Or were they searching for someone buried under the rubble?

A short distance beyond a crater was still smoking.

Nearer to the station, the crowd was thicker, people wanting to find a way to leave the city.

Two policemen blocked the way, directing them toward another street. In front of them was a large bomb that had not exploded, but was dangerous …

In one area on the side street, a clothesline had fallen, laundry still clinging to it, abandoned … two pairs of men's trousers, two women's skirts, some underclothes and socks. They stepped over them, trying not to tread on them. Elsewhere, a few discarded suitcases, one half-open.

They arrived at the railway station. Almost all the surrounding buildings had been bombed, as had the station. Craters at the platforms, half-fallen roofs and sheds. Destroyed train cars, some blackened by the smoke. An overturned steam engine, lying on its side.

'Stay close to me, children. Don't lose sight of me … don't get lost, hold hands,' Andromache said, opening a path in the crowd of civilians and wounded people that had to leave, soldiers and citizens loaded with provisions from the trains that had arrived.

The station was open. The rails had been repaired, the craters had been filled with earth and new rails had been laid wherever the older ones had been destroyed by bombs. Groups of soldiers and engineers as well as ordinary people worked day and night, without stopping, repairing, tireless as ants.

Andromache showed her papers to a police officer. He directed her to the platform for the train that would take them away.

They made their way through the crowds, Andromache cutting a path like an icebreaker. Arriving at the platform, Andromache showed her papers to an army officer who was overseeing the passenger train. Soldiers with guns pushed away anyone who tried to board without a pass.

The officer glanced at her papers, made sure that they were in good order and told the soldiers who were guarding the train to let her pass. Andromache supervised the children as they boarded the train and then climbed on after the last child. They squeezed themselves onto the seats. Andromache set Katerina down and counted the children. All there. She sat down as well.

The train started off with a lurch. It moved slowly at first and picked up speed as it left the station. It crossed the bridge over the Dnieper which was still unharmed. The Luftwaffe had not succeeded in destroying it. The train accelerated, black smoke curling upwards at times high, then low, small puffs entering the carriages, a smell of smoke and coal. Heat and perspiration

... uncomfortable seats ... But all the discomfort was nothing compared to the hope for salvation. The children rocked back and forth in their seats.

Andromache began to sing. After a brief hesitation, the children blended their voices with hers.

Labouring on its path, the train continued eastward toward Lubny, Myrhorod and Poltava. The road was still clear. Hopefully, it would remain clear, for a few more hours.

It was 150 kilometres to Lubny, about two and a half hours away under normal circumstances. But the circumstances were not normal. In a few places, the tracks had been severed by bombs and needed to be repaired as quickly as possible. Elsewhere, in some small, local stations, the train had to stop and enter a side track in order to allow a train carrying provisions for Kiev to pass.

Then, it started off again. The passengers rocked back and forth on the turns as if they were on a boat, riding the waves. Andromache doled out the few provisions that she had brought with them: some bread, some cheese. She kept some for later which they might need. There was no food on the train. But they might find something in Lubny ... when they arrived. If they arrived. If they arrived before the Germans ... There was information, rumours, that German tanks were approaching from the south and would cut the rail tracks ... But not yet. Proof of this were the trains that were coming to Kiev from the east.

Lulled by the rhythm of the train, most of the children fell asleep or dozed, their heads on their chests, some of them leaned on the backs of the seats, others leaned on the person next to them.

From the window, Andromache looked out at the monotonous plain with the small villages, the towns, the fields, some of which had already been harvested, others with stalks of corn, a deep yellow colour ... In the courtyard of a house in a small village, fruit trees and tall sunflowers with their yellow petals and black centres enjoyed the caress of the sun's rays. Far away, at various places along the horizon, smoke was rising …

Andromache closed her eyes, holding onto Katerina who was asleep with her head on her lap. She was exhausted. Sleep overtook her …

She awakened with a start. The train had slowed down, sliding for a little on the tracks and shaking before it came to a stop.

Andromache looked out. She couldn't see anything troubling. Why had they stopped? Another train? Damaged rails?

'Why have we stopped?' a child who had awakened, asked.

'I don't know,' Andromache answered.

Patience.

This was now the greatest, maybe the only virtue. And courage. Perhaps also faith, for those who believed in God, in a country that was officially atheist. And hope. Hope that they would reach Lubny, that they would find food and be able to pass through before the Germans encircled them. Hope that they would reach Myrhorod, Poltava, and farther away toward the east, toward safety … but where was it safe? Where would the Germans stop? Where was she to deliver the children? The orders had not been clear. Safely, in the east, they would be fetched. By whom? Where? When? And she, with her daughter, what were they to do afterwards? She remembered what Yiannis had told her when he saw her in August, when his unit had been in Kiev for two days, before leaving for the front: 'If the city is evacuated, try to go to Tbilisi. You'll be safe there. I don't think the Germans will go that far. I'll come to find you as soon as I can.' He had not added, 'if I survive.' But the thought crossed their minds as they said goodbye, when he held her tightly in his arms and she tried to hide her tears.

The train started again with a lurch, and then gained speed.

Five more hours to Lubny. It could have been worse. The train stopped at the station. It didn't appear to have been bombed. Not yet, at least. The Luftwaffe did not have enough aircraft to strike everywhere, Kiev, the bridges, to bomb groups of Soviet forces, in order to clear the road for the Panzers.

Andromache rose from her seat and told the children to wait. She sought out the sub-lieutenant who oversaw the train. She asked him how long they would be staying. He replied that they had stopped for coal and water for the steam engine. Perhaps half an hour … was there any food for the children? There was no food comrade, at least not on the train, not even for himself or his ten soldiers. Patience. They might find something at Myrhorod. Would she be able to find some food at the station? It was doubtful, but she could ask. But she should not go too far away or delay as the train might leave. Water? Yes, there should be water at the station. They might as well fill their canteens.

Andromache returned to the carriage, gathered all the canteens and took three children with her to the bathrooms at the station. They turned on the taps. There was water. They filled the canteens and returned to the carriage. She left the children and returned to the station and went outside.

She saw a middle-aged village woman holding a basket with peaches. Andromache approached her and asked the price. She bought them all. She gave a lot of money from what she had brought with her but what did it matter? Who knew when they would find food again? Where and when? She returned to the train and handed a peach to each child, keeping enough peaches for later. They ate greedily, skins and all, the juice running down their chins and cheeks, drops falling onto their clothes.

The train started to move. Myrhorod was close by, about 60 kilometres. A little over an hour. They arrived without any problems.

A stop. A small miracle. There were provisions, nothing special, only loaves of bread which the soldiers handed out to the passengers. It was not even fresh, but who cared? At least they had something to eat. Andromache approached with four children to help her. When it was her turn in the queue, she said to the person in charge:

'I am a teacher. The other children are on the rain.'

'How many are there?' he asked.

Without hesitating, she lied, 'Thirty.'

There were twenty children, but she hoped that the man wouldn't go to the train and count them. He didn't have time. And he wouldn't ask for her papers … there were so many people still waiting in the queue and the train would depart soon.

The man counted the loaves and gave them to her.

'Next,' he called out.

Andromache gave a sigh of relief. Together with the children who were carrying the bread she climbed onto the train. She handed out half the loaves … and saved the rest for another time.

The train started off. The next stop was Poltava on the Vorskla River, less than 100 kilometres away and then where to? Toward Kharkov? Behind the Donets River? Where was it safe? How far? How close? Andromache had no idea. Probably no one knew. It was a course toward the unknown … She might be able to learn something at the next station. Maybe they could help her … Until then, patience and courage. That's what counted. She had to save the children that had been entrusted to her, as if they were her own. And Katerina … Where was Yiannis now?

It was afternoon and the train travelled on with its familiar sounds.

They didn't hear the Stukas over the noise of the train's engine, only at the last minute did they hear the strident sirens as the aircraft began to dive.

The explosions were deafening when the bombs fall. The children cried out in fear.

'Hold on children,' Andromache shouted.

A bomb exploded on the rails, in front of the steam engine, bending them. Others burst next to the carriages in front, filling them with shrapnel. Fortunately, the carriage with the children was at the end of the train.

The engineer pulled the brake … The steam engine dragged, shrieking on the rails and throwing out sparks. There was not enough of a distance for the train to stop. The steam engine arrived at the twisted rails and derailed, falling to the left, throwing dirt and dust as it pulled the carriages, slowed down, leaning to the side and stopping.

The children screamed, grabbing hold of whatever they could find.

Andromache looked at each of them. Fortunately, no one had been badly hurt.

The carriage stopped, it was still on the rails, fortunately, it had not overturned.

The passengers crowded together and left the train. Andromache let them leave and then followed with the children.

'Stay close to me,' she told them, as they gathered around her, like chicks around their mother hen.

The passengers flocked around the train. Wounded people exited from the wagons in front. The Stukas had left and were not firing at the train.

But what was going to happen now?

Andromache found the sub-lieutenant who was surrounded by passengers. He was at a loss for words.

'I don't know,' he replied to their questions. 'A crane will have to come to lift the steam engine and an engineer is needed to repair the rails. I don't know if there is one in Myrhorod or Poltava, or how long it will take him to arrive.'

'What should we do?' someone in the crowd asked, the unspoken question on everyone's lips.

'I don't know,' the sub-lieutenant replied. 'It will be night soon. Spread yourselves around. The Stukas might return, and it's best if they don't see any targets.'

Andromache looked around her at the endless plain. The order sounded easy. 'Spread out'. But where? How far? How close?

She looked at the other passengers as they moved away in different directions, small groups of unarmed people, families, children, wounded soldiers who were able to walk, some of them supported by someone, others on crutches, some, more seriously wounded, carried on stretchers. About a kilometre away she could see a cluster of trees and bushes. It was far enough away should the Stukas return but close enough for them to board the train again when it was repaired.

'That's where we'll go,' she told the children and they started off.

They arrived. The ground under the trees was covered with leaves, soft as a mattress. They sat down, around her. She settled Katerina down next to her.

She gave the children some bread. One slice and one peach. Frugality. What would tomorrow bring? When would they find food again? Better to save some, even if it was only a small amount. She gave some bread to Katerina. There was no milk, which was more difficult to find than bread.

Nightfall. Fortunately, the temperature was still mild, not hot as in August, but balmy.

Andromache wanted to cheer up the children, before they went to sleep, to distract them from the frightening, inescapable, unknown present.

'Children, our next stop is Poltava. Who remembers what happened there?'

A boy raised his hand, as if he were in the classroom.

'Tsar Peter defeated the Swedes.'

'That's right Peter,' she answered with a smile. 'He defeated the Swedes who were led by Charles XII on 28 June 1709, opening the way for our country to become a great power. And what else did he do, Peter?'

A girl raised her hand.

'Yes, Anouchka.'

'He built St. Petersburg, in order to have a port on the Baltic Sea. We now call it Leningrad, in honour of our great leader of the revolution.'

'Correct,' Andromache answered. 'I'll tell you the history now. And then, it's time for sleep.'

Andromache began to relate the story and soon, the children's eyes began to get heavy and closed. They lay on the ground, close to one another with Andromache in the middle.

* * * * *

The Germans advanced. The Soviets defended themselves only sporadically, they had lost their military equilibrium. A sense of confusion pervaded as they were not certain of the objectives of the Germans. They sensed the danger, like trapped animals, but didn't know how to respond. The Germans captured the Seym River at Konotop and proceeded south toward Romny, on the southernmost tributary of the Dnieper, the Sula River.

The Germans advanced from the north, led by the 3rd Panzer Division under General Model which separated the Soviet forces of General Kirponos at the southern front at Kiev from those of General Eremenko at the northern front at Bryansk. A dangerous gap had been created and the German forces entered like water that finds a way to flow unhindered.

General Kirponos ordered the 21st Regiment to counterattack from the south against the Panzers so as to reconnect the two fronts. The attack began on 2 September.

Slusar and Tolmides didn't have a clear idea of what was going on and neither did the lesser commanders, nor any other Soviet commander, nor Marshall Boris Shaposhnikov, the Chief of Staff, nor the Stavka, not even Stalin. Information had been confusing and had arrived too late … it was the same with the orders.

What everyone in the unit knew was that they had to try to push back the German Panzers and tracked vehicles and to reconnect with the front at Bryansk.[32] They grouped all the remaining tanks, which were to lead the attacks, in front of the infantry.

They started off slowly, soldiers clinging to the rear end of the turrets so that the rest could follow on foot. The Soviet artillery fired on the German positions which could not be seen clearly … nor did they know exactly what they would be faced with, and where … Infantry and anti-tanks? Panzers? Tracked vehicles? All of these?

The Germans ruled the skies. The Soviet reconnaissance aircraft didn't fly, and when one dared to do so, it was immediately shot down. The attack was carried out almost blindly.

However, the Germans could see because their reconnaissance aircraft flew unobstructed and could aim at the Soviet counterattack … Nevertheless, in the immense plain, without enough cover, the clouds of dust raised by the tracked vehicles could be seen from afar.

Heavy German artillery began to fire. Flashes of light were seen and columns of smoke rose among the tanks and the infantry. Soldiers fell, some wounded, incapable of holding onto the handlebars of the turrets. The tanks didn't stop, they had no time, nor could they gather the wounded. Onward!

Before they could reach the German positions, the Stukas appeared and began to dive, their sirens screeching. Bombs fell on the infantry, large bombs from the bellies of the Stukas and smaller ones from under the wings.

---

[32] The Soviet "fronts" consisted of army groups, which corresponded to the German (Army Group) even though the Soviet groups were smaller than the German ones.

Streams of smoke, dirt, dust, shrapnel. A bomb struck a T-34 behind its turret, over the engine. The tank disappeared in a huge explosion as blazing fragments of the bomb entered the interior and set the ammunition on fire. It was so powerful that the turret was blown high, soaring a few metres before falling to the ground, far from the hull of the flame-wrapped tank.

The Stukas dove again, striking at the infantry, which fanned out, fell to the ground, trying to find shelter wherever it could. The infantry couldn't be protected from the Stukas. The Soviet anti-aircraft remained behind …

Tolmides' tank approached the German positions, which were temporary, machine guns scattered everywhere, anti-tanks, mortars, which nevertheless, together, formed a deadly wall of fire. Russian soldiers fell to the ground, others tried to find cover.

Through the driver's periscope, Tolmides could see a German machine gun in a makeshift trench. He called out the position to Mihail, the tank advanced quickly toward the machine gun which started to fire. The bullets that stuck the armour sounded like pebbles or hailstones. Yuri fired, raising a cloud of dust in front of the ditch. The Germans lowered their heads.

The tank passed over the ditch, the right track crushed the machine gun and continued on its way … Attack! Forward! Were the others following? The infantry? There was no way for Tolmides to be certain. He looked ahead. The enemy was in front of them. Danger! From an enemy he could not see. It was like a cowboy movie: the one to pull out his revolver first and shoot was the one that would survive and the second one, the slower one, would die. The orders were clear, as far as they could be in the general confusion. Charge! Stop the Germans! Recondition your conscience to think of the front at Bryansk!

Tolmides didn't notice the 88mm cannon, which was atop a small rise in the ground, a kilometre away. The projectile hit the tank at the centre of the hull, between the seats of the driver and the gunner. It pierced through the armour, filling the interior with fragments. Yuri was struck in the heart and instantly killed. Another, a larger one, blocked the rotating mechanism of the turret.

The tank was still moving but was badly damaged. A few damaged cables were smoking and sending out sparks. Slusar reacted instinctively, grabbed the fire extinguisher and directed the foam toward the sparks. They died out. A smell of foam, smoke, perspiration, blood. Tolmides started to cough and tried to clear his throat … Slusar bent over Yuri whose head had fallen on the handle of his machine gun. He confirmed that the gunner was dead.

Tolmides lifted the hatch. Despite the danger, he had to have a clear view. With the turret closed and without it being able to rotate, he was sightless.

The clamour of the battle continued, pummelling his ears, despite his earplugs. He raised his head cautiously.

The second projectile of the cannon hit the tank slightly to the right of the first strike, piercing through the armour again as shrapnel, various accessories and fragments flew about in the interior, hitting the walls, slicing through cables, some almost reaching the engine … a fuel supply line was punctured, fuel leaked out and caught fire from the flaming debris.

Slusar screamed and groaned. Shrapnel had crushed his ankle. The interior filled with smoke. The engine was on fire … losing power … The tank careened on an erratic course … slowed down … stopped.

'Abandon the tank!' Tolmides cried out. 'Mihail, help me!'

He exited first from the turret and stepped onto the grate of the engine which was beginning to burn from the heat. He could feel the heat through his boots. He grasped the semi-conscious Slusar by the arms and pulled him out while Mihail helped from below.

Mihail exited the turret and jumped to the ground. He lifted his arms and grabbed Slusar as Tolmides lowered him as gently as he could. Then Tolmides jumped to the ground. They each put one of Slusar's arms around their necks, holding him up and ran away as fast as they could.

Nearby, a solitary tree and a shallow depression in the ground. When they reached it, they fell to the ground, panting. Slusar, pale, groaned. Tolmides and Mihail bent over him. They saw the wound, bleeding heavily, in the lower part of the boot.

'We have to take it off,' Tolmides said to Mihail. 'Hold him.'

Mihail held Slusar in his arms. Tolmides pulled the boot as gently as he could. Slusar groaned. His eyes were half-closed. The boot came off. Blood. His sock was drenched in blood, it was wet and stuck to Tolmides' palm. When he removed the sock, Tolmides saw the deep wound, which was still bleeding. He took some gauze from his pocket and placed it over the open wound, then pressed down hard to staunch the flow of blood. He removed Slusar's belt which he used as a tourniquet. He had to clean and disinfect the wound. But with what? The first aid box had been left in the tank; they hadn't had time to take it with them.

The tank was on fire.

Thick smoke was curling above it, at times thick, at other times like a veil being dragged along the ground. It reached their hide-out, filling their nostrils and lungs. They coughed drily.

Carefully, Tolmides rose and looked around.

Smoke from burning tanks.

None were moving. Not even one Russian soldier could be seen. But the Germans were also invisible. Perhaps they had passed their own first line and were in a "no man's land" between the German positions and those to the rear, the artillery.

The sounds of battle continued, cannons, flashes of light, explosions, the incessant rattle of machine guns, some close by, some farther away. But he saw no one moving. Anyone who might have been out there was hiding.

'We have to move away from here,' he said to Mihail. 'The ammunition might explode any second now.'

He noticed another cluster of trees, approximately 100 metres away, and a shallow gully leading in that direction. If they could drag themselves, they might be able to make it without being seen.

They started off, dragging Slusar by his flak jacket.[33]

---

[33] The Germans laid siege to Romney between 10 and 12 September 1941. The two German pincers, one led by Colonel-General Heinz Guderian in the north and the other by Field Marshall Ewald von Kleist in the south, met on 14 September in Lokhvytsia, nearly half way between Romny and Lubny, closing the encirclement. The battle of Kiev ended with the surrender of the encircled Soviets on 24 September. The Soviet losses in the encirclement came to 685,212 prisoners, 824 tanks and 3,436 artillery, without counting the dead and wounded. It was the largest encirclement in the history of warfare. General Kirponos was killed. Commander Semyon Budyonny of the Southwestern Front, who confronted von Kleist, was replaced by Commander Semyon Timoshenko. Until the end of 1941, the Soviet Army suffered a total of two to three million deaths. After the fall of Kiev, the group of General von Roques, undertook the security behind the front lines with three German "safety battalions", one Slovak and five Hungarian brigades. One of their first campaigns was to round up all the Jews of Kiev at Babi Yar and to massacre them on the spot. By comparison, at Stalingrad, the Soviets imprisoned 90,000 Germans of the 6th Army.

CHAPTER 5

Escape, Soviet Union, Southern Front, September 1941

Break of dawn.

Andromache woke up, rubbed her eyes, and rose. The children and her daughter were still asleep. That was good. They needed energy. They had to be as rested as possible.

Looking toward the train, all seemed the same.

She saw a few people that had awakened.

She walked toward them and asked for the sub-lieutenant. When she found him, she asked for news.

'Last night I sent two soldiers to the next railway station. There was a telephone and they spoke to Poltava. They will try to send a crane and a crew to repair the rails. And a new steam engine if they can find one that is available.'

'When?'

'When? Unknown. There aren't many means. The same with the steam engines, many of which have been destroyed by the Stukas. I don't know,' he answered, shrugging in despair.

'What shall we do?'

'I really don't know,' he replied. 'I haven't received any instructions regarding you and the children. The situation is vague.'

'The Germans?' someone asked, from the crowd that had gathered around him.

'We don't know exactly but it seems that they have crossed the Dnieper at Kremenchug and are approaching from the south. When they'll reach us, if they reach us, if we push them back, no one knows.'[34]

'What shall we do?' Andromache asked.

The sub-lieutenant shrugged, his familiar gesture of despair.

'Whatever you want, whatever you think. We're obliged to remain here to guard the train. You ... maybe you should go on foot to Poltava. It's about 30 to 35 kilometres from here. Follow the tracks of the railway. A short distance away,' pointing out the direction with this hand, 'is the main road, Kiev to Poltava. You can take that road ... If they send us a train, you can board it. You'll see it coming ... by the smoke of the engine.'

'And if not?' Andromache asked.

'If not, you'll have to continue on foot. It's only 30 to 35 kilometres. It's a day's journey,' repeats the sub-lieutenant.

---

[34] The Soviet losses in steam engines and train cars, primarily from attacks by the Luftwaffe, were great, leading to severe shortages. For re-supplying, the Soviets increasingly were obliged to use carts pulled by animals. The Germans crossed the Dnieper at Kremenchug on 8 September. They destroyed the railway tracks between Myrhorod and Lubny on 13 September and seized Myrhorod on 17 September, arriving on the same day at the outskirts of Poltava.

'I'm accompanying children, not soldiers,' Andromache replied.

'Comrade, I'm sorry, but what can I do? It doesn't depend on me. It's your decision, either you walk, or you wait ...'

Andromache thought about it. Either they walk or wait. For what? A train? A miracle? The Germans?

'Is there any food?' she asked.

The sub-lieutenant gave a tired smile.

'Yes, comrade. The train is full. From blini to caviar. Where are you living? There is nothing. But you might find something on the road. There are *kolhoz* ... villages ...'

Andromache returned to the children. They were already awake. She had decided that they would walk. Even if it would be slow. It was better than waiting for a train that might never arrive or waiting for the Germans.

'Children, let's go' she said, pretending to be unconcerned and cheerful. 'It's a beautiful day and it's not very hot. It'll be like an adventure. We'll take the road. Stay together and close to me.'

Taking her daughter in her arms, Andromache and the children begin to walk. Toward Poltava. Toward the unknown. Toward salvation?

They walked across fields that had been harvested and found the main road.

It was crowded with people, civilians who had left their homes in the nearby villages and towns, even from cities farther away. Maybe even farther than that, maybe from Kiev. To save themselves from the bombings. From the Germans. Moreover, orders had been given. They must leave nothing useful behind for the invaders. Neither buildings, nor food, nor animals and, if possible, no people.

They travelled on, most of them on foot, carrying whatever they could, the most important, and whatever they considered to be the most valuable. They travelled with wagons and carts pulled by animals, oxen, mules, a few horses (most had been requisitioned by the army) and even a few camels … where had they come from? The carts and wagons were filled with a disorderly array of belongings: mattresses, blankets, suitcases, baskets, cages with chickens and geese, children and old people. In a few one could see furniture. In another, was it possible? A piano! Among the people and the carts, there were herds of animals, a few cows, goats, sheep, a cacophony of bleating, snarling, cackling, mooing.

A human river winding towards the east. But where in the east? No one knew. They might find some news at the next village, if someone was there who could tell them … otherwise, they would try at the next village. Otherwise at Poltava … maybe …

Andromache noticed a small opening in the crowd and passed through with the children.

'Stay close to me,' she repeated. 'Take each other's hand. We mustn't get lost.'

In front of them there was a cart driven by an old man and an old woman. Behind them was a middle-aged man with a few goats, about a dozen …

Andromache approached and asked: 'Do you have any food? Milk for my daughter and the other children?'

They had eaten the last of their food the night before.

The man looked at her indifferently.

'I can pay you,' she added.

'With what? Roubles? I don't want any. They might be worthless soon …'

Andromache took a moment to think. If not with roubles, then how? What could she give him that was of value?

Her ring, an heirloom of engraved gold with an amethyst that her mother had brought with her from Asia Minor. How could she part with it? She wouldn't give her wedding band. But neither she nor Katerina nor the children had eaten anything since last night

… and she didn't know when they would find food … how could they walk for more than 30 kilometres without food?

She decided.

She took off the ring and offered it to the villager.

He took it, examined it and nodded. The negotiations began and they came to an agreement. A few litres of milk, a head of dry cheese, four loaves of bread. He lowered them from the cart, all for a gold ring with an amethyst. But this little food, expensive, would give them some energy to carry onwards until they arrived, but where to? At least to Poltava.

Andromache and the children left the road, sat on the ground and she gave them some bread, sliced some cheese with a knife that she had brought with her, and gave them some milk from two metal cups. Frugally. She poured the remaining milk in some canteens that the children had brought with them. The food must last them all day … in the hope that later, somewhere (where?) they would find more. Or, the train might come.

But what was coming now, on the other side of the road from the east, was a Soviet unit going to the front. Infantry walking in two lines. Two vehicles that were pulling anti-tank cannons. Three carts with provisions, pulled by horses.

The officers walked ahead, trying to open a path between the refugees, like two opposing currents, fighting and colliding. Not at all easy. The civilians separated slowly, some crowded on one side of the road, others going into the fields. The convoy advanced, parallel to, but in the opposite direction of the people.

A droning sound was heard in the sky. Uneasy heads turned up toward the sky, uneasy eyes searched for the location of the sound. Specks. Black dots which meant aircraft … Probably German.

The officers shouted out orders. 'Spread out! Hide! In the fields! Far from the road!'

The soldiers obeyed, left the road and ran to the fields, falling face down on the ground. The civilians stood somewhat hesitant, without orders, not knowing what to do, and then many fled toward the fields on the other side of the road.

Andromache shouted to the children.

'Down! Fall to the ground!'

She lay down, protecting her daughter with her body. Frightened, Katerina began to cry.

The sobbing and the pandemonium of human voices and animals was concealed by the hair-raising shriek of the sirens of the Stukas which began to dive.

They dropped bombs from their bellies and wings. One Stuka was so close that Andromache could clearly see the bomb, green in colour, as it detached and fell to the ground. It exploded with a deafening noise next to one of the army vehicles.

The sound waves struck her ears like a blow, even though she had covered them with her hands. The children screamed, but fortunately, no one had gotten up … the shrapnel from the bomb had not reached them … More explosions on the road. Andromache felt something tickling her nose. She grabbed it with her fingers. A stalk of dry hay. How did it come here? She raised her head. The cart that was struck was carrying hay for the horses of the army. The bomb had tossed the hay in the air and now it was returning to the earth like a light, blonde rain.

The Stukas dropped their bombs. Two lorries were on fire and a thick column of smoke rose from them. But they still had their machine guns. They attacked again, not vertically and their machine guns rattled. The volley bursts struck the ground, scattering dust and dirt on the soldiers. Some volleys burst farther away, in the direction of the civilians, on the other side of the road.

Lying face down on the ground, Andromache could feel her heart leap, as if it wanted to escape, to fly out of her body. She felt so helpless when death was falling from the sky …

The Stukas dove again, dropping bombs. Andromache heard the strident sound over the noise of the engines. This was the sound of death, in 1941 Ukraine, for many: the drone of engines and the rattle of machine guns …

The Stukas rose, gained height, levelled off and left.

Deep sighs of relief. She could hear voices, groans, commands. She raised her head. Yes, the Stukas were gone. Yes, they had survived. All of them, she, her daughter, the children. Frightened, shocked, but alive, unhurt.

She gathered the children close to her and said firmly: 'Children, we will walk through the fields.'

Not on the road. It was too dangerous and attracted the attention of the Stukas. They were lucky this time, but they might not be so the next time. Under normal conditions, walking through the fields would have slowed them down, but with the road full of people, it was probably the best option now.

'Children stay close to me,' she told them as they walked parallel to the road, but about one kilometre away from it. Fortunately, it was not as hot as it was in July and August, the sun did not burn as much now, but it was warm enough to make them perspire, the sweat on their foreheads drippping to their eyebrows.

'We must be sparing with the water,' Andromache told the children. 'We don't know when we'll find more.'

They walked at a steady pace, synchronising themselves with the steps of the slower children. Fortunately, the ground was level and it was not difficult … later, they would rest under some shade … And, at the next village or *kolhoz*, they would ask for some water and food …

They were now walking through a field of corn that had been harvested. The pale yellow, dry stalks came up to her chest, up to the necks of the children. She wondered if there was any corn for them.

A droning sound in the sky. Uneasy, Andromache and the children looked up to the sky … Aircraft. Stukas?

No.

Two aircraft approached at great speed.

In front, a Russian Rata. Behind it, a German Me-109. The Soviet pilot attempted to manoeuvre away from the German who was more experienced and had a better aircraft. The German pilot fired a volley of blasts. Shrapnel struck the hull and the right wing of the Rata. The aircraft shook and caught fire, lost altitude and dove to the ground. From the height at which they flew, only 300 metres, the pilot, even if still alive, did not have time to jump with his parachute. The Rata hit the ground with a loud explosion, a ball of fire.

Major Günther Lützow flew over the burning Rata. Another certain victory. He had almost 100 victories and hoped to be the second German ace who would attain them. But what was that in the fields, a little farther away from the wreckage of the Rata? Was it possible? A woman surrounded by children? What were they doing there?

Lützow flew over them, circling around at a height of just 200 metres. He raised his right hand to his head in a gesture of greeting, holding on to the steering wheel with his left hand.

Andromache could see clearly the German raising his hand … Was he going to hit them? No, he wasn't! He was only greeting them. A German, who was only greeting them! Spontaneously, Andromache lifted her right hand and waved in return. The aircraft flew away.[35]

---

[35] Günther Lützow was the wing commander (*Geschwaderkommodore*) of the 8th Fighter Wing (*Jagdgeschwader*), who, together with the 77th Fighter Wing, flew over the southern front. On 25 October 1941 he became the second pilot in history, after Werner Mölders, to achieve 100 air victories. "Rata" (rat) was the nickname the Germans gave to the Russian Polikarpov I-16 (version 24), which was the most numerous of Russian fighter aircraft at the time. It had a 100hp engine, a speed of 326mph on the surface of the sea and 286mph at a height of 14,763 feet and could reach a height of 29,530 feet. It had two 20mm cannons and two 7.7mm machine guns. The German

But not the danger.

She could hear the crackling of fire. Smoke … The explosion of the Rata had set the dry corn on fire and the flames were coming toward them. Andromache realised that they were in danger.

'Quickly children. Run! We have to leave the field!'

They ran toward the opposite end of the flames, toward an area where there was no more corn. The fire raced after them, chasing them. Smoke filled their nostrils and throats as if from a dragon's breath. They coughed and choked. They ran. They stumbled. They ran.

The burning breath of the fire was at their backs … They ran … stumbled … ran… panting … Andromache carried her daughter in her arms.

They gained ground, left the cornfield behind and fell onto the bare ground far from the corn. They coughed and took deep breaths.

Andromache counted the children.

One was missing.

'Where is Sofia?' she asked.

She had been running with them but now she wasn't there. No one had seen her. She had been left behind … in the cornfield.

Andromache left Katerina on the ground.

'Anouchka take care of her', she said to one of the girls and ran to the cornfield, against the fire, now a new enemy. She was not going to leave Sofia behind. 'God, please help me!'

Her lungs filled with smoke, her eyes smarted, she coughed. Running, she tried to peer through the smoke. In some places, the

---

fighter aircraft, Messerchmitt Bf-109 (especially the F-3) was used by all the squadrons of the Luftwaffe in 1941. It had a Daimler-Benz engine of 1300hp with a top speed of 390mph at 22,000 feet, ascending speed of 3,320 fps at a height of 5,000 feet, top height of 37,000 feet. It had a 15mm cannon and two 7.9mm machine guns, all in the nozzle (see William Green).

flames had advanced, leaving ash behind. She could feel the heat on the soles of her feet, despite her shoes. Where was Sofia? Wasn't it through here that they were running?

Through the smoke she noticed a form on the ground. She ran, bent over the form and lifted it. Sofia had fainted. She gathered the child in her arms and ran from the field, toward salvation. It was a race for their lives against the flames and the smoke. A race against death, a race for life. Who would win? She ran as she had never run before … Where had she found such strength … such perseverance? No, I won't let the fire win. I will save the girl, or we will perish together. She ran. Her lungs were burning. She must go on. Just a little more. A few metres more.

They won the race. They had escaped from the field. Andromache fell to the ground, next to the children. But got up immediately, bent over Sofia, opened her mouth and breathed air into her lungs, as she had been taught … Sofia coughed, opened her eyes, sat up, coughed again.

Andromache gave her some water to drink.

Only then did Andromache, exhausted, lie down on the ground to regain her strength. Her clothes were black from the smoke. Some of her hair was singed.

But she had won the race with the fire.

* * * * *

Tolmides and Mihail, dragging Slusar, reached the cover of the trees. Panting, they lay on the roots, among the bushes. Slusar groaned softly. Tolmides took his canteen from his belt. Fortunately, he and the other two men had taken their canteens. They would have enough water. For a while.

He brought the canteen to Slusar's lips, who drank greedily.

'We must be careful, Valentin,' Tolmides said, taking the canteen gently from his lips. 'We don't know when we'll find water again. Are you in a lot of pain?' he asked, knowing that this was a meaningless question.

How could such a wound not hurt?

He examined it. Although it was bloody it did not appear to have opened again since the last time. But even if it had started to bleed again, what could he do? Should he tighten the belt? But if he cut the flow of blood toward the leg, it might cause gangrene to develop.

He took a map from his flak jacket, spread it out on the ground. He and Mihail poured over it.

'We are somewhere here,' Tolmides said to Mihail, pointing to a spot on the map. 'I think the best thing to do is to go northeast … in that direction, we'll meet the front at Bryansk.'

Mihail looked at him questioningly. Tolmides understood. Words were unnecessary.

'I don't know how far it is, Mihail. But what other choice do we have? If we go toward Kiev, we'll be walking into a trap. Should we surrender? If you want to, I can't stop you … But I'm not about to surrender. I don't believe that the Germans are kind to their prisoners. We have Valentin … you've heard the rumours. The Germans execute commissars on the spot.'

Mihail nodded.

'I'm with you, sub-lieutenant.'

'Let's leave formalities aside Mihail,' Tolmides said, trying to lighten the atmosphere. 'Call me Ivan. Let's see, what do we have: water, if we are frugal, should last us for one day. Food? Do you have anything on you?'

Mihail shook his head. Like Valentin and Tolmides, he had not taken any food with him. It was in the tank, which was now in flames.

'I have a compass, we have the map,' Tolmides said. 'That's something … let's wait for night … The darkness will provide us with cover. For now, let's rest and sleep, if we can.'

Tolmides approached Slusar whose eyes were open and told him what they had decided to do.

'How will you walk with me?' he asked.

'We'll support you, what else can we do? Leave you behind as a gift for the Germans?' Tolmides said, trying to joke.

'Of course, you can,' Slusar replied. 'That's what others might have done.'

'Others, perhaps. But not us.'

'Why not?'

'What do you mean, *why not*? We are fighting together. You're a member of our crew. We don't abandon our men.'

'And you and I have another bond,' Tolmides added in a whisper.

Slusar nodded.

'I don't know if I am worthy of it,' he said quietly.

'What do you mean *worthy of it*?

'Your devotion. I've done many things which weigh heavily on my soul. Are you amazed, Ivan? A commissar speaking of a soul? Confessing? And yet … at times like this I ask myself if I have a soul, if a soul exists, what I have done in my life. I served my party, thinking that it was the right thing to do … But was it?'

'Valentin, why are you confessing to me? I'm not a priest and I'm not judging you.'

'And, like a good communist, I don't believe in God,' he replied, trying to smile. But the smile transformed into a grimace of pain. He tried to control himself.

'But you're the right person to listen to me. I might die very soon. I need to talk to someone!'

'Do you have a premonition? Don't believe it. We aren't going to die!'

'Do you have an agreement of some kind with God? Or with one of the saints in your church? If you are a believer, that is?' Slusar asked without waiting for a reply.

'The Service has taught us to be ruthless, to obey orders without hesitating, whatever they might be. For the good of the revolution, for communism, for the Soviet Union. The authorities knew better, they were always right. We had to pursue the enemies of the people, of the revolution, the reactionaries. But what I discovered, and what you now know, has troubled me. It was the start of my doubts.'

Slusar stopped talking, took a sip of water, and continued.

'I was with a unit of the NKVD-GPU in Lvov. Our orders were to gather all the ethnic Germans in the city. There were many that had settled there, some of them many centuries ago, and all were Soviet citizens. But our leaders didn't trust them. For them, they were Germans, therefore, enemies and fascists. Potentially a fifth column, traitors. Of course, they didn't need proof. We gathered them outside the city, in fields. We dug open tombs and executed them all. Then we buried them without, of course, leaving any signs. After this, I applied to become a commissar, to be transferred to a combat unit ...'[36]

They heard the sound of numerous engines. Carefully, Tolmides raised his head and separated the branches of some of the bushes for a better view.

A motorised German convoy was approaching, raising clouds of dust. In the lead, to the right, left and in front, was an eight-wheel armoured reconnaissance vehicle. The main convoy consisted of

---

[36] The SS Wiking Division (comprised of Scandinavian volunteers) discovered the mass tombs on the tenth day of the attack against the Soviet Union (on 1 July 1941, when they occupied Lvov). This marked the beginning of a ruthless blood bath, with the pogrom of the Germans in Kiev and the Rumanians in Odessa. See Kirchubel, p.36, where a relevant photograph is published). Already, by the end of 1939, in the Katyn Forest, the NKVD had murdered 6,000 to 10,000 Polish officers that had been arrested during the invasion and partition of Poland. Years later, President Yeltsin formerly apologised for this event.

half-tracks bringing anti-tanks and 105mm cannons as well as lorries with infantry and supplies.

Tolmides, Mihail and Slusar lay down without moving, trying to become one with the ground. The main part of the convoy passed by them, approximately one kilometre away. One of the reconnaissance tanks was only 200 metres away. Tolmides could see the commander's head above the open hatch of the turret. He was wearing goggles to protect his eyes from the dust and a black beret. Tolmides could even see the colour of his hair, which was dark brown, almost black.

However, the German had his attention focused on the distant horizon, searching for enemy forces and had not looked toward the cluster of trees.

The armoured vehicle and the convoy advanced forward.

They sighed in relief.

They slept fitfully until nightfall.

* * * * *

How long had she lain on the ground to recover her breath? She wasn't sure. Perhaps only a few minutes, perhaps more. It didn't really matter. Time flowed differently now, not in seconds, minutes, hours, but with deep and shallow breaths, with faster, stronger and gradually more regular heartbeats. With thirst and trying to resist the temptation to empty the canteen. They would need water later; they didn't know when they would find more. Be frugal. Hunger, at first only a hint, now a growl in the stomach that grew stronger. They weren't starving, thanks to the provisions Andromache had managed to buy, but they were still hungry. Economise on food as well; they didn't know when they would find more.

Andromache got up.

'Let's go, children. We have to go.'

They walked on.

Parallel to the road and farther away from the railway tracks. The road was full of people walking eastward like a huge, endless human caterpillar. The railway tracks, however, were deserted. No smoke to announce the arrival of the steam engine of the train.

They advanced, keeping in step with the slowest children.

They advanced. Eastward, following the road.

Another cornfield. Should they walk through it or detour around it? She remembered the fire. But this time, she couldn't see any aircraft … The detour would slow them down.

'Children, hold hands,' she told them.

They entered the cornfield.

It was similar to the first one. Cornstalks as high as her chest, dry, yellow.

However, a few still had some ears of corn.

They gathered them quickly, leaving a few behind.

A precious gift.

'Children, gather as many as you can,' she said.

They walked more slowly now, gathering corn, putting it in their pockets, holding it in their hands.

They left the cornfield, stopped and counted what they had gathered. They had enough.

'Children, gather dry stalks, as much as you can. Bring them here.'

The children returned to the cornfield, cut as many stalks as they could carry and brought them to Andromache, who made a pile. She took a box of matches from her pocket. Fortunately, she had brought some with her. She struck one and lit a fire. The dry leaves and stalks caught fire easily. Andromache showed the children how to place the ears of corn on the fire, holding them from the small stalk at the one end and turning them slowly until they were cooked. When the corn was ready, they bit into the kernels. Since they had cut and roasted it themselves, they thought that it was tastier than usual. For the time being, their stomachs stopped making gurgling sounds. She gave her daughter some milk and then they set off again.

They reached the buildings of a *kolhoz*, a small village.

It had been burned to the ground. Some buildings were still smoking. The Germans must find only scorched earth, but, the same was true for the civilians.

At the edge of the buildings there was a well. They stopped. Andromache lowered her daughter gently to the ground, lifted the protective cover over the well and looked inside. She thought she could see water. Fortunately, the bucket was hanging from its rope, the end attached to a lever over the opening.

She threw it into the well. She heard a splash as it hit the surface of the water. She lifted the bucket, turning the wheel with her hand.

The bucket rose to the surface, full of water. Andromache tasted it. It was clean and cool.

'Children, fill your canteens with water, have a drink and wash your faces.'

They filled their canteens and drank.

Andromache threw the bucket into the well again and pulled it back up. They threw water on their faces, rinsing off the perspiration and smoke. The children helped her throw the bucket back into the well and to pull it up. The water, which they splashed carelessly on their faces, necks and even their clothes, was cool and refreshing.

'Okay, children, let's go.'

They walked at a quicker pace now, revived by the cool water.

The sun began to sink behind the horizon.

They saw aircraft overhead. Fortunately, they were not diving, they didn't bother them.

What time was it? She assumed that it would soon be dark. How many kilometres had they walked? How much farther was Poltava? She didn't know. But they had to find a place to sleep.

Outdoors?

She looked around for a suitable place.

She noticed some farm buildings which appeared to be undamaged. It was possible that they hadn't been bombed because they were somewhat remote.

They approached the buildings to see.

Andromache entered the house and looked around.

Everything was untouched. A few pieces of furniture, open drawers, no clothes because the owners had taken them when they left. But there was no food. The storeroom was full of items for agricultural use. There was no food there, either.

There were no animals in the stable but it was full of hay. And in one corner, there was a basket full of apples … perhaps meant for the animals, which they had taken with them. Andromache took one and examined it. It looked alright. She took a bite. Perhaps a little overripe, but delicious!

She decided that they would sleep here tonight. The children gathered around her. They ate the rest of the food that Andromache had bought and an apple each. Not more than that as they were overripe, and she was afraid that this might create stomach problems. But tomorrow, they would take the apples with them.

They lay down on the hay in the stalls of the animals. Better mattresses than last night! Their stomachs were full and they fell sleep, exhausted.

Andromache woke up.

The children were still asleep. It was quiet. What woke her up? The rays of the sun entered through the slits between the wood panels of the walls; were the rays curious to see the temporary residents of the stable?

No.

It was the sound of a motor.

A motorcycle. Andromache listened closely.

The sound became louder. It stopped. The motorcycle must have stopped outside the stable. Russians? Germans? What should she do? She was frightened, her heart pounding in her chest.

She had no choice. The large door of the stable creaked as it opened.   Andromache could see a shadow in the opening, but the sun was in her eyes, blinding her.

A soldier … she could not see the colour of his uniform nor the shape of his helmet. But she saw the gun and rose.

'Wer ist da?'[37]

The voice removed any doubts from her mind.

She rose and raised her arms. Fortunately, she spoke good German as she also taught foreign languages at the school.

'Kinder!' she called out loudly. 'Nicht schiessen!'[38]

'Raus!'[39] the German called out and made way for them to leave.

'Children get up. We're leaving. Don't be afraid,' she said, trying to reassure them.

They left the stable. A motorcycle with a sidecar had stopped outside. A second German was standing next to it. He had removed his helmet and was wiping his brow.

'Who's there, Klaus?' he asked the first man.

'Children,' he replied as he removed his helmet.

He caught Andromache looking at him. He was very young, only 20 years old. Blond, freckles, rosy cheeks. The other one had the same features. Close up, the face of the German army, which she saw for the first time, was not at all frightening.

The corporal lowered his gun.

'Where are you going? Where are you coming from?'

---

37 'Who's there?'
38 'Children! Don't shoot!'
39 'Out!'

'From Kiev. We were ordered to leave the city and go east,' she replied.

'Have you seen any soldiers?'

Obviously, they were scouts.

'No, not since we left the train,' she replied.

In her arms, Katerina looked at the German with her large eyes. His grey uniform with the metal buttons looked curious. She reached out her hand and touched one of the buttons. She laughed.

The German was startled. This was unexpected. Then he smiled. He stretched out his hand and caressed Katerina's hair. The child laughed again.

'Fritz, let's go,' he said to the other German, as young as himself. 'There's nothing here.'

'Do you want some apples?' Andromache asked him boldly. 'I'll go fetch some for you.'

She returned to the stable, came out with four apples which she offered to him.

The Germans took them.

'Do you have any food?' she asked.

The corporal took out his knapsack, put the apples inside, searched and found a large salami which he gave to her.

'Fritz, do you have anything?' he asked.

He searched in his knapsack and took out a loaf of bread which he gave to Andromache.

The two Germans climbed onto the motorcycle, put on their helmets and goggles. The corporal started the engine.

'Auf Wiedersehen!' he called out, raising his hand.

'Auf Wiedersehen!' she replied.[40]

The motorcycle left, raising a cloud of dust.

---

[40] 'Until we meet again!'

Andromache regained her senses. The encounter seemed like a dream. 'Until we meet again!'

They had greeted each other as if they had met at a social event, almost like friends before parting … Was this war? Maybe it was, just like the Stukas, the bombs, the machine guns, the dead and the wounded, the burnt farms, the fire, the wreckages of aircraft, the fear, the hunger, the thirst, the perspiration.

'Children, let's go,' she said.

They left.

Toward the east.

* * * * *

Night.

Tolmides rose from their hiding place and took a careful look, 360 degrees around. After the German convoy, they hadn't seen a single person or vehicle. It was as if they were shipwrecked in an endless sea.

'Let's go,' Tolmides said.

Supporting Slusar on the left and right, they started off. Slusar could only step on his good leg, making their pace slow and awkward. Walk, jump, stagger. From afar, they must have looked like a three-headed animal with five legs.

It took them three times more than normal to proceed. Clenching his teeth Slusar grimaced in pain.

They continued walking. Fortunately, the heat was not overwhelming and at night the air was pleasant. They walked toward the northeast. Tolmides looked at his compass every 15 minutes, when they stopped briefly to catch their breaths. Despite the mild temperatures, their strenuous efforts made them perspire. Occasionally, when they stopped for a rest, they sipped some water from their canteens. They were careful as they didn't know when they would find water again. They had no food. When had they last eaten? Yesterday morning, before the start of the attack. Without food, they could last for at least 24 hours. A second day would be more difficult. It would have been easier if they did not have to expend so much energy carrying Slusar.

They continued walking at their tortuous slow pace until daybreak without meeting a soul, only burnt and abandoned villages and *kolhoz*, where they found nothing.

'We have to find a place where we can spend the day,' Tolmides said as he looked around him in the dark, which was dimly lit by the moon. On the almost flat plain, with the harvested wheat and corn, the trees loomed like dark forms.

He noticed another grove of trees, not far away. It was the best cover that they could see. They walked toward it and when they arrived, they sat down under the trees.

Striking a match, Tolmides took out his map and looked at it. He could see better with the light. Where were they? If he had known exactly where they had been hit, he would have been able to judge their current position. But he didn't know. How many kilometres had they covered? Judging by their slow pace, their frequent stops, he estimated 10, at the most 15, kilometres.

'We must be close to the banks of the Psel River[41],' Tolmides remarked. We should be there by tomorrow ...'

They were exhausted and sleep overtook them as soon as they lay down.

Tolmides awakened with the first light and the rays of the sun that caressed and warmed his face.

He got up and looked around. The terrain was quite regular with a few furrows in the ground resembling frozen waves but they were almost unnoticeable which made it difficult to be seen. There was no point of reference such as a mountain, a town, or a river.

---

[41] A tributary of the Dnieper River, which flows into the Dnieper at Kremenchug.

Only fields and burnt *kolhoz* and villages. He could see smoke in various places on the horizon, some far away, some closer by.

What time was it?

It was past noon. He had slept five hours, but his companions were still asleep.

He looked around once more.

Not far away, he could see a dirt road, one of the dozens that crossed the plain, from north to south. Burnt farms, *kolhoz*, villages

A few kilometres farther away, microscopic because they were so far away, but nevertheless distinguishable, he saw motionless forms. Damaged vehicles and tanks, the signs of battle.

Then, looking toward the dirt road, he saw a phalanx of German infantry approaching. He looked around him quickly. Was there a better hiding place close by?

No, there wasn't. At its point closest to them, the dirt road seemed to be about a kilometre or more away. Far enough. If the Germans didn't send out scouts, if they stayed hidden and didn't move, they would probably not be seen. It was all he could hope for.

He lay face down behind a tree trunk, watching as the infantry approached. He made sure his companions were not visible among the trees and vegetation.

The Germans approached.

A motorcycle was at the head, followed by an eight-wheel armoured vehicle. Coming behind was the infantry in rows of three, an unending grey caterpillar that was interrupted only by a few cars, half-tracks and carts drawn by horses.

They approached close to them, but without leaving the road.

When they passed close by their hiding place, they continued without seeing them.

Tolmides gave a deep sigh of relief. He looked at his comrades who were awake now. Slusar's eyes were glazed, there was perspiration on his brow. Tolmides put his hand on Slusar's forehead. He didn't need a thermometer to know that he was burning with fever … There was nothing he could do. All he could do was to give him some water.

The German convoy had moved farther away.

Tolmides looked around again.

He was beginning to feel pangs of hunger. The others must be feeling the same … it was almost noon. They had been without food for almost 30 hours … They needed to eat something for energy and strength, especially since they had to carry Slusar. But he saw nothing to give him even the slightest hope that they would be able to find food.

Now that it was daylight and he could see far, it seemed as though, toward the east, toward the horizon, he could see something that resembled reeds. Reeds meant a marsh or a river. In other words, water. Water, which they would soon need.

'Mihail, look!' he cried out, pointing toward the reeds. 'What do you think? Are those reeds?'

Mihail nodded in agreement.

'We'll walk in that direction,' Tolmides decided.

He searched the horizon again. It was empty.

Should they wait for darkness? Or should they dare to leave their hiding place and walk now that it was daylight?

With the light of day, they could walk faster and reach the water quickly.

'Mihail, Valentin,' he said. 'Let's go now. There are some areas of cover. We're only three people and from afar we're not as noticeable as a convoy. We'll either see or hear them before they notice us. Let's go!'. They lifted Slusar who grimaced in pain.

'You'll have to leave me behind,' he mumbled faintly.

'Why? Does our company bore you?' Tolmides asked, jokingly.

They proceeded to walk, somewhat faster than they had at night, the perspiration dripping from their efforts. Their mouths and throats were dry, they were panting. They stopped every 15 minutes and lay on the ground to catch their breaths. Then they got up and continued walking. Every time they stopped for a short rest, it seemed harder to carry on. Their minds and their will commanded them to continue walking but their exhausted bodies were increasingly unwilling to obey … Soon, they arrived at a battle scene. A Soviet tank unit must have been struck by the Stukas. They arrived first at a burnt-out BT-5 tank. Farther away there was another one, its turret blown ten metres away. Wreckage of lorries. A burnt-out T-34. Among the equipment and broken tracks, there were the dead, some burnt, others appeared to be without injuries, having fallen in different positions. They could smell the stench of death. The battle must have taken place two or three days ago and the bodies had decomposed quickly in the summer heat. Flies and other insects buzzed around them.

'If I were a fly, I would be satiated by now,' Tolmides thought, completely irrationally.

But what they had noticed from afar were, indeed, reeds. They could see in the reeds, half sunk, a heavy Klim Voroshilov tank.[42] It seemed undamaged. It had probably fallen into the marsh while attempting to escape the bombardment and was trapped. The water of the marsh reached almost to the upper section of the tracks, lapping against the hull. But what was important was that it seemed to be untouched. Maybe, inside, they could find something useful.

'Mihail, stay here,' he said, pointing to the dry ground at the edge of the marsh.

'What are you going to do?'

---

[42] In 1941, the Klim Voroshilov 1 tank was the only heavy tank in the world. It had the same 76mm cannon as the T-34/76, a five-member crew (unlike the four crew members of the T-34) but stronger frontal armour of up to 100mm, with a weight of 43 tonnes (unlike the 26 tonnes of the T-34) and a top speed of 35 km/h (unlike the top speed of 55 km/h of the T-34).

'I'm going to check out the tank. There might be something we can use.'

Tolmides removed his boots, undressed. The water was quite deep, judging from the level it reached on the tank. His clothes would only hinder him and anyway, why get them wet? He would dry faster if he entered the water naked.

The water reached his knees, then his waist, his chest. Now he had to swim for the remaining five or six metres. He reached the tank, grabbed hold and climbed up. The turret's hatch was open. He clambered onto the turret and entered. The light that entered through the open hatch was enough for him to see the interior.

Tolmides looked around and found a few treasures.

A half-full bottle of vodka. A small, portable first aid box. Five tinned goods. Fortunately, the crew had abandoned the tank quickly, leaving behind valuable items that Tolmides took to his friends in two trips.

First of all, a good slug of vodka for each of them. It burned but revived them. Then, one tin of food each that they devoured greedily.

Finally, they took a close look at Slusar's wound. They washed it with water from their canteens. At least, it wasn't bleeding. Then Tolmides poured vodka over it and sprinkled sulpha powder from the first aid box to disinfect the wound. Then he wrapped it with gauze. Even though it was probably too late, they were able to provide some first aid.

'Let's sleep here,' Tolmides said.

They were exhausted and it was not wise to cross the marsh at night. Or to detour around it. However, the marsh was an encouraging sign that the Psel River was not too far away, although they still couldn't see it.

'If necessary, we'll hide in the marsh,' he added.

'The river is not far,' he thought out loud. 'When we cross it, we might be safe. Perhaps our side still controls its banks, Sumy and the railway track.'[43]

Perhaps.

Too many "perhaps" issues. But what else was there, aside from "perhaps"? Abandonment was not an option.

'I don't know how to swim,' Mihail said quietly.

Great! He would have to cross the river with one wounded man and another who couldn't swim. He would have to deal with the problem when they arrived. If they arrived …

They closed their eyes and fell asleep, the deep sleep that came with exhaustion.

Tolmides woke up suddenly and opened his eyes. It was dark … what had awakened him?

He heard a droning sound … Aircraft? At night?

He roused himself. It wasn't aircraft.

The sound came from mosquitoes. A swarm of mosquitoes thirsty for blood, buzzing in his ears, invisible in the dark, attacking like the Stukas. He felt itchy. His ears, his forehead, his cheeks. They had bitten him … one was sitting on his cheek. He hit it with his hand, a loud slap.

But there were many determined mosquitoes … He scratched himself, tried to shoo them away with his hand. All in vain. They couldn't stay here any longer. The mosquitoes would not let them have a moment's peace …

He heard Mihail turning, slapping himself. Was he awake or asleep?

'Mihail,' he said softly, 'are you awake?'

'Yes, Ivan. Damned mosquitoes … they've turned me into a sieve. How can I sleep?'

---

[43] Sumy is a little over 100 km east of Konotop.

'Me, too. We have to leave. Otherwise, we'll get no rest.'

'And go where?'

'We have to go inland, wherever we find a suitable place.'

They woke up Slusar, got him up and, supporting him, they left the marsh.

They arrived at the battle site again. The masses, the shapes of the damaged tanks and vehicles appeared darker at night. The first one they came across was a T-70 tank. Crushed tracks, two supporting wheels were missing, thrown far away by the explosion of a bomb that had immobilised it. It didn't appear to have any other damages and there were no dead crew members in the interior or outside somewhere. They could tell because there was no stench from bodies.

'Let's lie down here' Tolmides said. 'The tank will provide us with cover.' They lay down next to the tank and quickly fell asleep.

* * * * *

Andromache and the children began to walk toward the east, using the sun as their guide.

A uniform landscape, with few variations. Harvested fields, burnt villages and *kolhoz*, smoke rising in some parts of the horizon, the road farther away, full of civilians ... was the steam of people never-ending?

Furrows in the ground, which sometimes sloped, thus alleviating the monotony of the level ground.

Dust and flies. Insects. A few butterflies lent some colour and beauty. What did they eat? Andromache saw no flowers; they had all dried in the summer heat.

The children were beginning to lag, dragging their feet as if the ground did not want to release their shoes as they plodded onward. They were not used to such long walks and were beginning to tire, especially the younger ones. But they continued, following their teacher, following her example. There was the fear of getting lost, of being alone in the unknown. They knew and trusted their teacher Andromache, perhaps they also loved her. She was the only known factor of the unknowns of the day. The only thing stable in a new world, one that was chaotic and frightening. Only a few weeks ago they were at home with their families and in school.

Now they were walking in an endless plain. They had heard and seen bombs exploding, the rattle of machine guns, houses that had collapsed, burnt houses, dead and wounded people. And their first Germans. They would not forget them, they had not been frightening at all … nor were they two metres tall, with red eyes, who killed whoever they meet … They would remember and tell their families when they saw them again, they would tell the other children, when they arrived. 'We saw Germans. They gave us salami and bread.'

They continued to walk.

They stopped.

Food. Andromache gave each child some salami, a thin slice of bread and an apple. It was not a royal feast and not even satisfying but enough for them not to feel the pangs of hunger and to provide them with enough energy to reach their next stop, wherever it might be, until they found, perhaps, hopefully, some more food. Enough, at least, to last them until they reached Poltava. She thought that without anything unexpected happening, they would arrive before nightfall.

They continued to walk. Dust and perspiration.

Their clothes stuck to them like a second skin. The dust and perspiration had penetrated their clothes and had created a clay-like layer on their bare skin wherever their bodies, hands, legs, necks, foreheads were not covered by clothing.

But it was not important. When they arrived, they would wash up. When … If…

The important thing was to keep walking, not to let fatigue and fear defeat them. They were the enemy: fatigue, fear, abandonment.

Cavalry on the horizon, coming from the east.

They stopped short. The cavalry approached them. Cossacks. In a hurry. They passed by them, indifferent, on some assignment.

They resumed walking. It was noon. The sun was directly overhead.

They saw some farm buildings. They seemed untouched. They detoured a little in order to get closer. They might find food there, like before …

But they were greeted by a stench. A short distance before the farm they saw a Soviet lorry that had been hit, full of holes and bullets from machine guns. The German aircraft … A few soldiers were on the ground, fallen where the bullets had struck them … the stench came from the bodies.

A pack of dogs feasted on the bodies. Perhaps they had once guarded the farm and other neighbouring farms. When the farmers left, they were left behind. They had formed a pack and hunger had transformed them into wild dogs trying to survive in any way they could. In September of 1941 the Ukrainian plain was filling with the bodies of animals and humans.

A dog smelled the people approaching, lifted its head and looked at them. The enemy! Did they want to take away their food? The dog growled threateningly, baring its teeth which were red with blood and had bits of meat hanging from them.

Andromache froze. She trembled.

She raised her hand to stop the children. With her other hand, she clutched Katerina tightly to her.

'Back away,' she told the children quietly. 'As you are, don't turn your backs. Pick up some stones but don't throw them.'

They obeyed her and collected some stones. Andromache bent her knees and reached for some stones.

They backed away slowly from the dogs.

The dog growled again but didn't attack them. It followed them with its eyes. Since they were leaving, they were not enemies and wouldn't take away its food.

When they had gone far enough away, the dog lowered its mouth over the body, its teeth in the open stomach, it bit and dragged out an intestine, chewing it. It was tasty and filling.

Andromache let out a deep sigh. They were safe.

They walked away from the farm. They stopped for a rest. She gave Katerina the last of the milk. There was no more food. But they had water which they drank.

They started off again, dragging their feet.

'Courage, children,' she said, trying to hide the fatigue in her voice. 'We're almost there.'

The next *kolhoz* had been burned but at the entrance there was an abandoned cart with a broken wheel. A little farther away was a large basket with bread on the ground. She lifted it excitedly. Bread! Food!

It was dry and dusty. It must have fallen when the villagers were hurriedly leaving.   Andromache wiped off the dust as best she could, cut slices with her knife and passed them out to the children.

Dry and bland, with the taste of dust. Delicious when you're hungry.

They rested for a while and then took to the road again. When it began to get dark, they saw the houses of Poltava.

They had arrived!

Without any urging, without a word, they quickened their pace. The hope of salvation gave them strength, a sudden burst of strength they did not know they had.

Poltava was still in the hands of the Soviet army. A few officers and soldiers were trying to put some order in the crowd that was gathering, going toward the railway station.

When they arrived, Andromache, by prodding and pushing, managed to open a pathway to the bench at the entrance to the station. Three seated officers, with documents spread out in front of them and by the light of two kerosene lamps, tried to impose some order. Behind them, about a dozen soldiers with guns raised, prevented those who had not received permission by the officers from entering the station.

Andromache approached the men and stopped in front of one of the officers, a young blond captain. She gave him her papers.

'Where are you coming from, comrade?' he asked.

'From Kiev. I have children with me. Our train was hit … we've been walking for two days and nights,' she replied somewhat incoherently.

The captain glanced at the papers and then looked at her. Did she see something like respect in his eyes?

The captain stood up and put out his hand.

'Bravo,' he said. 'What you have done is remarkable. You have saved these children … Congratulations!'

'What will happen to us now?' she asked.

'A train is leaving in one hour for Izyum and Voroshilovgrad.[44] I will put you on it. It will be somewhat crowded, but there is nothing I can do about that. At Voroshilovgrad you'll be safe. From there they will direct to you wherever necessary.'

'Thank you,' Andromache said with relief as the captain sat down to complete a document. He handed it to her together with her papers.

'You may go,' he said, showing her the entrance to the railway station.

'Is there, by any chance, some food for the children?' she asked.

The captain smiled.

---

44 Cities on the Donets River which flows into the Volga River.

'We'll find something,' he replied.

He gave an order to a soldier who led them to the station, to the train, to a carraige where he ordered those who were inside to make room and for some of them to stand.

Some of them protested, but the soldier reproached them.

'Shame, comrades! The teacher and the children have come from Kiev and have walked 50 kilometres. They deserve to have seats.'

Andromache and the children sat down.

The carriage smelled of the unwashed people who were crowded inside. But for Andromache it was a welcome smell that implied safety and human warmth.

She felt exhaustion overcoming her as she relaxed.

The captain entered the carriage with a soldier. From a large sack that he was carrying, he took out eggs, one for each, and loaves of bread, which he handed out. The captain gave her a bottle of milk.

'Thank you,' she said as she took it.

'You deserve it,' he replied and saluted.

The train began to move.

* * * * *

Tolmides opened his eyes. His left eyelid felt heavy, half-covering his eye. He nudged Mihail gently to awaken him. He opened his eyes and looked at him.

'Do you see something in my eye?' Tolmides asked him.

'Your eye is swollen, Ivan,' Mihail said. 'Perhaps from a mosquito.'

His forehead and cheeks were covered in red spots and small bumps from mosquito bites.

Tolmides smiled.

'It seems that the mosquitoes have done more harm to us than the Germans. Do you suppose that they connived with the Germans against us?'

Mihail was taken aback but then smiled. Where did Ivan find the nerve to joke?

Tolmides turned serious.

'What do you think we should do? Should we wait until dark or leave now?'

'We can't go through the marsh at night, nor can we cross the river when we reach it,' Mihail replied.

'The longer we delay, the farther away our people might be getting,' Tolmides added.

Mihail nodded in agreement.

They awakened Slusar.

Before starting off, Tolmides climbed onto the tank which was close to where they had spent the night. He found nothing useful. The crew had taken everything of use when they had abandoned it.

Walking, they followed the banks of the marsh from a distance. At some point they would meet the river.

As before, they stopped every so often to rest. Slusar had a fever, his hands and forehead were burning, he was perspiring, more so than the others and his eyes were glazed. But they kept on. They continued to walk.

At noon they stopped for a longer time, they shared the last two tins of food and sipped some vodka. When would they find more food? Unknown. How long can a person walk when he's hungry? Unknown, but Tolmides preferred not to think about it.

Early in the afternoon, Mihail noticed some shapes in the distance.

They looked like infantry combing the plain. Faint at the beginning, the figures started to look sharper as they got closer and then they heard dogs barking.

They exchanged uneasy glances. It was a second-line battalion, which followed in order to clear the rear of the enemy's first-line battalion. They weren't Soviets, the barking dogs were proof of that.

They looked around. Where could they hide?

A few clusters of trees. Some bushes. Some furrows in the ground. If there were only men, they could possibly escape being noticed. But the dogs would certainly smell them.

'We must reach the marsh,' Tolmides said, 'and enter the water. In the reeds, the dogs will lose our scent. Let's move quickly!'

The walked faster. However, walking faster with the lame Slusar was impossible. They walked slower than the normal pace of a person.

The reeds were approximately two kilometres away. The enemy was about the same distance away but getting closer. Had they been seen? Had the dogs smelled them?

The plain offered no protection. It was certain that they would be noticed. The dogs would be able to smell them at any moment now.

They could now hear loud voices and the dogs barking.

Tolmides cast a quick glance behind him. They had been seen. Some of the enemy ran after them, together with the dogs.

They had to hurry, but how?

They were bathed in perspiration and they breathed deeply, heavily, panting. They were losing the race.

'Leave me,' Slusar said. 'We can't make it! Leave me!'

'Do you know that they execute commissars?[45] Tolmides said, between breaths.

'I don't have papers on me showing that I'm a commissar. I'm only an ordinary crew member of a tank. I'm not in any danger.'

---

[45] Hitler had ordered that commissars that were arrested were to be shot on the spot.

Did he really believe what he was saying?

They could hear the cries of their pursuers as well as gunshots.

Mihail stumbled, slipped and fell, dragging them all down as they fell in a heap. Slusar groaned in pain when his leg hit the ground.

'Are you hurt?' Tolmides asked Mihail.

'No, I only stumbled.'

They got up and lifted Slusar.

Gunshots. A bullet hit the ground a few centimetres from Tolmides' right boot, raising some dust. Running, the pursuers were getting closer. They could see them clearly. Judging from the shape of their helmets, they must be Hungarians.

'Leave me,' said Slusar. 'It's an order! There's no sense in all of us being captured. You can escape. Let them catch only me!'

Tolmides hesitated. Slusar was right, but how could they leave him?

Slusar removed his gun from its holster and pointed it at Tolmides.

'Leave me,' he ordered them once more. 'I'll delay them. Leave me!'

Mihail was the first to obey.

Tolmides wavered again but obeyed as well. He put Slusar down on the ground.

'Ivan, there's something I must tell you,' Slusar whispered. 'In case we don't meet again.'

He whispered a few hurried words.

Tolmides was surprised. He would have liked to ask for an explanation, but time was running out. The Hungarians and their dogs were coming closer.

'Go!' Slusar ordered them. 'Good luck!'

Ivan grabbed his hand and shook it. He was deeply moved, as was Slusar. But there was no time to lose if they wanted to save themselves. No time for any more words. One final glance of farewell.

Mihail left first, running toward the marsh. Tolmides ran behind him.

They could hear more gunshots.

Slusar shot with his gun. The Hungarians closest to him hid.

Mihail and Tolmides gained valuable seconds, perhaps even a full minute. They ran with a new-found strength that came with the thought of self-preservation, of hope and of despair ... Where this sudden burst of energy came from, they didn't know.

Slusar had emptied his gun.

The Hungarian soldiers, together with their sub-lieutenant surrounded the fallen Slusar. One of them was holding a dog that was snarling, baring his teeth, pulling at his leash.

The sub-lieutenant looked at the Russian and saw his bloody leg. Another wounded Russian. What could they do with another wounded prisoner? They had arrested already hundreds of thousands and didn't know what to do with them ... How could they escort another one to prison, to which camp, with what food? Wounded enemy soldiers were useless.[46]

The sub-lieutenant gave an order. A soldier aimed his gun at Slusar's head and pulled the trigger.

When Mihail and Tolmides reached the bank of the marsh, they ran into the water, separating the reeds, and proceeded until the water reached their waists when they were farther away from

---

[46] The Soviet Union had not signed the Treaty of Geneva regarding prisoners of war, which was another reason, aside from the ideological war, that made the war at the eastern front so ruthless. The treatment of the Soviets wounded by the Germans was brutal, contrary to their treatment of western prisoners such as the French, British, American, etc. The Soviets treated German prisoners in the same way. Of the 90,000 that were taken as prisoners at Stalingrad, only a few thousand survived to return to Germany at the end of the war.

the bank. They could hear the Hungarians coming closer, but the thick, tall reeds concealed them. The dogs lost their scent in the water and couldn't follow them.

Making their way through the reeds, they crouched in a thick cluster of reeds, up to their chins in the water. They remained still with only the sound of their heart beats, which to them sounded like a drumroll.

The Hungarians stopped at the edge of the marsh but couldn't see them. The dogs sniffed around but they had lost all trace of the men's scent on the banks.

The sub-lieutenant decided that it was not worth their while to lose time searching for two Russian soldiers in the immense marsh. They would have to cover too large an area. Time was short.

He ordered his men to turn back and to continue combing the plain. The sounds of their presence weakened. The voices and barking faded away.

It was twilight before Tolmides and Mihail dared to emerge from their hiding place. They were soaked, covered in mud from the marsh. They looked like two strange beings, like men made of clay.

'Mihail, let's walk along the bank of the marsh. If necessary …'

He didn't have to finish his sentence. They might have to hide again in the reeds.

As for the mosquitoes, they were extremely bothersome, but less dangerous than the Hungarians.

They continued to walk, casting frequent glances toward the plain to spot any enemy. It was deserted now except for the permanent smoke in the distance. Strange how the landscape changed so quickly, at times empty and then filled with soldiers, artillery, lorries. Like an ocean where, on some days, you can't see another ship, and on others, it is full of ships.

When it got dark, they stopped and lay down in a cluster of trees, not far from the edge of the marsh. They were exhausted, physically as well and mentally. They shared the same thoughts: What had happened to Slusar? Would they be able to save themselves?

They were hungry. They hadn't eaten anything since the morning and the two tins shared between the three of them had not been enough. They still had the bottle of vodka. They each took a sip, leaving some for the morning. The alcohol burned their throats but it revived them.

They could hear the croaking of frogs, invisible in the marsh, and the buzzing of errant mosquitoes which fortunately, were not many. They closed their eyes and fell into a deep but troubled sleep.

The first rays of the sun that sneaked through the leaves fell on their faces and awakened them with a caress. They got up with difficulty, their legs and bodies stiff. They drank the last of the vodka which invigorated them.

They started off.

The same landscape. Deserted, burnt farms where there was nothing for them, burnt or harvested fields, smoke in the distance.

They reached the end of the marsh.

They saw a continuous line of trees which blocked the horizon.

They looked at each other.

They were thinking the same thing. Those must be trees growing along the banks of the river. They walked faster.

This was how the Myrioi, the mercenary troops of the ancient Persians, must have felt in their descent, when they first sighted the sea.

This was how they felt now that they could see the river through the trees.

They reached the banks of the river.

The Psel was wide and its calm waters flowed gently toward the south, but it was not the Dnieper. The water was so deep in the middle that they would have to swim.

They sat on the bank to gather some strength, basking in the warmth of the sun. Then they got up.

'Mihail, when we reach the deep water where we can no longer touch the bottom, you'll have to float on the water and I'll drag you. Just stay calm, it's nothing. Okay?'

'Okay,' Mihail replied, although Tolmides could tell that he was apprehensive.

They entered the water, walking carefully so as not to slip. The water reached their knees, their waists, their chests. When they could no longer walk, they would have to swim.

'Let yourself go, Mihail,' Tolmides said. 'Hold onto my shoulder with your right hand and I'll drag you. It's not far.'

Mihail followed instructions.

Tolmides began to swim, pulling Mihail who tried to float and to keep his head above the water. Suddenly, he made an abrupt move, gulped water and choked, coughed, kicked in panic and, clutching Tolmides, dragged them both under the water.

Tolmides swallowed water but reacted instinctively. He freed himself from Mihail's clutches and hit him on the chin with his fist, dazing him. Tolmides rose to the surface, spat out water, and pulled Mihail up by his flak jacket to the surface of the water. He continued to swim, dragging Mihail.

His feet touched the riverbed and after three strokes he steadied himself. Mihail also stood on his feet. Supporting each other and staggering, they reached the opposite bank, fell down, coughed, spat water, and lay down.

After a short rest, they continued their walk toward the east.

In the afternoon they met up with a patrol from the Bryansk front which picked them up.

PART II

Exodus

CHAPTER 6

Operation Bagration, June 1944 and London

At the end of spring and the beginning of summer in 1944, the Soviet Army could not be compared to the defeated and retreating army of 1941. After three years of war, a new generation of field marshals and generals, more experienced, capable and decisive, had assumed the leadership, men such as Georgy Zhukov, Ivan Konev, Konstantin Rokossovsky, Nikolai Vatutin, Ivan Chernyakhovsky and Ivan Bagramyan. An air of optimism and trust blew from headquarters to the soldiers. The equipment had also changed. The basic tank remained the T-34 though with a larger turret and heavier 85mm cannon, reinforced with SU-85 and SU-100 machine guns. The new, heavy Josef Stalin tanks as well as the American Shermans and the British Cromwells and Churchills now joined the fray.[47]

---

[47] They used the hull of the T-34 tank, without the turret with 85mm and 100mm cannons respectively. All the British tanks (even as of today, with the

Tens of thousands of American lorries manufactured by General Motors, Ford and Chrysler provided speed and flexibility to the Soviet advance, with plentiful petrol from the oil fields of Baku, which had at one time supplied fuel to the Germans during the twilight period between the two dictatorships. Now, the Soviets were prepared to surpass their German mentors in applying the blitzkrieg tactic. In the air, the Soviets, under the capable leadership of General Alexander Novikov, ruled the skies, with an overwhelming superiority in numbers and types of fighter aircraft, equal to the German ones, such as the Lavochkin La-5 FN, Yakovlev Yak-9 and Yak-3, the two-engine aircraft bombers, the Petlyakov Pe-2 and Ilyushin Il-4 and their answer to the Stuka, the ground attack aircraft, the Ilyushin Il-2. The German veteran pilots were always extremely dangerous but now there was a new generation of capable Russian pilots who were experienced in battle, such as Ivan Kozhedob and Alexander Pokryshkin.[48]

Moreover, a large number of fighter aircraft of the Luftwaffe had been withdrawn for the defence of the Reich from the American daytime bombardments.

Challenger) have names that begin with a "C" which indicated the cruiser type, such as the Crusader, Cromwell, Churchill, etc. At the beginning of the war, the British had two categories of tanks, the infantry tanks Valentine and Mathilda and the cruisers. This differentiation was abandoned, thus creating a slight confusion because the Churchill was a heavy and slow infantry tank and not a cruiser. The type IS/JS-2 tank weighed 45 tonnes and had a 122mm machine gun.

[48] Kozhedob piloting the LA-5IN aircraft claimed 62 victories, Aleksander Pokryshkin piloting the American-made Bell P-39 Airacobra aircraft claimed 59. In 1944 the Luftwaffe had the JG 1,3, 5, 6, 11, 51, 52 and 54 on the eastern front of which a part (Gruppe) was at the western front. For example, five were in Norway, which faced off with the Soviets and the Anglo-Americans.

Captain Ivan Tolmides was also a veteran now. He had fought during the Soviet counteroffensive of Moscow during the winter of 1941-42, at Kharkov and Rostov in the summer of 1942, at the Soviet defence of Stalingrad in the winter of 1942-43, at Kursk in the summer of 1943 where he was awarded the medal, "Hero of the Soviet Union", and at the military operations on the banks of the Dnieper in the autumn of 1943.

At the beginning of June 1944, he had received a new squadron with a T-34/85 tank that belonged to the 1st Guards Tank Army,[49] a unit of the 1st Tank Corps under Major General Mihail Panov, a unit of the 1st Belorussian Front under General Konstantin Rokossovsky.

On 23 June 1944 a large Soviet invasion codenamed Operation Bagration began under Rokossovsky, whose main objective, after Bobruysk on the Berezina River, which joined the Dnieper farther south, was Rogachev. The objective was to liberate Belorussia and defeat the German Army Group Centre.[50] It would be, from one point of view, an 'anniversary gift' for the Germans because it would have begun exactly three years after the German invasion of the Soviet Union.

Tolmides examined his tank one last time before the battle. He thought to himself that although it was a machine of destruction, it had a certain strange beauty. He felt a kind of pride that he would be directing it into battle, much like a medieval knight riding on his horse. On the side of the turret, in large white letters was written the slogan, "For the Soviet Union".[51]

---

[49] The Guard Units were selective. And the title was an honorary one.

[50] Prince Bagration was a hero of the Napoleonic Wars. By giving his name to the Operation, the Soviets wanted to associate the fate of Hitler with that suffered by Napoleon.

[51] Such slogans were commonly found on tanks and airplanes and served to strengthen morale. In winter they were written with black letters on a white background, and during the rest of the year, white letters on green.

The day before, on 22 June, the Soviets had begun their reconnoitring attacks. The major offensive began on the 23rd of June.

Five o'clock in the morning.

The battle commenced with a barrage by the Soviet artillery. The flashes of light had been so constant that it appeared as though dawn had arrived from the opposite direction, from the earth to the sky. The noise was frightening, continuous. The German lines disappeared in a cloud of explosions, smoke, dust, earth, shrapnel, damaged anti-tanks and mortars, human bodies and limbs that spiralled upward as if the earth wanted to shed itself of bothersome insects. Katyusha rockets added to the hubbub with whistling sounds, flaming tails and explosions.[52]

Seven o'clock in the morning.

With the sun rising behind them and blinding any surviving Germans, the Soviet infantry attacked with small, flexible groups, with the support of the machine gunners whenever necessary. The first German defence collapsed. A breach in the German lines.

It was time for the tanks to take advantage of the moment and to penetrate deep into the rear lines of the enemy, throwing them into disarray.

Tolmides and his crew climbed onto the tank and took their places.

The tanks started off toward the west and the Rogachev-Bobruysk axis with their engines groaning, leaving behind them a cloud of smoke.

They didn't meet with any resistance at the first German line of defence. The Soviet infantry had occupied and cleared the

---

[52] It was the most intense initial bombardment by artillery up to that time on the Eastern front. Each 122mm machine gun fired 160 rounds, a total weight of six tonnes (see Zaloga 1996, pp.44-45).

centres of resistance. The Soviet tanks advanced toward Bobruysk. Tolmides looked at the scene, which had become familiar by now: A wild, semi-dark frightening picture of smoke, dust, flashes of explosions, destroyed tanks, armoured vehicles, trenches and strongholds, dismembered bodies. A scene that he had witnessed so many times it had become almost intimate, if one could say that about death and destruction.

Tolmides' unit advanced toward Slobodka, a town south of Bobruysk.

Explosions!

A T-34 tank was on fire.

Tolmides and the other commanders observed from their hatches. Where were the shots coming from? There were only a few buildings in front of them, a village or *kolhoz*, among some trees.

More explosions. Another T-34 caught on fire.

Tolmides noticed German Panzers, painted in camouflage colours of ochre and green, concealed among the buildings and trees.[53]

'Mihail,' he called out to his gunner, as he rotated the turret. 'Projectile!'

He had a German tank in his sights. He stopped the turret and aimed with the machine gun. Mihail tapped him lightly, a gesture which they had repeated dozens, hundreds of times all these years and which meant that the projectile had been placed and the cannon was ready to fire.

---

[53] From the summer of 1943, the German Panzers, armoured vehicles, etc., were delivered from the factories to the units painted in a colour called "yellow" but which was really a beige-ochre (the hue of the soil in summer) instead of the former *feldgrau* (dark grey). The units were painted in camouflage colours of brown or green, in spots or stripes, etc.

Tolmides fired. The projectile struck the German tank in the centre of the hull, under the turret. A flash of light and smoke. Without waiting for orders, Mihail had loaded another projectile and tapped Tolmides lightly once again, who fired another round. He saw the round striking at about the same spot. The German tank was smoking. Its crew opened the hatches, climbed out and ran for cover, abandoning it. It was the 20th tank that Tolmides had destroyed.

The tank battle appeared to be disorganised, as tanks advanced, stopped and fired as the turrets rotated. Some were hit, some were ablaze, smoke and flames billowing, trees and buildings burning. There was a cacophony of groaning engines, fires crackling, the roar of cannon, the sharp blasts of explosions, the stuttering of machine guns.

Tolmides noticed another German tank concealed in the trees. Its turret and cannon were turned toward another target, its exposed flank just 500 metres away.

'Stop!' Tolmides cried out and the driver braked abruptly as if it had struck an obstacle, jolting them.

Tolmides turned the turret, bringing the enemy tank into his sights now that the T-34 was not moving and was stable.

Fire!

The Panzer was struck at the centre of the turret. Smoke and flashes of light. Then, a second, blinding explosion. The projectile struck the ammunition stored in the turret. As if unreal, the turret broke off from the hull, flung into the air from the explosion and rising two metres high, then falling upside down three metres away from the hull, which was burning with a thick black smoke.

Victory number 21.

The tank battle ended.

The surviving German tanks retreated in disarray. The Soviet tanks advanced.[54]

A few trenches and foxholes of the German infantry. The Soviet tanks passed over them, firing their machine guns, crushing with their tracks barbed wire as well as machine guns and soldiers who had not had a chance to escape.

Tolmides and his crew were so blinded by the smoke that they did not see a German who rushed out from a hideout concealed by tree branches. He aimed and shot a shoulder type anti-tank weapon, the *Panzerfaust*.[55]

The rocket struck the turret on the side of the tank, where Tolmides sat. There was an explosion that sounded as if they had been struck by a huge hammer, a powerful jolt and loud thud. It opened a crack in the armour, sending fragments into the interior of the tank. Tolmides felt a sharp pain in his right thigh and his chest. The interior of the tank filled with smoke and sparks. The

---

[54] In the tank battle at Slobotia the Soviet tanks encountered 71 type IV Panzers of the 20th Panzer Division. The 20th had only one of its squadrons there because the second one was in Germany to receive the new Panther Panzer. The Soviets lost 60 tanks, the Germans about half of theirs and were unsuccessful in stopping the Soviet advance. The Panzer IV was the must numerous of German tanks used in the war. During 1939-1941 it was a support tank with a short-barrelled 75mm cannon. In 1944, it was in service in versions H and J with a long-barrelled 75mm cannon, the L-48 (Laenge (width) 48 meant 48 times the bore of the barrel, in other words, 3.6 metres). It weighed 25 tonnes and had a frontal armour of 80mm. From the point of view of armour and machine gun, it was equal to the T-34/85 but it was slower and less flexible.

[55] *Panzerfaust*, meaning, 'tank fist', was a single shot, recoilless anti-tank weapon consisting of a disposable, pre-loaded launch tube that fired an explosive warhead. It could penetrate the side hull of a tank, but its range was only 60 metres. The Germans had their own version of the bazooka, the *Panzerschreck* (meaning, 'tank fright').

tank was on fire and it stopped. The crew jumped out, pulling the semi-conscious Tolmides with them.

He did not regain consciousness until much later.

He found himself in a temporary hospital at the front line, inside a tent.

A military doctor was bending over him.

'You've recovered, comrade captain! You're lucky! I removed shrapnel from your thigh. It was deeply imbedded but fortunately, it had not hit the main artery. I took out four smaller pieces of shrapnel from your ribs. Three are broken. You'll be in pain, but you won't have any permanent damage. Your recovery will take time. Perhaps months. For now, the war is over for you. You'll stay here for a few days until you feel better, and then I'll send you behind the lines until you're fully recovered.[56]

* * * * *

---

[56] Operation Bagration was a victory for the Soviets and led to the collapse of the German Army Group Centre. Seventeen German divisions were totally destroyed and another 50 suffered severe losses, which meant they were out of the war. Belorussia and Minsk were liberated. Approximately 100,000 Germans were taken prisoners, somewhat more than the 90,000 captured at Stalingrad. On 23 August, the Soviets reached the Vistula River at Warsaw and the frontiers of Rumania. On 29 August, Rumania changed sides, abandoning the Axis. On 4 September, Finland asked for and succeeded in obtaining a truce which led to a permanent truce two weeks later and its exit from the war. Finland ceded the territories that it had lost in the Russo-Finnish war of 1939 and the city of Petsamo that the Soviets had not occupied. Stalin accepted Finland's independence because he knew that capturing it would involve a heavy cost that outweighed the benefits and because he needed the forces that would be released from the Finnish front for the final attack against Germany (see Zaloga, 1996).

London, mid-August 1944

Before looking at the man sitting opposite him, Stewart Menzies, the head of MI6, was enjoying his pipe, rings of smoke drifting languidly toward the ceiling.

'We are faced with a rather delicate matter. The war is approaching its end and our victory is assured. The German front in Russia has collapsed as it has in Normandy.[57] I don't know how many more months the Germans can last, but I don't give them much time. Nor does the Prime Minister. He's already thinking about the future and what the situation will be like after the war.'

Sir Stewart enjoyed another puff on his pipe before continuing. Sitting across from him, Lieutenant Andrew Bond waited patiently. He was fully aware of the man's habit of summarising the situation before coming to the topic that he wanted to discuss.

'I can tell you, confidentially, that I met with the Prime Minister. He confessed his worries to me. Perhaps, more accurately, his fears for the future of Europe after the war. He's concerned. The Soviets are emerging stronger. Depending on how each party perceives the matter, either Poland has been liberated or it will be occupied once again. The same is true for Rumania, Bulgaria, Hungary, Czechoslovakia, and perhaps Austria.[58] Will it become an independent country after the fall of the Reich, or will it become a large part of Germany? The Prime Minister doesn't

---

[57] The British and American forces had broken through the German front in Normandy. They met at Chambois on 19 August 1944, encircling the Falaise Pocket. The captured 60,000 Germans, destroyed hundreds of tanks, machine guns, etc. By 23 August, Paris had been liberated, the Germans had crossed the Seine and were in complete retreat, fleeing toward the German border and abandoning France.

[58] Austria had lost its independence after the Anschluss and its incorporation into the Third Reich in 1938 was enthusiastically accepted by the great majority of the Austrian population.

know how the world will be apportioned after the war. He is trying to convince President Roosevelt to maintain a common stance. But he knows that some Americans are suspicious. They believe, and perhaps not unjustly, that we want to hold onto the empire. The negotiations will be difficult. The Prime Minister needs every negotiating advantage that he can get his hands on.'

Sir Stewart fell silent, puffed on his pipe again and continued, looking straight at Bond.

'And this is where we come in. Just a short while ago, we received some extraordinary information from our office in Teheran, from an Azerbaijani warlord and smuggler. He claims that a Soviet officer has important information, fully documented, regarding a highly-placed official in the Soviet Union. The Azerbaijani has told us roughly who it is, but we will receive the documents only if we reach an agreement regarding the transaction. Isn't it strange?'

'Who is this Soviet officer, sir? What kind of transaction?' Bond asked.

'He's not asking for payment. He's asking for safe passage from the Soviet Union for himself and his family, his wife and small daughter, and to provide them with permanent residency in Great Britain. As for the highly-placed official, he seems to be the 'father of his people.''

Bond, who was not easily surprised, was left with his mouth open from this startling information.

'Exactly, Bond,' Sir Stewart said, with one of his rare smiles. 'My reaction was exactly like yours when I found out. Fantastic! Unbelievable! It sounds like a fairy tale! But you can imagine what a trump card this will be in the hands of the Prime Minister - if it is true, if we can get it.'

'I fully understand, sir.'

'I don't doubt it. But as you can imagine, before continuing, I asked the Service to find out more. What we learned is that the informant is a decorated Pontic Greek, a Soviet citizen, a commander of an armoured unit of the Soviet Army. He grew up in Tbilisi in Georgia, to where his parents fled after the Greek-Turkish war of 1920-1922. The Azerbaijani has told us that the Greek, let's call him that, acquired the information from an agent of the NKVD. It seems plausible. Our next step was to examine the archives of the Foreign Office. And what do you think we discovered? A report from our ambassador in Moscow in 1938, Aretas Akers-Douglas, 2nd Viscount Chilston, which seems to confirm the information that has been given to us. It appears that, I assume, the same people tried to sell the information to the Greek ambassador at that time,' ... Sir Stewart cast a glance at a document on his desk, 'a Mr Dimitris Nikolopoulos. But something went wrong, and some believe that the ambassador may have been assassinated by an agent of the NKVD. Viscount Chilston wrote his report and you will find a copy in the file. He could not find out more, which is perfectly understandable, considering the situation at that time.

'I met with Viscount Chilston,' Sir Stewart continued, 'and he confirmed everything that is in his report. He added that the Greek ambassador was a cultured man, full of *joie de vivre*, and was anything but a storyteller. The Viscount believes that Nikolopoulos really did have knowledge of a significant secret, and this put him in danger of his life, rightly so, as it turned out for him. Perhaps, it was the same information that has been offered to us now. There are too many coincidences for it to be merely coincidental.'

'I agree, sir,' Bond replied, sensing a thrill, the familiar thrill of each new assignment, the stimulation of challenge and danger.

'My next step was to meet with Churchill with this information. The matter is exceedingly delicate, as I said before. We would not be able to proceed without his approval. You can imagine his reaction.'

'Since I am here, sir, he must have been interested.'

'Bond, "interested" is an understatement. Churchill's expression was like that of the cat who had just swallowed a canary! We have his approval. This is where you enter the scene.'

Bond was surprised but didn't show it. This was the first time that he had heard the director speak in metaphors.

'We've received approval to have one of our men bring the Greek man and his family to England with the documents. The terms of the Greek are that he will not attempt the escape if one of our men does not pick him up in Georgia. As a guarantee and for safety. Do you realise what this means? One of our men must secretly enter the Soviet Union, which is an ally, and assist in the escape of a Soviet citizen. The nature of the assignment is such that, if something goes wrong, we know nothing, we have not approved anything. Whoever goes will be on his own until he returns. That is why we need a volunteer. I am not giving you an order. You are my first choice but you are under no obligation to accept. You can think about it until tomorrow. The prize is so great that it's worth taking the risk. The Soviet Union is an ally, at least for the time being. What we are about to do, if it's discovered, might be interpreted as a hostile act. Therefore, the secrecy and our complete, supposed ignorance, as I've told you … These are muddy waters,' Sir Stewart said, becoming somewhat incoherent.

Recently, Bond had been feeling restless from the lack of action. At last – now he felt alive, eager for action. Danger revived him; it was like an intoxicating drink.

'I accept, sir. I don't have to think about it.'

Sir Stewart looked at him with ill-concealed relief.

'Okay,' he said. 'Thank you.'

'How will we go about it, sir?'

'From Iran, at the border with the Soviet Union. There the Azerbaijani will meet you and will bring you back. Of course, he will be heavily compensated. As you know, there is a large population of Azerbaijanis in northern Iran who communicate with their fellow countrymen in Azerbaijan in the Soviet Union. This is how smuggling is carried out and it makes it easier for us. You will find all the details here,' Sir Stewart said, pushing a file on his desk toward Bond.

Bond picked it up and stood.

'Is there anything else, sir?'

'Yes. Let your moustache and beard grow. You're dark complexioned and from afar, with a beard and moustache and the right clothes, you'll look like an Azerbaijani.'

'I'll do it, sir.' Bond said, smiling as he said goody bye.[59]

That evening, Bond met with Amanda Clark and went to the Bar and Nails in Soho which had become their favourite haunt. While they sipped their first drink, he told her that he was leaving soon on an assignment.

'Where will you be going?' she asked, somewhat anxiously.

'Nowhere particularly dangerous. Iran. I have to investigate something there,' he replied with a half-truth.

He had complete trust in her. Moreover, Amanda belonged to the Special Operations Executive. In 1944 she had been inducted into the Special Operations Executive, a secret organisation which trained wireless operators and saboteurs (both men and women) and had been set up at the instigation of Churchill and his orders

---

[59] Sir Stewart Menzies was director of MI6 (Secret Intelligence Service) throughout the duration of the war. He signed as "C", keeping the tradition that had been started by Captain Sir Mansfield George Smith-Cumming, the first director of MI6, during World War I. Iran, formally independent, was a British protectorate during the war. The southern axis of supplies from the Allies to the Soviets passed through there, via the Caspian Sea and the Caucasus. Of course, at that time, the Russian oil deposits had not yet been exploited as the Allies did not need Russian oil since the British had sufficient supplies from Iraq, Iran, Kuwait and Saudi Arabia, and the United States from Texas and South America.

to "set Europe ablaze" (meaning occupied Europe). Amanda had gone to Normandy in May 1944, just before the invasion.

Bond never told her about his assignments before they were completed, and she never insisted on more information other than what he was willing to tell her. It was a silent agreement between them that they upheld unremittingly. It was the same with their relationship. For the duration of the war their relationship would remain open, without ties. Theirs was an intense and erotic relationship (volcanic, he felt), possibly because of wartime, a relationship of *carpe diem,* since they did not know what tomorrow would bring. Bond had met Amanda in July 1943 prior to an assignment in Italy. One of his first assignments had been in Singapore, Malaysia from November 1941 to February 1942. When the war was over, if they survived, they would discuss the future. For the first time in his life, after knowing her for only one year, Bond could envision a life together after the war.

But for now, he felt only his familiar edginess after so many months of sitting at his desk, waiting for a new assignment. Every so often he had to drink from the glass of danger to feel reinvigorated.

They returned to her flat. Whenever Bond was in London, they spent every night together but maintained separate flats as part of their silent agreement.

'Andrew, please pour two drinks,' she said. 'I have something for you.'

Bond poured some whisky in each of two crystal glasses.

Amanda entered the room and gave him something. A brown scarf.

'What's this?' he asked.

'A present for your birthday. It was going to be a surprise but I'm giving it to you in advance. You might need it in Iran.'

'Amanda, you're amazing,' he said, visibly touched, and hugged her. 'Don't tell me you knitted it by yourself?'

'Of course! What did you expect?'

'You're full of surprises! I didn't know you could knit. Did you learn it in SOE?' he joked.

'You don't know how calming knitting can be! It helps release nervous tension when you're waiting, bored and idle, concealed somewhere from where you can't and don't dare to move. It distracts you from anxiety and fear … and the knitting needles can become a weapon if need be,' she replied half-jokingly.

'Perhaps you should suggest to Gubbins[60] to introduce knitting as necessary training for SOE agents?' he joked.

'Do you want to try a friendly game of self-defence? You with your martial arts and me with my knitting needles?' she replied in the same tone of voice.

'It would be an uneven competition.'

'For whom?'

'For now, I prefer another kind of game,' he replied slyly.

He drew her gently toward him, put his right arm around her shoulders, bent his head and searched for her lips.

The merged in a warm kiss, their tongues searching for one another. Bond put his hand on her breast, caressing her as she sighed deeply between kisses.

They rose, still embracing.

They went to the bedroom. Bond lay down on the large bed while Amanda remained standing. They turned off the ceiling light, leaving only the lamp on the table next to the bed turned on, throwing the room in semi-darkness.

Amanda began the ritual that she performed on certain nights, which Bond enjoyed and excited him.

She started to undress slowly, swaying her body. Cardigan, blouse, skirt, shoes, bra and knickers fell to the floor. She stood

---

[60] Sir Colin Gubbins was the director of the SOE (see M.R.O. Foot 1984, "The Special Operations Executive", a BBC publication).

naked except for her black garter belt and black silk stockings which accented her rosy body in the semi-darkness. Bond sat admiring her beautiful body, curvaceous and firm, like a statue of Aphrodite.

Amanda came to the bed, lay on him and placed her hands next to his face, to support herself, her breasts provocatively over his face.

He raised his arms and embraced her body, his mouth and tongue kissing her nipples.

'Since you did not accept a friendly competition, how about trying a new Kama Sutra position?' she asked slyly and playfully. From one of his earlier assignments, Bond had brought a copy of the *Kama Sutra*.

'Whatever my personal goddess Kali commands,' he replied.[61]

When their erotic skirmish was over, bringing them to climax, panting and exhausted, and still embraced in bed, Bond thought how fortunate he was that he had met her, that he had a Penelope, beautiful and strong to return to.

Perhaps not a Penelope, certainly patient, but not crafty for fooling non-existing suitors.

Strong and a little wild when she wanted, she was more like the beautiful Amazon queen, Penthesilea, or a Boudica,[62] a woman full of life who had shown bravery and endurance in battle.

'I think I will call you Antiope instead of Amanda,' he murmured.

'You can call me what you like. Antiope! What made you think of her?'

'From Eton. You can't imagine what one learns there,' he replied. 'But it suits you,' he added with a smile.

---

[61] Kali is the Hindu goddess of creation and death.

[62] Boudica was the queen of the Iceni tribe and a British national heroine, who led an uprising in 60-61 AD against the Romans. She was killed in battle.

'If I remember correctly, the Amazons fought with bows and arrows, spears and swords, not with knitting needles,' she joked.

'It's never too late for a battle with a bow and arrow!'

She bent over him.

'Take your scarf with you,' she murmured.

'I will, even though it will be summer …'

'Iran has mountains. You never know,' Amanda said as sleep began to overtake her.

CHAPTER 7

Rahman Mustafayev

Tbilisi, end of August 1944

Tolmides took long walks around the city to strengthen his leg. He could now walk without crutches and a cane, having almost completely recovered from his injuries.

He would soon be re-examined by a military doctor who would confirm his complete recovery and would sign a certificate stating that he could return to active duty.

But he had no intentions of returning.

If his plan succeeded.

He had served selflessly and, as the citation for his awards stated, he had served his country with the utmost courage. He had shed blood for it.

The Soviet Union did not always reward those that had fought for their country. Stalin and the party were suspicious of minorities, exiling, imprisoning or sending to Siberia or gulags entire families, entire villages, Tartars, Cossacks, Poles, Muslims of every nationality, Pontic Greeks.[63]

---

[63] For the persecution of the Greeks, see Ahtzides, chap. 5, and the bibliography.

In spite of the war, the situation did not seem to be changing. Tolmides doubted that anything would change, as long as Stalin was alive. It remained a repressive regime.

Tolmides and his family did not want to live any longer under such conditions. He had discussed the matter with Andromache and she had agreed.

Now they had a unique opportunity to escape. They were in Tbilisi, not far from Iran. The borders were not guarded as closely as they had been before the war because there was a lack of guards due to the war.

He had in his hands a trump card, the secret gift that Slusar had whispered to him before ordering them to leave him. Slusar had not destroyed the original document. He had entrusted it to someone that the NKVD would never suspect, an Orthodox Christian priest, one of the few that remained, in the mountains. The priest had hidden it in the crypt of an old Byzantine-style church that had been built during the reign of Tamar.[64]

Moreover, he trusted the Azerbaijani warlord Rahman Mustafayev who had delivered his offer to the British. He had met him on a previous leave of absence from the front.

From day to day, Tolmides waited for Mustafayev to bring a reply.

Mustafayev and his band, or perhaps it was more correct to say, band of smugglers, went in and out of Iran and the Soviet Union taking footpaths that only he and his men knew about, although they also took ordinary roads. Furthermore, Azerbaijanis on both sides of the border made his movements easier. He felt as much at ease in these parts as a fish in a large ocean. In the Soviet Union he

---

[64] Tamar was the Queen of Georgia (end 1184-1213 AD). She had a good relationship with Byzantium and Trebizond and was successful in repelling the Seljuk Turks. Byzantine masons built many churches in Georgia that still exist today.

could pass as a Soviet citizen and in Iran as an Iranian. Smuggling was particularly profitable for him. To the Soviet Union he brought American and British cigarettes, Scotch whisky and even, as special requests, western fashions and silk underclothing for the wives and mistresses of highly placed officers of the communist nomenklatura. To Iran he took war booty provided by Soviet officers and soldiers on leave: watches, medals and pistols taken from wounded or dead Germans. The watches were in high demand by the Iranians and even in lower Mesopotamia which was under British control. The value of the medals rose accordingly, from the simplest to the more important ones, and pistols such as Lugers, Parabellums and Walters, were in high demand by British and American support agencies that supplied military material to the Soviet Union from Iran. An Iron Cross was worth one gold sovereign, a Knight's Cross two or three, a Knight's Cross with Oak Leaves, was worth much more, according to demand.[65] Those who bought them could boast, when they returned to their homes, families, wives and girlfriends that they had fought heroically, offering them as proof the trophies of war.

* * * * *

Azerbaijan, end of August to September 1944

Bond arrived in Teheran on a military aircraft by way of an itinerary organised by the Service. From London to Paris (now liberated), from Paris to Malta and from there to Cairo. From Cairo he flew to Baghdad and then on to Teheran. He arrived somewhat bedraggled, not having slept very well on so many flights, in spite

---

[65] The German medals were the *Eisernes Kreuz* (Iron Cross), 1st and 2nd class, the Knight's Cross (*Ritterkreuz*) with Oak Leaves (*mit Eichenlaub*), or with Swords (*mit Schwertern*), or with diamonds (*mit Brillanten*).

of the fact that he was accustomed to the discomfort, having flown on previous assignments to and from Singapore and Australia, India, North Africa. At least, nothing unexpected had occurred.

After a day of rest which consisted mainly of sleep, Bond was provided with a jeep and a guide by the head of MI6 in Teheran. They set off for northern Iran where he was to meet with Mustafayev.

After a lengthy drive of many hours they reached the Soviet Republic of Azerbaijan, above the northernmost of Iran, on the border with the Soviet Union.

They stopped at a village and waited. Mustafayev arrived at night with his men. Bond's driver knew them and made the introductions.

Mustafayev was tall and lean, with black hair, a beard and moustache, eyes that were so dark that the cornea could barely be distinguished. He was dressed in military attire, which was without national insignia, boots and from his belt hung a Luger, obviously war loot. His air of pride and bravery made him appear even taller, as tall as the mountains of his homeland. His band consisted of twenty men, dressed like him, armed with pistols, British, German and Russian rifles. All were bearded, upright with an air of determination, like their leader. With them they had ten mules loaded with provisions.

Mustafayev extended his hand which Bond grasped warmly. The Azerbaijani grinned, showing his white teeth, and said, 'Greetings, Shota.'

Shota, which was a Georgian name, was the name that Bond was to use on this assignment. He had chosen it because it was the name of the 12th century Georgian poet Shota Rustaveli who wrote the national epic, *The Knight in the Panther's Skin*. Another nugget of knowledge that he had picked up during his studies at Eton.

'If you're ready, we'll start off in an hour, as soon as we've finished our work here.'

"Work" consisted of the trade with the British and Americans who oversaw the flow of supplies. A convoy filled with provisions was lined up on the road, one vehicle after another, like a mechanical caterpillar which stretched out for almost a kilometre. The British and American drivers would hand it over to the Soviet drivers for the remainder of the journey.

Mustafayev's men unloaded the mules and handed over everything they had brought and had agreed upon with their British and American friends. In exchange, they received other goods in crates which they loaded onto the mules.

When they were finished, Mustafayev turned to Bond and said: 'Let's go.'

They started off.

Like the Azerbaijanis and Georgians, Bond carried a knapsack on his back with necessary items and a Beretta in a holster, a gift from the Italian Navy from a prior assignment. He also had with him a commando's knife.

They arrived at the border guard's hut.

Mustafayev greeted the Soviet officer, an old friend. The men unloaded a few boxes of American cigarettes and two bottles of whisky which they gave to the Soviet soldiers.

The Soviet officer and Mustafayev shook hands, exchanged a few words and a smile and passed over the border. As easy as that!

They walked for two hours until twilight when they arrived at a small village. They stopped at the central square and while the men looked after the mules, Mustafayev knocked on the door of a house.

'They are friends and are expecting us,' he explained to Bond.

He spoke reasonably good English, thanks to his relationship with the British and Americans.

A middle-aged man opened the door.

They embraced and Mustafayev introduced him to Bond, saying something in Azerbaijani. The man bowed slightly and stepped aside so that they could enter. He led them to the sitting room and dining area of the house, which resembled an oriental-style room, an *onta*. They sat on pillows around a low table, which stood on a beautiful hand-woven carpet.

'Shota, in your honour, my friend has prepared an Azerbaijani meal,' Mustafayev said.

'Please extend my thanks to him,' Bond replied.

'My country is at the crossroads of civilisations and religions,' Mustafayev said proudly. 'Zoroastrianism flourished, which left us honouring fire and the hearth of every house, the *otzak*,' he said as he pointed to the fireplace, which was lit with a small fire, in spite of it being summer.

'Christianity and Islam, which came later, were influenced by Zoroastrianism and influenced our life and national cuisine, even today.'

Two women appeared who, as Mustafayev explained, were the wife and older daughter of the host. They carried glasses and dishes, knives, forks and spoons and two carafes that they placed on the table.

Their host filled their glasses, two each, one for water and the other for another drink.

'We distinguish between two types of water, white and dark,' said Mustafayev. 'The white is clean and we use it for drinking and cooking.   The dark water contains many minerals. This other drink in front of you is called *iskenderjebi* which is a refreshing drink as well as a digestive. Try it.'

Mustafayev, the host and Bond raised their glasses and drank.

It had an unusual taste, different from any other drink that Bond had tasted. Sweet and sour, rich, stimulating and refreshing.

'It's delicious,' Bond remarked. 'What is it?'

'A mixture of water, grape juice, honey and vinegar,' Mustafayev replied. 'It is one of our many local beverages.'

The daughter returned carrying a basket with bread. Their host gave some to each. Mustafayev touched the bread, closed his eyes and whispered a few words in his language. The host nodded.

Mustafayev opened his eyes and explained, 'I made a vow over the bread to be always your friend and protector. For us, such a vow made over bread is as sacred as a vow made over the Koran.'

Bond nodded, touched his bread and said, 'I would like to make the same vow. Forever a friend, in peace and in war.'

The two Azerbaijanis smiled.

The women brought platters with food and set them on the table.

As their host served, Mustafayev described each dish.

'These are *gutab*, triangular pies filled with chopped meat and dusted with ground pepper and nutmeg. *Han kebab, shaslik,* souvlaki are all made with lamb's liver and spices. *Doghramaj,'* he said, pointing to a dish with a white-coloured food.

'This is made with yogurt, finely chopped cucumber, coriander, basil, green onion, dill, eggs, garlic, and some pieces of cubed beef. A refreshing summer salad.'

'And of course, rice,' he said, pointing to the last platter. 'We have 80 ways of preparing rice. This is *shah pilaf,* the emperor's rice. It's prepared in a flatbread crust, like a pie, with chestnuts, butter, *albouhara* – a type of dried plum – raisins, meat, and a puree of cherries. It's cooked for two and a half to three hours over an open fire. It's a dish that Evliya Çelebi loved. Do you know who he was?'

'He was the great 17th century Ottoman explorer who wrote about his voyages,' Bond replied, silently thanking Eton for the remarkably trivial knowledge that it had imparted to him.

They began to eat. Everything was exceptionally delicious. Bond once again felt the familiar twitch of guilt. He was about to consume as many calories at this meal as four London meals with ration coupons, even though the situation had improved vastly since the dark days of 1940-41. He recalled the long queues of women of all ages at food shops, sometimes after rumours that a particular shop had something, without knowing what that "something" was. On one occasion, it was a single fresh orange for each woman, so precious that it was worth waiting an hour for.

After the meal was over, more drinks. Tea, without which an Azerbaijani meal could not end, and *bekmez*, a digestif made from mulberries, watermelon, sugar cane, beets, grapes and wild persimmons.

He thought back on previous assignments. "Join the Secret Service and get to know the world. And the food and drinks of each country."[66]

They slept on mattresses which were laid out in the sitting room.

They awoke at dawn, ate freshly baked bread, cheese and drank milk. Thanking their host, they left. The men were waiting for them in the square with the mules and horses.

'We'll leave the horses here before crossing the border. Do you know how to ride?' Mustafayev asked.

Bond nodded.

They mounted the horses and rode off, taking a dirt road, not the main road to the north which was full of British and American auxiliary assistance vehicles. They left the Aras River, the ancient Araxes River, and followed the Kura River which flowed in the valley between the main or Greater Caucasus to the north and the Lesser Caucasus to the south.

Green meadows dotted with autumn flowers such as large pink cyclamen, and forests with various types of trees, such as the argan with yellow-green leaves that created a carpet on the ground where they had fallen, among the flowers.

---

[66] A paraphrase of the well-known poster of the British Navy, "Join the Navy and see the world."

'The argan is a tree in the Caucasus that lives for two centuries. Its wood is so compact and hard that it is impossible to drive a nail through it,' Mustafayev explained to Bond. 'Nature is particularly splendid here. There are dozens of different kinds of trees, hundreds of plants, dozens of animals and birds, brown bears, gazelles, deer, wolves …'

Bond was amazed.

The landscape was exceptionally peaceful, the war and his assignment seemed so distant.

They passed through meadows and forests with trees such as the tall Mondell pine, whose trunks and leaves intermingled. He saw small villages, steep hills and mountains that rose like rocky guardians of the plains, and which were occasionally crowned by medieval castles.

Flowing northwest toward Georgia, the Kura River, serpentine and blue, shimmering in the sun, had small islands with white sands in some areas of its riverbed. Meadows stretched out from its banks with forests, small sandy coasts, small marshes with reeds. In some areas, dotting the landscape, were bird refuges with herons, pelicans and flamingos with their incredibly long and spindly legs, their long serpentine necks, their black and white wings and curved bills with black tips. There were many others whose names he didn't know.

Villagers tending their flocks of sheep, goats and cows waved at them as they passed by.

He was overcome by this idyllic landscape of such magnificent beauty and serenity and he thought of Amanda and how she would have liked it here, if she could have been with him …

Even time flowed slowly, at a leisurely pace, with the gait of the horses and the mules, their stops to eat and rest, spending the night at welcoming villages homes. Mustafayev and his men had made this journey many times before and their stops were reminiscent of caravans from the past …

The presence of the Soviet Union in the countryside was not perceptible on the paths that they were following. No soldiers, no police … and why would there be? Even collectivisation seemed far away. Here the villages seemed to live in the past, in the age of the Khans or the tsars, with their small vegetable gardens, orchards, their animals, a few sheep and goats.

He estimated that they were travelling about 45 kilometres a day which meant that they would reach Tbilisi in 10 days.

At times Bond was impatient but didn't say anything. Mustafayev was not worried, obviously he had organised their arrival time accordingly and Bond could not intervene. All he could do was to enjoy the journey which, at times, was on foot so that he could stretch his legs after a long time on horseback. Fortunately, he was in top physical condition.

Keeping them company was the beautiful countryside, such as the small miracle of nature, Lake Göygöl, an impounded lake surrounded by forested hills. Its sparkling blue colour and its forested banks, the colours colliding and blending: the blue of the sky with some white clouds, the darker blue of the lake, the dozens of green hues of the forests, the yellow-green of the grass in the valley farther away, the grey of the mountains beyond the valley.

'The lake was created by an earthquake in 1139 by our calendar,' Mustafayev explained, always the proud guide of his country. 'The clarity of its waters is such that you can see to a depth of 13 metres. But the strange thing is that there are three levels of water which don't mix. There is clean, drinkable water on the surface, a second layer and then there is a poisonous sulphurous layer of water near the bottom that contains sulphur.'

Bond, from the remote dirt road that they were on, could see no difference. The Kura River continued to flow toward its source in Turkey, unaware of borders created by men. But there were no man-made borders within the countries of the Soviet Union. Furthermore, the borders were invisible in another way, by the diverse languages, religions (which in some places were very much alive even though they were not officially recognised), manners and customs, Party members or not, Party members and ordinary people, police patrols on the main roads, blockades of the secret police who, if they considered it necessary, could position themselves anywhere, not only at the borders.

A lorry that had obviously seen better days, was waiting for them farther away.

They were greeted by a young man who looked like Mustafayev's men.

'Roustem, this is Shota,' Mustafayev said, as he introduced them.

The warlord gave his men some orders, said goodbye and gestured towards the seat in the driver's cubicle next to Roustem. Bond climbed onto the truck and sat next to him. The large seat fit them comfortably.

'My men are going to deliver some goods. We'll go to our meeting.'

Bond did not say anything. He was beginning to feel something akin to admiration for the Azerbaijani's organisational abilities. Everything was smoothly planned as it would have been for a successful business … for that matter, Mustafayev was exactly that: the owner and executive officer of a successful business even though it was illegal according to Soviet laws. He smiled as he thought about it.

The lorry turned onto an asphalt road and after a while, turned into a dirt road.

'Aren't we in danger of being stopped?' Bond asked.

'Only a slight chance. This is a farmer's lorry, so it's legal. Our documents are in good order, as are yours, in the unlikely chance that we are stopped. You're an Azerbaijani, we have come to meet some friends, you don't speak German or Russian …'

'Nor Russian? Isn't it compulsory for all Soviet citizens to speak Russian?'

'It is,' Mustafayev said with a smile. 'However, even today, there are many people who have not learned to speak Russian well, especially older people. In any case, you will not speak, leave it to me to do the talking. Just smile.'

'And what if we encounter someone who speaks Azerbaijani?'

'Then pretend you're a mute,' Mustafayev said with a laugh and Bond laughed as well.

Later, Bond asked him, 'aren't we going to Tbilisi? I saw on the map that it's about 65 kilometres from the border with Azerbaijan. We should have been there by now.'

'No, we're not going to Tbilisi. Be patient. You'll be safe where we're going.'

It was afternoon by the time they arrived.

They were surrounded by grey-black, rocky, bald mountains with abrupt cliffs, and dotted with the openings of dark caves.

'We've arrived,' Mustafayev said and climbed down from the lorry. Bond followed him.

Roustem turned the lorry around and returned to the road they had been on.

Bond wondered where it was that they had arrived. The place looked absolutely deserted.

'Where are we?' he asked.

'We're in Geghard,' he replied, which meant nothing to Bond.

'You'll see,' he added.

They took a narrow path leading uphill, following its winding trail among the stones.

Suddenly, they stopped.

The view was otherworldly, captivating, even for Bond who had travelled widely and was not easily impressed.

Stones which were the grey-brown colour of the surrounding boulders. Two-storied buildings with windows presented a unified front with two semi-circular towers at the outer fortification walls.

'Where are we?' Bond asked.

'We are at the Monastery of Geghard in Soviet Armenia. The monastery is closed now. It was built by Georgians during the reign of Tamar after the Seljuk Turks were thrown out of the region. The first one that was built is even older, when Gregory the Illuminator introduced Christianity in the fourth century.[67]

'At first, it was called Ayrivank, the Monastery in the Cave, now it is called Geghard or Geghardavank, the Monastery of the Spear. Supposedly it was here that the Apostle Thaddeus brought the spear that pierced the side of Jesus. Am I tiring you?'

'Not at all,' Bond replied, impressed by the warlord's knowledge. He was always interested in learning more about the places that he visited, even if it had nothing to do with his assignment. Curiosity was an aspect of his character that had been cultivated during his student days at Eton. In an event, curiosity was a basic trait of every good spy.

'I believe that, after the war, you would make an excellent tourist guide,' he said with a smile.

'Who will come to the Soviet Union for tourism? Do you think that even after the war foreigners will be welcomed here?' Mustafayev said seriously. 'But you, as the sole tourist in the area, please enjoy it!' he added with a smile.

They entered the monastery through a large stone archway.

'Aside from the main church, there are chapels inside the caves and one of them has a sacred spring. The main church was built in

---

[67] Saint Gregory the Illuminator is the patron saint and first official head of the Armenian Apostolic Church. He was a religious leader who is credited with converting Armenia from paganism to Christianity in 301. He illustrated the Gospels.

1215 by the brothers Zakare and Ivane, who were Tamar's generals and overthrew the Seljuk Turks.'

Within the monastery walls there was a church.

On a small plateau at the foot of the rocks, on the side of the mountain, there were some buildings. The main church was built of stone from the mountain, an equal-armed cross inscribed in a square-in-plan with triangular arched roofs over each opening of the cross. From its centre there rose a tall cylindrical dome with slender pilasters that terminated in an embedded semi-circular moulding. Between them were tall and narrow embrasures like openings for archers. The dome was a tall white cone topped by a black cross.

Attached to one side of the church was a small belfry supported on slender columns which terminated in a small polyhedral cone with a black cross.

All around were caves whose entrances were protected by stone archways.

'This is one of the oldest Orthodox monasteries in Georgia. It is closed now, as are almost all monasteries in the officially atheist Soviet Union,' Mustafayev explained.

'However, it is not completely deserted. There are some people who keep their belief in God alive. Are you a believer, Shota? Are you religious?'

It was a strange question and Bond didn't know how to reply. He was not particularly religious and had never thought about it seriously before. If he believed in something it was performing his duty, living intensely, and enjoying, as much as possible, every moment … *carpe diem*, as they had been taught at Eton. His life during the war and his assignments had been always, or almost always, a breath away from death because of unexpected, sudden events. Death had become something familiar, almost like an invisible friend …

And, in spite of everything, he had survived, against all odds.

He had survived the Battle of Britain when so many young pilots had died. He had survived in the jungles of Malaysia and the Amazon, on the Java Sea and the Atlantic, murderous attacks by Thugs heretics in India, twice in occupied France, being pursued a few months ago in Germany and the Bavarian Alps, intrigues in Italy … It was as if he were protected by an invisible force, a guardian angel.

If he believed in something, now that he thought about it, it was in an invisible force, a god, not necessarily as religions defined him, but a god that protected him so that he could successfully conclude his assignments in this huge war, a war that, as Churchill had said, was a war of Good against Evil or, as Eisenhower put it, a crusade against the forces of Darkness, which was Nazism.[68]

'Andrew Bond, Crusader of Good,' he thought to himself, with a smile. But if he was a crusader, even metaphorically, he had to believe in something.

Mustafayev was not expecting an answer. He stood in front of the entrance to a cave that had a wooden door and called out.

'Father Nicholas!'

Bond realised that the caves were the cells of monks that had lived there centuries ago.

The door opened with a small dragging sound.

A slender man around 50 years old dressed in civilian clothes stood at the door.

'May God be with you, Father Nicholas,' Mustafayev said in Georgian.

'And may God be with you,' he replied, making way for them to enter.

---

[68] The memoirs of Dwight D. Eisenhower, leader of the Allied Forces in North Africa, Italy and France, and later President of the United States, are entitled *Crusade in Europe* (see bibliography).

'Our guest, Shota,' Mustafayev said, introducing Bond. The priest clasped his hand with a warm, strong grip.

The interior of the cave had been transformed into a cell which looked like a tall stone dome. It was partially dark as the only light that entered the cell was from the open door. Bond could see a wooden bed with a mattress, a wooden table, two chairs, and an iconostasis with icons in an alcove that had been carved into the rock. In front of it hung an oil lamp with a faint, trembling flame.

They sat in chairs around the table.

Another figure appeared at the door, carrying a tray with three glasses filled with water and three small plates with a sweet, and spoons.

'This is Kyria Maria, the Father's wife,' Mustafayev said, introducing them. The woman smiled and Bond smiled back. He recalled that Orthodox priests were allowed to marry.

'They don't speak English,' Mustafayev said. 'They are Pontic Greeks. The sweet, which is made from grapes, was made by Kyria Maria.'

Bond tasted it. The sweet was delicious.

'Father Nicholas is one of the few priests in the Church that still conducts services, in a small church in a nearby village. The regime tolerates the existence of a few churches as well as some Moslem mosques in Azerbaijan, allowing some freedom of religion. Georgians, Pontic Greeks, Azerbaijanis are firm believers even though some practice their religion in secret. The regime is afraid of greater opposition, especially now, with the war … It wants peace in Azerbaijan and Georgia so as to be assured of the flow of oil,' Mustafayev explained.

Bond nodded.

'Will the meeting take place here?' he asked.

'Yes, here. Roustem will bring the family from Tbilisi and they'll be here before nightfall.'

Father Nicholas took them on a tour of the area. Kyria Maria was cooking something in the built-in oven of the monastery.

Father Nicholas unlocked the church while Mustafayev explained.

'When the regime closed the monastery, Father Nicholas was a very young priest. He managed to keep one of the church keys and once a year, on the nameday of Saint George, he conducts a service with a few of the faithful.'

Father Nicholas lit a few candles, thus shedding light on the Byzantine frescoes on the walls of the church. Warrior saints, medieval Georgian and Byzantine soldiers with austere faces, ready to escape from the walls, to come alive and take up arms for a new battle … On the dome, an image of Christ blessing all those inside the church.

In the silence, with the trembling light of the candles and the scent of the incense that had been lit by the priest, Bond felt something akin to awe, a feeling that was unusual for him.

They went outside and Father Nicholas locked the door. They walked for a while, as the sun was setting, its rosy rays bathing the rocks.

A dog appeared and approached them hesitatingly, wagging its tail. A half-breed German shepherd that was black with light brown hair on the underside of his tufted tail, dark brown eyes, one ear raised, the other half bent.

'Is the dog yours?' Bond asked the priest.

'No. It must be a stray. Who knows how it got here?'

Bond had grown up with dogs on the family farm in Scotland. He extended his hand to the dog who took two steps, smelled it and wagged his tail. Bond patted its head and scratched behind its ears. The dog wagged its tail enthusiastically.

'You've made a friend,' Mustafayev said with a smile.

Father Nicholas said something which Mustafayev translated for Bond.

'Whoever shows love for animals is a person with a good heart. You must be a good Christian. The Orthodox Church has a saint named Modesto who was the protector of animals.'

Bond was amazed. They had called him many things on his assignments, but never a "good Christian"!

Four figures appeared on the path: Roustem, a young man, a young woman and a little girl, about five years old.

They reached the men and Mustafayev made the introductions.

'This is Captain Ivan Tolmides, his wife Andromache and their daughter Katerina.'

The two men shook hands. A strong grip and they met each other's eyes. Their first encounter, with an unspoken question: 'Can I trust you with my life and my loved ones?'

'Lieutenant Andrew Bond, of the British Secret Service,' Bond said, giving his real name.

He then shook hands with the graceful woman with the beautiful face.

'Sprechen sie Deutsch?' she asked.[69]

'Jawolh,'[70] he replied with a smile, considering the irony of the situation. He would be conversing with these people in the language of the enemy!

The little girl curtsied and smiled. Bond leaned over, smiled and said to her mother in German so that she could translate.

'I'm particularly pleased to meet you lovely miss!'

Katerina laughed happily at this tall, manly foreigner with the beard, wearing military clothes, a gun and a knife in his belt. He could have been dangerous and threatening ... but his smile inspired trust.

Kyria Maria called for them to eat. Father Nicholas brought ceramic dishes, knives and forks from the cell. They sat on the

---

[69] 'Do you speak German?'
[70] 'Of course.'

ground close to the oven. Kyria Maria brought a large loaf of bread that she had made and baked in the oven. Father Nicholas sliced it and gave some to everyone.

It was warm and smelled wonderful.

Bond tasted it. Perhaps because he was hungry or maybe because he was eating outdoors, in a Georgian monastery, it seemed to be the most delicious bread he had ever tasted. He cut a piece and gave it to the dog that had sat down close to him, as if he were a part of the dinner party. Katerina also cut a piece of her bread and gave it to the dog, who took it and came closer to them.

Father Nicholas brought some copper cups and Mustafayev took a bottle of wine from his bag.

'Georgian *giuaani*,' he explained. 'In spite of the fact that it is red, they call it the "pearl of the Caucasus". A very old variety, perhaps dating from antiquity, it was standardised in 1894 from Saperavi grapes, from the village of Manavi, in the Caucasus region of Kakheti.'

He poured some in everyone's glass and lifted his own in a toast.

'May everything go well, with the help of God,' he said.

They drank.

Bond tasted the unusual flavour and the bouquet, which was strong, earthy, almost peppery and fruity with the taste of sour grapes and plums.

'Are you surprised, Shota, that even though I am a Moslem, I'm drinking wine?' Mustafayev said, replying to an unspoken question on Bond's mind.

'We Azerbaijanis are faithful Moslems and follow the spirit but not the letter of the Koran. Yes, some of us drink wine. We produce wine.[71] We illustrate our books and carpets with human

---

[71] A distillation device dating from the 17th/18th century has been found in the region of Gabala. After the fall of tsarist Russian, Azerbaijan became

figures, animals, birds and plants. Furthermore, we are the first Moslem democracy in the world.'

The first platter of food arrived.

'Eggplant with tomato, onion, garlic, baked with oil. The dish is called *imam*, and it is well known in Greece, Turkey, Georgia, and Azerbaijan,' Andromache explained to Bond.

Bond tasted it. Delicious!

The main dish arrived, *satzistsi*, meat with vegetables, tomatoes, sweet peppers, potatoes, eggplants, onions and pumpkin, baked in an open cylindrical pan. It was accompanied by rice, this time with olives, saffron and peas.

Kyria Maria spoke in Greek and Andromache translated.

'This dish is offered by Mr Mustafayev who provided the ingredients. On our trip we might not have the opportunity to eat hot food.'

'It's wonderful,' Bond said, and thanked her.

They ended their meal with baklava.[72]

They collected all the leftovers and Bond spread them out on a flat stone for the dog to eat.

---

independent, held elections and functioned as a democracy for two years (1918-1920) until the invasion and its violent capture by the Soviet army when the communists took over in 1920.

[72] Even during the period of the Soviet Union, the Caucasus produced an abundance of vegetables and fruit which were difficult to find in Russia. On the author's first visit to Georgia in 1983 with his father, Kostas Kyriazis who, at the time, was president of EOT, the Greek National Tourist Organisation (essentially, the Ministry of Tourism, because Greece did not have a Ministry of Tourism then), they were accompanied by an agent of Intourist of the Russian Ministry of Tourism. It was believed that she was a member of the KGB, the successor of the NKVD. When they took their flight to Moscow, Larissa was carrying bags of vegetables and fruit with her. The reason for this trip was to sign, for the first time, an agreement for touristic cooperation between Greece and the Soviet Union.

Then it was time for a serious discussion. Bond wanted to learn about the general situation. Father Nicholas was the first to speak about the persecutions of the Pontic Greeks and the church. All Greek organisations had been abolished, almost all the churches had been closed and many priests, both Georgian and Greek, had been arrested, imprisoned, exiled or even executed.

'But when our faith is challenged it becomes even stronger, just as it was with the first Christians,' he added.

'Stalin is a Georgian and his surname is Jughashvili,' Tolmides said. 'But in spite of this, in spite of the fact that he was born in Gori, he loathes, almost detests Georgia.'

'Why?' Bond asked.

'It's rumoured that he's illegitimate. His mother was from Ossetia and had an affair with a famous author named Vazha-Pshavela, who she did not marry. When she married Besarion Jughashvili, he adopted Stalin. However, Stalin knew this and never overcame the hurt of being illegitimate. Perhaps this affected his personality,' Tolmides said, while Andromache translated.[73]

'Do you have the documents for the asylum and the residency permit in Britain?' Tolmides asked.

'Not with me. The documents are in Teheran. It would have been too much of a risk to carry them with me. You have to trust me. Mr Mustafayev can assure you that I truly am who I say I am,' Bond replied.

When Andromache translated, Tolmides nodded. It was understood that it would have been a risk to carry the documents with him.

'The documents?' Bond asked, meaning the papers that were the object of his trip.

---

[73] I owe this information to Ms Marina Amirajabi who told me that it has been written many times in the Georgian press.

'They're here. I'll give them to you now!' Tolmides replied, saying something to Father Nicholas.

'Come,' he said and got up and walked toward the church.

It was already night. Mustafayev gave the priest a torch.

They entered the church. Father Nicholas entered one of the openings of the iconostasis. He motioned to them to follow.

In the apse there was a marble altar, with carved legs, perhaps as old as the church. The priest gave the torch to Tolmides, speaking to him in Greek. He knelt down to the base of the altar while Tolmides shone the light on the floor tiles.

The priest grabbed one of the tiles with both his hands, lifted it slightly and put it aside, revealing a space underneath. He put his hands in and grasped something which he lifted. It was wrapped in cloth to protect it from the dampness under the floor. He unwrapped it and revealed a metal box. There was another piece of cloth inside which he unwrapped carefully, exposing some documents.

He gave them to Tolmides who handed them over to Bond.

He glanced through them quickly by the light of the torch. He was unable to read the Cyrillic script, but the seals, the numbers and the face pictured, both in profile and frontally, were recognizable even though the photograph showed a man more than 30 years younger. Black, unruly hair, a thick moustache, a straight pointed nose and eyes with slightly fallen eyelids.

He looked at Tolmides in agreement, wrapped the documents in the cloth and placed them in a pocket inside his jacket.

The priest replaced the empty box in the space under the floor, placed the tile over it and they left the church.

'We'll sleep here tonight,' Mustafayev said, 'and we'll leave tomorrow at sunrise. Roustem will take us on the first leg of our journey.'

They slept with their clothes on, lying on wooden beds in the cells and wrapped in blankets that Roustem had brought with him in the lorry. The temperature fell in the evening, but even though it was almost the end of summer, it was still comfortable. During the day it was pleasant, around 23° Celsius.

Bond was the first to wake up, a little stiff, but feeling rested. He got up, splashed some water on his face at the fountain and took a few steps. He heard a slight bark and saw the dog coming toward him, wagging its tail.

'Have you adopted me?' he asked, petting the dog.

The others woke up, ate a simple but satisfying breakfast of milk, bread and cheese. Bond and the others said goodbye to the priest and Kyria Maria.

'May God be with you,' the priest said to them. "May His will be done!'

Bond had learned not to be left to anyone's will, only to his own. However, he knew that the priest meant it and so the wish was a welcome one. He understood the spiritual grandeur and power of the priest's faith. It would be one more vibrant memory of the people that he had met and admired during the course of the war.

He took three gold sovereigns, which he carried with him in case of need, from a secret pocket in his belt and offered them to the priest.

The priest shook his head.

'I did not do this for payment,' he said.

'I know,' Bond replied. 'It's for the church, please accept it.'

Andromache translated and then Father Nicholas nodded.

'Then, I'll accept it. I'll pray for you.'

They climbed onto the lorry. Andromache and Katerina sat in the cabin next to Roustem. The others, with their few belongings, sat in the back of the lorry.

Before they started off, the dog jumped onto the back and settled next to Bond.

'Shall I chase it away?' Mustafayev asked.

'Leave it, it doesn't matter,' Bond replied. 'When we reach Iran, we'll see.'

He didn't have the heart to leave the dog behind.

'You're getting soft,' he said to himself. What has happened to the tough agent Andrew Bond? Had the atmosphere of the monastery and the previous evening with the priest affected him so strongly? Are only a few hours necessary to have an impact on us, to shape our character and decisions? But aren't these very fleeting moments and spontaneous decisions that sometimes influence our lives?

Another thought, a different one, passed through his mind and made him smile. How was he going to justify the three gold sovereigns that he had given to the priest in his report regarding the finances of his assignment? 'A business dinner in a Georgian monastery.' Surely the Finance Director would raise his eyebrows. But C would understand. Besides, he believed that gold saves lives.

CHAPTER 8

Vladimir Miralamov

Moscow, August 1944

The headquarters of the NKVD in the Lubyanka Building in Moscow, which had been a department store at the beginning of the century under tsarist Russia, was a beehive of activity for those who entered (some unwillingly), exited (some dead) or worked in dozens of offices. For most of them, the building emitted an air of fear and mockery, as if it were the cavern of a dragon or a monster that devoured flesh and souls.

The Lubyanka and its residents were feared by everyone, even the decorated field marshals and generals of the Soviet army who had been fearless when facing the Germans. In the past, some of them, such as Marshall Konstantin Rokossovsky had been a "guest" there. He was one of the lucky few because in 1938 he had suffered only a few broken teeth when he was interrogated by NKVD agents. He had replaced them with gold teeth, thus earning the nickname "Golden Smile". He had been reinstated and was now the director of one of the Front Guards that marched against the heart of the Third Reich. Many others had not been as fortunate.

For the men of the NKVD, such as Vladimir Pavlovitz Miralamov, the Lubyanka was the strongest centre of power in the Soviet Union. Miralamov had undertaken a new assignment directly from the chief of the NKVD, Lavrentiy Beria, which indicated how important it was.[74]

Now that the war had taken a decisive and positive turn and the end was in sight, the file with the information that had been leaked to the Greek ambassador in 1938 had been re-opened. At the time, the NKVD had stopped the leak but had not discovered the source. The NKVD and Miralamov had to guarantee the leak would not be repeated otherwise, if it fell in the hands of their adversaries, it would be dangerous and damaging. Miralamov and his team had to uncover the source of the leak.

They looked through old files and interrogations, searching for the names of those that had been involved in the matter, and obtained statements from whomever they could find. Some had died, some of natural causes and others in the purges, or during the war. Their task was a very difficult one.

Miralamov and his team had made a list of names that had been involved in the matter in 1938 and were now investigating those who were no longer alive.

One of these was Valentin Slusar, who had handled the matter in Georgia and Tbilisi, had served as commissar in 1941 and had been lost in the retreat, unaccounted for, perhaps a prisoner or more likely, dead.

Miralamov and his team now searched for survivors who might have known Slusar and had possibly worked with him.

---

[74] Lavrentiy Beria was the chief of the NKVD and confidant of Stalin and responsible to a great extent for the 1938 purges. After Stalin's death and de-Stalinisation under Khrushchev, he was arrested, convicted and executed.

He had no information that made him suspect Slusar. However, he had no information about anyone and this was his main problem. They were in the dark and essentially investigating without any evidence, which meant that they had to consider everyone, dead or alive. Miralamov knew that the investigation was critical for the Soviet Union, the Communist Party and for himself … If he succeeded, it would be a very important step for his career, a step toward an almost certain promotion to general. If he failed… he preferred not to think of the consequences.

Slusar, therefore, the missing Slusar.

This one thought preoccupied him. There was no special reason for this aside from his trustworthy instinct. Slusar had undertaken the investigation of a possible leak in Georgia. And earlier, he had been examining the files of OKHRANA in Georgia.

Since Slusar was missing, Miralamov and his team investigated all those who had known him when he was alive. Paying close attention to detail, as always, they had prepared lists with names which Miralamov studied carefully. Among the names one struck him like an alarm: Sub-lieutenant Ivan Tolmides. In 1941 he had served in Slusar's battalion where Slusar was a commissar. Some of the men in the battalion who had survived had reported that Slusar had been an unofficial crew member of Tolmides' tank. In the archives of his battalion, they discovered Tolmides' report from the time he had succeeded in reaching behind the lines of the Soviet Army. He had reported the capture of the injured Slusar.

He was now Captain Ivan Tolmides. Twice a hero of the Soviet Union, the second time very recently for being wounded at the beginning of Operation Bagration. Above suspicion … But in the Soviet Union, when even highly placed officers such as Leo Trotsky, Mihail Tuhachevsky, Nikolai Yezhov, Nikolai Bukharin, Lev Kamenev, Grigory Zinoviev and so many others had been judged guilty, no one was above suspicion. Not that Miralamov suspected Tolmides. However, he thought that since he had been

Slusar's colleague in 1941 and was probably the last person to see him alive, it was possible that Slusar had told him something that might be useful … possibly.

His team also discovered that he was now in Tbilisi where he was recovering from his injuries. Tbilisi, Georgia, where Slusar had conducted his research … A coincidence? Perhaps. But Miralamov had no further evidence, no facts for his research.

He decided to go to Tbilisi, to meet with and interrogate Tolmides. Perhaps not an interrogation at this point, more of a friendly conversation with a hero, who might be able to assist in the research … however, he was curious. Did Tolmides know something about Slusar?

* * * * *

Armenia, Soviet Union, September 1944

They drove for about an hour.

They stopped and got out of the lorry

'From here we'll continue on horseback,' Mustafayev said. 'It's too risky to continue with the lorry having Tolmides with us, so far from Tbilisi. I can't be sure that we won't be stopped on the main road by the NKVD or by the army. Nor can we officially leave from the border where we entered. Tolmides' family would raise questions.'

'What's the plan?' Bond asked.

'We'll head south taking footpaths. We'll cross the Lesser Caucasus and re-enter Soviet Azerbaijan at Nakhchivan. From there, we'll enter Iran at the 46th meridian,' Mustafayev said, smiling at the trivial information he had just provided.

'It's not a difficult trip in the summer, nor is it difficult now, at the beginning of autumn. Of course, it's different in winter …'

They said goodbye to Roustem who drove off in the lorry.

Leaving the main road, they took a small dirt road that led toward some scattered houses, not even a village.

Five of Mustafayev's men waited for them there with ten horses.

Mustafayev asked Tolmides if he knew how to ride, who said no.

'I thought so,' Mustafayev murmured. 'I'll give you a calm horse and your wife can climb behind you … but your daughter …'

'I'll take her,' Bond said readily.

'Okay, this way we'll have extra horses to alternate with the horses that have two riders so that they can rest when necessary,' Mustafayev said.

'Let's go!'

They mounted the horses, helping Andromache and Tolmides. An Azerbaijani raised Katerina and placed her behind Bond on the horse.

'Hold onto my waist,' he told her. 'Don't be afraid.'

Andromache translated. The girl put her arms around Bond's waist, saying in Greek, 'I'm not afraid!'

They started off. With a joyful bark, the dog began to trot next to Bond's horse.

'It seems that you're a member of the team until the end,' Bond said with a smile. 'This means that we'll have to give you a name. What shall it be? How about Wolf?'

'Wolf!' he called out to the dog who turned its head toward Bond, barking twice as if in agreement.

They started off, without hurrying, giving Tolmides a chance to get used to riding his horse. With its steady, unhurried gait, he realised that this was a smoother means of transportation than a tank that lunged for attack on uneven ground.

It was an uphill climb, ascending hills with meadows and forests, before arriving at the Lesser Caucasus. It was idyllic, with an occasional, isolated house and flocks of grazing sheep and goats.

Bond thought how it was when one looked at the landscape with the eyes of the soul. The same place can appear serene when one is at peace with oneself, when one is not filled with fear and anxiety. But the same place can seem wild and threatening when one is uneasy, when being pursued. Like those slender pine trees. So beautiful, a place where one can rest under their shade, close one's eyes and dream … or can it also serve as a refuge to hide from one's enemies? Or an obstacle that must be detoured when in a hurry, when one feels the breath of the enemy coming from behind?

He smiled. These were strange thoughts that were not characteristic of him.

'Are you okay?' he turned his head and asked the girl behind him.

She understood and nodded.

At noon they stopped under some trees, dismounted and took a few steps to stretch their legs. Then they sat down for their simple but satisfying meal of bread, cheese, tins of corned beef (Bond read the labels and saw that were American products, probably from Mustafayev's commercial dealings). They finished their meal with apples.

'What made you decide to leave the Soviet Union?' he asked Andromache.

She translated and Tolmides answered.

'When the war ended, we decided that we didn't want to live again what we had lived through before it began …'

'And yet you fought hard for this country that you are now abandoning,' Bond observed.

'I fought for my family, my honour, my comrades. I did not fight for an idea, for the Party, or for Stalin. I fought for the people I love. It's for them that I am abandoning the country. So that they can have a better future, a future that is safer, a future with freedom. You have lived in a free country. You will find it difficult to understand what life here is like.'

Andromache translated and added fervently, 'You don't know what it's like to live in terror. I'm not talking about the war, somehow you find ways to deal with it, no matter how terrible it is. You think that someday it will end and perhaps you'll survive. You fight with all your might to stay alive. But how can you fight against the uncertain regime in your country which you cannot control but which controls you, stalks you, terrorises you, never knowing how it will deal with you, what decisions it will make for you. Not knowing if your loved one will return from work or will disappear without warning, without explanation, without a reason. Do you know that the NKVD, like the GPU in the past, but even more so now, can arrest, exile, imprison or execute anyone without a trial, even children over the age of 12? I don't want our daughter to live in such an environment. This is why we've decided to leave. So that she can live free. Do you understand?'

Bond remained silent.

He understood, even though it was difficult. He knew enough, like everyone in the Service, about the regime in the Soviet Union. He knew that the demands of war had transformed Stalin from an unfeeling dictator to a well-intentioned, "good father" for, at least, a people (or many people) somewhat too simple to accept western ways and democracy. The leaders were aware of this and tried to cultivate this idea in public opinion. Would this change after the war? When conditions were different? And what about vested interests? And the judgement of those who made decisions? Whether they were right or wrong? What, in the final analysis, was the greatest evil? The Nazis? Stalin's communists? He thought of the politicians in his country, of Neville Chamberlain before Churchill came to power, and his Munich Agreement with Hitler, and Chamberlain's declaration of "peace for our time". And the vivid words of Churchill, "An appeaser is one who feeds a crocodile

— hoping it will eat him last." Who was the crocodile? Hitler? Stalin? Would one crocodile replace another? Can you fight one evil by joining forces with another? How was it that ordinary Soviet soldiers fought so heroically, with such self-denial? Did they fight for their country, but which country? What did it offer them, what did they expect?

'Every meaning of dignity and humanity has been lost,' Tolmides added quietly as if reading his thoughts. 'We are all slaves of the NKVD … and its leaders. At first of Nikolai Yezhov, a drunk and salacious man … and now of the "golden" Lavrentiy Beria. They can do whatever they want with us. Terrorizing, blackmailing, threatening women and daughters to give themselves sexually to save their fathers, husbands, brothers … displacement of minorities for the sole reason that they were not born Russians but Chechens, Tatars, Pontic Greeks, Uzbeks. This is why we want to leave.'[75]

Mustafayev interrupted them.

'Time to go,' he said.

* * * * *

When they reached Tbilisi, Miralamov and his men went to Tolmides' flat. They knocked on the door but no one opened. It was possible that Tolmides was away, perhaps he had gone for a walk. Nothing unusual.

Miralamov left two of his men and went to the offices of the local NKVD. He spoke to the director, asked a few questions, received a few answers that added nothing to what he already knew. He returned to the flat. It was late in the afternoon.

Tolmides had not returned. Nor had his wife, nor his daughter.

---

[75] Stalin wrote that "a single death is a tragedy; a million deaths are a statistic".

Miralamov felt a nagging suspicion. He sent one of his men to the school where Andromache worked. It was closed at this time but the guard would give him the address of the school's director. He would know where Andromache and the little girl were.

In the meantime, he decided to inspect Tolmides' flat. It was within the jurisdiction of the NKVD. He asked one of the men to force the lock. For the time being, it wasn't necessary to break down the door. Anyway, the old lock did not present much of a problem.

They opened the door and entered the flat. It was a small, cramped place, like most in the Soviet Union. There was a small living room, a bedroom with three beds, a small kitchen and an equally small bathroom. Only a few pieces of furniture. Nothing in comparison to the comforts that party officers and highly placed officials of the NKVD enjoyed.

They took a quick look around. Nothing suspicious. Some clothes, many books, all of which were approved by the regime, nothing that was banned.

Miralamov sat on the only couch. What the devil was going on? Something was bothering him, but what? Where was the family? Where was the man that he had sent to the school?

He felt like a hunter waiting for his prey. But the prey was not showing up and seemed to be making a fool of him.

What showed up a while later was the man that he had sent to the school. He had found the director who told him that Andromache Tolmides had not gone to school that morning; she had asked for a leave of absence the day before, saying that her daughter was sick with a fever and she wanted to stay home and take care of her.

His suspicions were confirmed! Leave of absence! A sick daughter! But they weren't in the flat nor was Tolmides. Sick enough to be in the hospital? Perhaps, but he didn't think so.

Miralamov flew up from the couch. He barked out orders. The men were to search all the hospitals in the city. They were to awaken all the residents of the building!

The men left quickly to execute his orders.

A little while later, he was talking to the awakened and terrified residents. A middle-aged woman remembered that she had seen the family leaving the flat the previous morning. A sick child? They were leaving the flat. Had she noticed anything unusual? Unusual? Probably not … or, perhaps, yes. They were carrying something … bags … as if they were going on an excursion, or a trip.

He was right to have been suspicious! He felt the blood rising to his head.

Furious and without a word, he left with his men, leaving behind the stupefied residents. Just in case the family showed up, he left two men at the flat. But he was certain that Tolmides would not be returning. Just as he was certain that they would not find them in any hospital.

He returned to his office at the NKVD and ordered a general search to be conducted.

He began to think things out.

He decided that the family was trying to leave the Soviet Union. There was nothing to explain their disappearance and the fake illness, the fake leave of absence.

There were two questions. Why and where to? Regarding the first, he had some suspicions, but no answers. Regarding the second, he had to think and make a plan. If he found them and arrested them, he would receive an answer to his first question.

Together with his men and the local leadership of the NKVD he began to study a large map of the area.

As was his habit, he tried to get into the mind of the person that he was searching for. What would he do if he were Tolmides? Where would he be heading?

Obviously, he would be trying to leave the Soviet Union. He would have to cross the border … Where to? Turkey or Iran? Turkey or neutral Iran which was under Anglo-American protection?

Toward the Black Sea and some port in Georgia, Batum or Kobuleti, and then a boat or caïque to Turkey? Probably not. The distance from Tbilisi to the coast was long. The ports were being checked. It would be difficult for them to find passage with a boat. It was too risky …

Traveling inland from the Lesser Caucasus was a shorter distance. Easier, toward either Turkey or Iran.

Turkey or Iran?

Turkey was neutral and from the time of the agreement between Lenin and Kemal[76] the country was on friendly terms with the Soviet Union. Turkey would not welcome fugitives.

On the other hand, Iran was under the control of the Allies. Accepting fugitives depended on their willingness. If they had something to offer, if there was some prior arrangement, the country would accept them.

Had there been some kind of arrangement? Did Tolmides have something to offer? Was there a reason behind his escape? A specific reason? Miralamov felt something like an inner knife jab. He did not want to admit it, but his suspicions were turning into certainty. There was a connection between Slusar, Tolmides and his investigation. He had to find Tolmides and prevent him from leaving the Soviet Union.

---

[76] At the end of the Russian Revolution, Lenin had agreed that the Soviet Union would give arms and gold to Kemal, which he later used against the Greeks. In return, Kemal would withdraw his support of the newly established Islamic Republic of Azerbaijan which, in 1920, was violently seized by the Soviets. This was Kemal's betrayal of the Azerbaijanis (see Rahman Mustafayev, ambassador of Azerbaijan to Greece until 2017, *Azerbaijan between the Great Powers 1918-1920*, Enalios 2016).

But how?

He had to cover all possible escape routes. Set up blockades on all the main roads. But that was not enough. He also had to consider the dozens of footpaths in the mountains. Difficult … he would have to find a lot of men. He would have to ask for reinforcements from the army … which would take some time. Tolmides already had an advantage of 15 hours. How far could he get in that time? On foot? By car? Was he familiar with the roads and footpaths in the mountains? To some extent, probably yes. He had grown up in Tbilisi.

He had to organise a search that would be successful. More than just the blockades. He needed a team under his supervision, and a local guide that knew the mountains. He gave orders for a search team to be organised and for a mountain guide to be found.

Where would the search begin?

He needed information. Quickly and safely.

How?

Reconnaissance from the air in the morning.

He began making telephone calls, giving orders, threatening when necessary. Yes, he needed reconnaissance from the air. Immediately. Where would they find the aircraft? A problem for the local air force command. Should he, perhaps, inform Comrade Beria that the local Soviet Air Force refused to participate in a matter of utmost importance to the state? Would the Commander understand? Wouldn't Comrade Beria need to be informed? Would he do what was needed? Would he agree to grant all the necessary means to the Comrade Colonel? Okay, okay. Comrade Colonel would emphasise in his report that the air force had cooperated.

Miralamov hung up the telephone.

He had done everything that was needed. Now he had to wait until the next day, to be ready as soon as his prey was spotted.

He tried to sleep so that he would be rested. It was difficult.

The men returned from the hospitals. There was no child by the name of Tolmides in any of them.

Of course. Just as he expected.

* * * * *

They continued their way uphill on paths that wound up the sides of the Lesser Caucasus, now more forested with a variety of trees with intertwining trunks, branches, leaves and colours.

It was almost like an excursion in beautiful and friendly natural surroundings.

Then, suddenly, they heard the quiet hum of a light engine aircraft. Before they had a chance to wonder what it was, or to run for cover, a U-2 biplane[77] appeared from behind a mountain peak, flying at a height of about 60 metres. They turned their heads to look at it, holding onto the reins of the horses.

The aircraft flew over them and left, then turned around and returned to the place from which it had appeared.

Bond directed a mute question to Mustafayev, who understood what it was and replied.

'It's a training and reconnaissance aircraft. It might be on a training flight. However, I don't like it. It might be a coincidence or it might not be. Training flights over the mountains are unusual.'

'Do you think they're searching for us? They may have discovered that Tolmides has fled,' Bond said, voicing his concern.

---

[77] The Polikarpov U-2 (Po-2). At first this two-seater biplane was used for training and was produced in 1929. It was used during the war for reconnaissance, as a bomber (primarily at night) and as a medical aircraft. Over 20,000 were manufactured. When its designer Nikolai Polikarpov died in 1944, the aircraft was given his name as a tribute, Po-2. It had a 110-125hp engine, top speed of 93mph, lowest flying height of 40 miles and landing capability of 200 metres. It occasionally carried a machine gun for defence in the rear and up to 250kgs of bombs.

Mustafayev shrugged fatalistically.

'God only knows. But we should hurry. We'll spend the night in an isolated medieval castle, an eyrie. At night the aircraft won't see us, even if it flies overhead.'

They quickened their pace. At times, they cast a worried look at the sky. Mustafayev sent a man to scout ahead and another behind them, in case they were being followed.

A light rain began to fall, cooling the atmosphere. The earth smelled pleasantly of damp soil, fallen leaves and autumn flowers. It was about 22° or 23° Celsius, very agreeable, neither the suffocating heat of summer nor the unbearable cold of winter.

It was twilight when they saw the ruins of a castle at the top of a rise. It had once guarded the Christian kingdoms of the Caucasus from the invasions of the Seljuks and Ottomans.

Circular towers rose from the sides, now deserted and silent, with ivy and small trees growing near them. However, the towers and the wall connecting them, over five metres in height, were still well-preserved.[78]

They entered the grassy inner area, dismounted and took a few steps to relieve their stiffness after riding for so many hours. Mustafayev's men left the horses to graze on the grass and gave them water to drink. Two others lit a fire with wood that they had gathered. The walls concealed the flames and the smoke could not be seen in the dark.

They sat around the fire and ate food that had been warmed. The man that Mustafayev had sent as rear guard arrived and reported that they were not being followed at close range.

'We are close to the border,' Mustafayev said. 'We'll be there tomorrow night or the day after at the latest. This path is not guarded ...'

---

[78] The Caucasus has many medieval fortresses, or eyries, such as Chirag-Gala, and Alinja in Azerbaijan.

Exhausted, they fell asleep. One man kept guard from the top of one of the towers, just in case.

Bond woke from a curious feeling. Something wet on his nose.

He opened his eyes. Wolf was standing over his face, licking him. As soon as he realised that Bond was awake, he wagged his tail and growled softly, baring his teeth.

Bond got up, listened and looked at the dog. Wolf wagged his tail again and growled as if wanting to warn him.

Bond shook the sleep from his eyes. He climbed on the tower where the guard sat. He listened closely, trying to discern something in the dark, to hear something … But he could see nothing nor hear anything unusual, aside from the sounds of the night, the rustle of leaves and branches, the calling out of a night bird, perhaps an owl.

He climbed down.

The dog growled again, louder.

'What is it, Wolf?' Bond asked.

Wolf barked once, softly.

Bond decided that it was best to play it safe, even if they had to wake up. The dog had smelled and heard something. It might only be an animal, a deer or a bear. But it might be something more threatening.

Bond nudged and awakened Mustafayev.

'Wolf is uneasy,' he said. 'He's heard something and is warning us. Let's play it safe, just in case.'

Without answering, Mustafayev flew up. He woke up his men while Bond woke up Tolmides.

'Get ready,' he said. 'Something might be going on. Let's be careful.'

Mustafayev's men prepared the horses. One stayed with them while Bond and the others, with their weapons, climbed on the wall and the towers and took positions.

They tried to spot something in the dark, between the trees, to hear something ... Expectation and anxiety ... his heart was beating heavily ... they might be taking precautions without cause. Were the leaves of the trees moving slightly? The bushes? A breath of air? Or was it something else? That sound ... what was it? Not a night bird, not the growl of an animal ... a muted, choked cough?

He felt the perspiration on his forehead and his palms. He gripped the handle of the Beretta in his hand.

He noticed shadows in the bushes and trees. There was no doubt.

It was almost daylight and the first rays of sun were chasing away the darkness.

The figures were entering an open area that separated the forest from the walls of the castle, about 60 metres away. Now they could see them clearly. Human shadows. Soldiers that were approaching as quietly as possible.

Mustafayev spoke softly to one of his men who climbed down from the wall.

'I told him to take the family and leave right away. We'll detain them for a few minutes,' he said to Bond.

That was a sound decision. As long as the enemy had not already encircled the castle ... and as long as it was approaching only from one side, the northern side. The dog's early warning had given them some valuable time.

Bond heard the horses leaving the castle. He cast a quick glance. Tolmides, Andromache and one of Mustafayev's guards with Katerina behind him were leaving together with the horses that carried the supplies.

He watched them for a short while until they disappeared beyond the castle walls. Would they be able to proceed without anything unexpected happening? How many seconds, minutes until they reached the path farther away?

How many breaths, how many heart beats?

No gun shots.

They must have reached the path …

Bond looked again toward the outer side of the wall.

The soldiers had left the cover of the forest and were approaching slowly, trying not to make a sound.

There were about 20 to 30 men.

'Let them come half-way', Mustafayev murmured.

Unseen and without making a sound, Mustafayev's men eyed them, their guns aimed …

A little more, a little more …

Mustafayev fired and his men fired right after him, with rapid shots, emptying their guns. A few soldiers groaned and fell, the rest fell to the ground to protect themselves. Voices and commands were heard. The soldiers tried to seek out the enemy at the walls. They began to shoot but without aiming because Mustafayev's men were well hidden behind the embrasures.

They loaded their guns once more and continued to fire, intermittently now, just to nail the enemy.

A machine gun began to fire from the forest, scattering fragments and mud from the wall.

'Time to leave,' Mustafayev said.

They had slowed the advance of the enemy by about five minutes. By the time the enemy attempted to encircle the castle, to regroup and realise that they had already left the castle, they would have gained some additional time.

Mustafayev, Bond and the men climbed down from the ramparts and ran toward the inner area of the castle. They mounted their horses and left from the second gate, behind the castle. They galloped at a fast clip with Wolf running next to Bond's horse.

They reached the path farther from the castle without mishap and only then did they slow down. A short while later they met up with Tolmides and his family and the guide.

'What do we do now?' Bond asked.

'We continue as quickly as we can. We have gained some time but they'll catch up with us soon. They probably also have horses. The reconnaissance aircraft must have spotted us yesterday. If necessary, we'll delay them with ambushes ...'

Mustafayev ordered a man to scout ahead and one behind them as a rear guard.

One of Mustafayev's men took Andromache behind him on his horse so that the other horse could rest from its double load. Bond took Katerina with him.

They continued on the upward path as quickly as they could on the rough and uneven ground and with Tolmides who was not accustomed to riding a horse. The path took them through a forest which offered them some cover.

They proceeded with the monotonous trotting of the horses on which they swayed as if they were in a boat riding the waves. Bond could feel Katerina's hands around his waist and he occasionally turned around to say a few encouraging words even though he knew she could not understand. But the tone of his voice was important as was his smile, which Katerina returned with a grin. The brusque, strong man inspired confidence in her. Katerina gritted her teeth. She would show him that she, too, was strong, like a true Greek, like the ancient women of Sparta, or Bouboulina, the Greek woman naval commander and heroine of the Greek War of Independence in 1821, whose stories her mother had told her.

They continued without a stop until noon, struggling with fatigue and exhaustion, while the horses panted, foaming at the mouth and began to slow down.

At noon they took a brief rest to loosen their stiff joints, to drink some water and give some water to the horses. A break that could not be avoided. Without even a short rest, the horses would not be able to continue.

Fortunately, till now, the guards had not spotted anything suspicious. Nor had they heard any gunfire. Their pursuers were not close.

But as soon as they had started on their way again, the scout arrived on his panting horse and spoke quickly to Mustafayev.

When he finished listening to him, Mustafayev, uneasy for the first time, turned to Bond and spoke to him.

'There is a blockade on the path, about two miles ahead of us,' he said.

Bond felt a tightening in his chest.

The road ahead blocked and their pursuers behind them … Caught in a trap so close to the border and yet as far away as the moon!

He didn't have a chance to ask what they should do next before Mustafayev spoke.

'There is only one escape route.' he said. 'From there!'

He pointed to the peaks of two mountains and the col between them.

'Behind the pass is Iran,' he said. 'A little farther down there is a path, perhaps not even a path, something more like a trail created by flocks of animals when they pass through. It's passable, but only on foot. It's too steep and rough for the horses. It's the only solution there is.'

Bond nodded.

'Let's go,' Mustafayev said. 'We'll have to leave the horses as soon as we arrive.'

A short time later they came to the place where the path branched off. Bond couldn't see it. All he saw was an upward slope between the trees, although he had noticed, from a different angle a little while ago, that it gave way to a bare area higher up, with vegetation and rocks as far as the pass.

They dismounted.

Mustafayev's men took some necessary provisions from the horses, whatever they could carry with them. Then they let the horses go free.

'They might see their tracks and get confused, even if it's only for a short while,' Mustafayev said. 'Every minute gained is valuable,' he added.

They started off, Andromache holding Katerina's hand.

Tolmides looked at his wife and smiled.

'We'll make it,' he told her. 'We've managed before and we'll manage again. We're close to freedom!'

She smiled, trying to look calm and not show her fear, saying a prayer to herself, as she had done when leaving Kiev.

Tolmides remembered the summer of 1941, his escape from Kiev. What an irony! At that time, it was the Germans who were chasing him as he tried to reach the battalions of the Soviet Army. Now they were being pursued by Soviet soldiers in their attempt to abandon their country, a country which had become more of an immense prison than a real country …

* * * * *

Miralamov entered the abandoned castle. The prey had escaped … How had it noticed their approach at night? He had lost two soldiers and another four were wounded. However, he still had enough men to continue the chase.

Although he had lost precious time, they would not elude him. He had arranged for blockades by frontier units along all the paths that led to Iran. And he was coming behind them with his team. The trap that had failed at the castle would simply succeed a little farther away.

They mounted their horses and followed the path as fast as the animals could gallop.

Later, among the trees, they saw horses without riders.

They stopped. Some of Miralamov's men caught them and brought them to him. They must be the fugitives' horses. The reconnaissance aircraft had not seen any other horseback riders in the region. But where were the riders?

Miralamov called for their scout, a hunter who knew the mountains well.

'Where can they have gone?' he asked.

The man shrugged his shoulders.

'Since they left the horses behind, they must have abandoned the path. This means that they're going toward the border on foot.'

'Where?' Miralamov insisted.

'There are no paths, only trails made by animals. Toward the pass.'

'Can you find their tracks?'

The hunter did not reply, feeling offended, but not daring to show it to this abrasive and intimidating colonel of the Secret Service.

'Well, can you?' Miralamov insisted.

'Of course,' the hunter replied. 'A group of so many people moving quickly always leaves tracks.'

Indelible traces, discernible only to an experienced eye like his, much clearer even than the tracks of a deer or a bear.

The hunter began to walk on the path while the others followed him.

Suddenly, he stopped, kneeled, and looked closely at the ground. Then he said to Miralamov, 'This is where they left the path. They're heading toward a pass between two peaks. Iran is on the other side.'

'How far ahead are they?'

'It's difficult to say. I think about one or two hours,' the hunter replied.

'Is there any other way that we can reach the pass without following them?'

'Yes, but only for one or two strong men who can clamber up the farthest places and rocks. It's not for everyone; one person would be in the way of the other.'

Miralamov made a quick decision. He ordered his second-in-command to follow the path taken by the fugitives. Then he ordered the hunter to lead him.

He slung a rifle with a scope over his shoulder.

The hunter cast a quick glance at him before turning away. The colonel looked fit and tough, but was he really?

Not important. How fit he was would show later. The colonel's endurance would determine their speed. The hunter would simply serve as his guide and would follow orders.

CHAPTER 9

Wolf

They climbed or, to be exact, clambered up the uphill path through the trees and fallen leaves as quickly as they could. Mustafayev's men and Bond were in excellent physical shape. But Tolmides was not and his wound, although it had healed, had left him somewhat weak. His leg had become numb now and he felt shooting pangs of pain because of the exertion. He gritted his teeth and walked on. Freedom was near, only one last effort …

Andromache walked but lagged behind because she had to hold onto Katerina's hand. The girl's steps were small and her endurance just as small. They were holding back the rest of the party.

Mustafayev kept looking back at them, without saying anything. But Bond understood what he was thinking.

He paused, letting Andromache and Katerina reach him. When they were next to him, he said: 'Andromache, let me take Katerina on my shoulders.'

Without waiting for an answer, he said to the girl: 'Do you want me to be your horse?'

She smiled at him.

He took her in his arms and put her on his shoulders. Her legs hung over his right and left shoulders.

'Are you alright up there?' he asked without waiting for a reply.

They continued to walk. The child was light, much lighter than the 30 kilos that he had to carry on training hikes with the SAS, when he was in training.[79]

It occurred to him that he had told Amanda that he was not going on a dangerous mission. The "not dangerous mission" had turned into a deathly pursuit … What would Sir Stewart say if he could see him now, a little girl on his shoulders, clambering up the inaccessible slopes of the Lesser Caucasus?

They kept climbing. Step by step. From breath to breath. Heartbeat to heartbeat. Perspiring from the effort. Tolmides panted, limping slightly, half-stopping for seconds at a time to catch his breath.

Mustafayev approached him and offered his hand. Tolmides hesitated at first but then took it.

They continued to climb toward the peak. The forest ended at the foot of the pass. Stones and dirt, open, unprotected ground for a few hundred metres and the pass between two steep peaks with rocks like teeth or natural ramparts. On the other side lay Iran and freedom.[80]

They stood for a while under the protection of the last trees. Mustafayev scanned the pass and the rocks with his binoculars.

He saw nothing suspicious. The pass was clear, as if it were welcoming them.

'Let's go,' he said, letting a scout go first, about 100 steps ahead of them.

---

79 The Special Air Service, the special forces of Great Britain that was formed by David Stirling in North Africa in 1941.

80 Such regions are characteristic of the Lesser Caucasus, such as Mount Kapaz in Azerbaijan.

They left the forest, climbing the steep ground which was slightly slippery from the rain. The dirt was dotted with large stones and rocks. The expectation of freedom so near gave wings to Tolmides, casting off his exhaustion for one final effort.

Less than 1,000 metres to the pass … less than 900 … don't count steps and breaths, keep your mind focused on freedom, on the pass which you are approaching … 800 metres … 700 … you can do it, you can do it, you can do it … you're getting closer, you'll make it, you'll succeed, a little more, a little more, 600 metres, a little more, what are 600 metres compared to the kilometres from Tbilisi, what are 500 metres compared to the kilometres you walked in the summer of 1941 in Ukraine, without food, almost without water?

The shots resonated suddenly and echoed on the mountain.

Mustafayev's scout, who had walked ahead of them, fell to the ground, struck in the head. He was dead before he even touched the ground.

'Down!' Mustafayev shouted, pulling Tolmides to a shelter behind a boulder.

Bond fell to the ground carefully so that Katerina would not be hurt.

'Stay here,' he told her, pointing to the boulder that protected them. Andromache and Mustafayev's men had also found cover. The uneven ground offered protection from the unseen sniper.

But they were trapped. If they stood up, they would be easy targets. The enemy had only to wait for either a sudden movement or for the pursuers to reach them from behind. Bond had no doubts that their pursuers had not abandoned their efforts. They were trapped.

Cautiously, he lifted his head and cast a quick glance. Nothing. The sniper was invisible, concealed somewhere among the natural ramparts around the pass.

'Do you see anything?' Mustafayev asked.

'No,' he replied.

The minutes ticked by. Inaction. Anxiety. Perspiration. Inertia. Trapped. Time was against them.

Miralamov was alone now as the hunter had left him. Face down between two boulders, he looked through his rifle's telescope. He was patient. They would be an easy target if they made any movement, but he wanted to capture them alive. He wanted to arrest them, to interrogate them, to discover how the documents had been leaked. He could wait. His men were climbing behind them on the mountain. When they arrived, they would encircle and trap them. Miralamov was going to snare them!

The minutes ticked by. Tortuously slow. Freedom was so close and yet so far away.

Something had to be done, but what?

Next to Bond, Wolf growled.

Bond turned his head and saw the dog that had stayed close to him. Wolf looked at Bond with a piercing expression, as if wanting to say something.

Bond understood, or thought he understood. Completely crazy, but what other option did they have?

'Rahman, can you push your rifle to me?' he asked the Azerbaijani who was lying face down about five metres away.

Mustafayev didn't ask why.

He pushed his rifle, a British Enfield, toward Bond.

He moved slightly, stretched out his hand, caught hold of the barrel of the rifle and pulled it close to him.

He loaded it.

'Wolf, get him,' he called out to the dog. 'Find him, grab him!'

Wolf wagged his tail and barked twice.

Bond steadied the barrel of the rifle on the rock that protected him and fired without raising his head, without aiming, but only to distract the sniper. He fired again and two of Mustafayev's men did the same.

The dog leaped over the rock and began to run.

Miralamov did not notice the dog behind him until he felt its teeth digging into the thigh of his right leg.

Piercing pain.

Without wanting, he let out a scream that echoed over the mountains, just as the shots had done previously.

Wolf dragged him by the foot.

Miralamov let go of his rifle, trying to free himself from the dog's teeth and to rise from his prone position. He tried to kick the dog with his free foot but from his prone position, it was not easy and he did not have enough strength.

With great effort, he managed to turn upright. He kicked again with his left foot, harder this time. He hit the dog in the ribs with his boot but the dog would not let go, digging its teeth even deeper into the flesh, trying to drag him. Miralamov screamed again. He succeeded in kicking Wolf twice in his muzzle. Wolf opened his mouth, his teeth dripping with blood, he howled in pain and took a step back.

But, as Miralamov attempted to get up, he immediately pounced again. Wolf fell on the man's chest, trying to get at his throat. Miralamov managed to raise his hands to protect himself. Wolf's teeth closed around his left wrist. Miralamov screamed again, falling to the ground together with the dog. Wolf would not let go of the man's wrist.

Miralamov hit him with his right hand but Wolf would not release his wrist. Miralamov grabbed the rifle with his right hand, struck Wolf in the ribs with the barrel. But the dog continued to hang on to his wrist.

Stumbling, leaning on his rifle, Miralamov succeeded in rising.

He was more stable now and his right hand had a wider range. He hit Wolf on the right front leg with all his strength, using the butt of the rifle.

Wolf opened his muzzle, yelped and fell to the ground, holding up his injured leg. However, even limping, he prepared to pounce again on his enemy. Miralamov loaded his rifle quickly and brought it to his shoulder to fire.

As soon as Bond heard Miralamov's first scream, he leaped from his hiding place and began to run toward the place from where he believed the shout had come. A few seconds, a dozen or so steps. He noticed movement behind some rocks without, however, having a clear field to shoot.

He continued to run, without panting, in spite of his efforts.

Suddenly, he saw the sniper getting up from behind the rocks, his back turned to Bond. Bond stopped and with a quick move, brought his rifle to his shoulder, aimed and fired. Miralamov was about 300 metres away but Bond was an excellent marksman.

The bullet struck him in the heart. His rifle fell from his hands before he collapsed to the ground.

When Bond reached him, the man was dead.

Bond cast a look around him. There was no one else. The sniper had been alone.

'Come!' he called out to the others, gesturing with his hands.

Then he turned to the dog who looked at him with expressive eyes, as if waiting for the man to speak.

Bond kneeled and scratched behind the dog's ears.

'Bravo, Wolf. You're a hero. You saved us.'

Wolf licked his hand. Bond noticed that he had lifted his right front leg. He took it and held it carefully, feeling the bone. It was broken.

The others came up to them.

Mustafayev saw the dog's leg and understood.

'He won't be able to follow us,' he said. 'the first village is about 15 kilometres away … If he stays here, the wild animals will devour him … there are wolves and bears … or he'll die of hunger.

We have to kill him … Do you want me to do it?' he asked, taking hold of the handle of his pistol.

Katerina understood and cried out, 'No!'

Bond stopped Mustafayev.

'Go on,' he said. 'I'll catch up with you. Go!' he said to Andromache telling her to take the girl who was in tears.

Andromache took her daughter's hand gently and pulled her.

They left, walking to the pass, to freedom.

Bond took out his knife.

Wolf looked at him with a sad face, almost human in its expression.

* * * * *

The Kremlin, Moscow, October 1944

The aircraft with the British representatives landed at the airfield in Moscow on the afternoon of 9 October 1944. Molotov, together with other Soviet officials and a military detachment, rendered honours to Churchill, Foreign Secretary Anthony Eden and their entourage.

Limousines took them to their accommodations, a perfectly appointed house for Churchill and another, close by, for Eden. They ate alone, rested and, at 10 o'clock in the evening, they went to a meeting at the Kremlin.

Stalin, Molotov, Churchill and Eden were present together with their interpreters, Major Arthur Birse and Vladimir Pavlov.

After the formalities of greetings had taken place, Churchill spoke, while Birse and Pavlov translated.

'Let us settle about our affairs in the Balkans. We have interests, missions, and agents there. Don't let us get at cross purposes in small ways. So far as Britain and Russian are concerned, how would it do for you to have 90% dominance in Rumania, for us to have 90% of the say in Greece and go 50-50 in Yugoslavia?'

While Pavlov translated, the Prime Minister took a half-sheet of paper and wrote:

Rumania: Russia 90%, the others 10%

Greece: Great Britain (in agreement with the USA) 90%, Russia 10%

Yugoslavia: 50% and 50%

Hungary: 50% and 50%

Bulgaria: Russian 75%, the others 25%

Churchill slid the paper toward Stalin.[81]

A small pause.

Then, Stalin took his blue pencil and made a tick on the paper as if he were trying it out and returned the paper to Churchill. Everything was settled in a very short time, only as long as it had taken Churchill to write the note.

A short silence.

The paper with the blue tick, which decided the fortunes of people and countries, lay on the table.

Once again, Churchill was the first to speak.

'Might it not be thought rather cynical if it seemed we had disposed of these issues, so fateful to millions of people, in such an offhand manner? Let us burn the paper.'

Stalin replied, 'No, you keep it.'

The Prime Minister then brought up the matter of Germany.

They agreed to have the matter studied further by the two Foreign Secretaries and the American Ambassador to Russia, Averell Harriman.[82]

---

[81] This was the "Percentages Agreement" drawn up by Churchill and Stalin concerning the Balkans in Moscow in October 1944 (see Winston Churchill, *The Second World War: Triumph and Tragedy, vol. VI*, p. 198).

[82] Churchill, vol. VI, p. 198.

Back at his residence, Churchill was alone with Eden. The Prime Minister smoked one of his cigars and they each had a whisky, which they had brought with them. Of course, the Russians had offered them wines from the Crimea (pre-war production) and vodka but they didn't know that they had brought whisky with them.

'What will they say about me Anthony? Regarding today? Of course, it was not an inspiration of the moment, we had planned it. I was surprised that Stalin accepted it so readily …'

'Will he keep the agreement?' Eden asked.

'I agree, Anthony. I don't trust him at all. But I haven't said my last. We will have another meeting.'

Eden raised his eyebrows with an expression of doubt.

The Prime Minister smiled.

'The day after, Anthony. Allow your old Prime Minister to surprise you.'

He changed the subject once more.

'What will they say about me Anthony? That I am cynical? A realist? Both? That I won the most difficult war in the history of Great Britain and lost peace? Is there a future for the Empire? How I helped my country find itself on the right side of history? How I gave so many countries to a dictator? To an autocracy? That I did nothing more, nothing less than Chamberlain did with Hitler. What do you think Anthony?'

Eden had rarely seen the Prime Minister in such a state of mind.

'Did we give him too much?' he asked.

'No, Anthony. We did not give him too much. We gave him nothing more than what he already had, whereas we secured something that he could have made his own. The Soviet Army already has Rumania and Bulgaria. The same will happen to Hungary. All three were on the side of the Axis, they were enemy countries. But Greece … our traditional ally. Who would have prevented the Soviets from invading Greece from Bulgaria with the support of ELAS and KKE, the Greek Communist Party, in order to "liberate" the country? No one. I tried to open a front in the Aegean in September 1943 with our landings on Samos, Kos, Leros. We failed. My greatest fiasco, my critics said. The Americans never supported us then, they were afraid of our imperialist motives. They were short-sighted. Now, only diplomacy can save Greece.'

'And my little surprise,' he added.

Churchill sipped his whisky, took a puff of his cigar and watched the smoke as it curled upwards, before continuing his monologue.

'How will history judge me? I hope that I have given the Greeks the glorious and great decoration of freedom.'[83]

'I want them to write about me that I kept Greece free and that I gave the Jews a country. No two cities have counted more with mankind than Athens and Jerusalem.[84] They will become capitals once again of two free countries. This is what I want my legacy to be. I don't want them to write about me what I said about Chamberlain. "To England you offered the choice between war and dishonour. You chose dishonour and you will have war."[85]

'I chose war to the extreme. I encouraged the British in their darkest hour. I did not promise them "peace for our time". I promised them blood and tears. But also victory at the end. I kept my promise. The British rose to the occasion. Whatever might happen in the future, the world will not forget it. From June 1940 till December 1941 we alone kept the flame of freedom alive against the phenomenal might of Nazism. At the time when the

---

[83] From the lost theatrical work of the poet Timotheus of Miletus, *The Persians*.

[84] Churchill, *The Second World War: Closing the Ring*, vol. V, p. 471.

[85] Said by Churchill to Lloyd George when Chamberlain signed the Munich Agreement with Hitler on 13 August 1938 in Moscow.

Luftwaffe was bombarding and destroying our cities. With Soviet fuel. I won't forget this, Anthony. But we held on. We did not yield. Just as the Greeks did not yield when they fought the Italians for six months. I won't forget this, either, Anthony. They made a fool of Mussolini. Even more so, they probably helped us hold onto Egypt. What would have happened if the Italians had sent 300,000 soldiers and the aircraft of the Regia Aeronautica[86] against us in Egypt instead of to the Albanian front? I won't forget this. Perhaps they think that I am cynical and that I think only of the interests of the Empire. It is true. But I do not forget. I remember our moral obligation to the Greeks. Fortunately, this time, morality and interest go hand in hand!'

The Prime Minister emptied his glass.

'Anthony, I have kept you long enough. Let's go to sleep. We still have a lot to do tomorrow and the next day.'

Moscow, the British Embassy, 11 October 1944

On the evening of 11 October Stalin went to the Embassy of Great Britain for dinner. The police and the NKVD had taken its measures and hundreds of men in uniform and in civilian clothes had closed off the surrounding streets but also, with the permission of the embassy, the interior. Passing in front the armed guards that were protecting the central staircase of the embassy, one of the dinner guests, Vyshinsky, said, 'It is said that the Red Army has claimed a new victory. It has seized the British Embassy.'

Churchill smiled at this display of Soviet humour.

Sometime later, he approached Stalin together with the British interpreter, Birse.

---

[86] Regia Aeronautica, the Royal Italian Air Force.

'I'd like to talk to you in private for a few minutes,' he said. 'Come.'

Birse translated.

Stalin was about to call for his interpreter, Pavlov.

Churchill said to him, 'What I have to say is entirely confidential. The fewer people that know about it, the better. Let us rely only on Mr Birse.'

Stalin did not show any surprise when Birse translated Churchill's words, or else he managed to hide it. With a wave of his hand, he sent off Pavlov and followed Churchill to the ambassador's office.

Birse closed the door behind them.

Churchill took the envelope that he had left earlier, opened it, removed the contents and gave them to Stalin.

Churchill studied him.

No expression. No reaction, as if it was the most innocent matter.

Or perhaps not?

He noticed a slight tremble of his thick moustache. Like a rat sniffing food.

Or danger.

Without a word, Stalin gave the document back to Churchill.

Churchill said to him, 'I assure you that your secret is safe with me, so long as you keep your side of our agreement.'

They returned to the reception.

When the guests had left, Churchill found himself alone with Eden. He told him about his meeting with Stalin.

'What do you think of my little surprise, Anthony?'

'I admit, I am speechless. Who would have thought it?'

'My secret trump card, Anthony,' Churchill said with a smile. 'I think that I won my diplomatic duel with Stalin. I blackmailed him openly, I admit, but what counts is the end result.'

'Stalin, an informer of OKHRANA! Who could have imagined it!' Eden exclaimed.

'Truly. But if you think about it, for someone as unscrupulous as Stalin, what could be more accommodating? Safe from the tsar's secret police and, at the same time, informing on political and personal enemies, he was able to clear his way of potential opponents.'[87]

'Will he honour the terms of the agreement?' Eden asked.

'I think he will,' Churchill said with certainty. 'Because it's to his advantage. Can you imagine the reaction if this information was to become known? The communist parties in France, Italy, The Netherlands, all the leftist intellectuals including our own, even the Soviet Communist Party and the Red Army? He won't risk it, Anthony! Fortunately, MI6 gave us the trump card for victory!'

London and Kent, mid-October 1944

The police in civilian clothing did not stop C and Bond at the entrance to the neo-Gothic residence that was surrounded by a forest, roughly 50 kilometres from London.

C was not unknown to the men and since he was accompanying someone, this meant that the other man was above suspicion.

They were led to the Prime Minister's office.

Churchill got up from his chair and extended his hand.

'Sir Stewart, thank you for making the effort to come to my office. And you must be Mr Bond. I told Sir Stewart that I wanted to meet you in person in order to thank you.'

---

[87] The document that revealed that Stalin was an informer for OKHRANA was published in *Pravda* on 30 March 1989 and was re-published in Ahtzidis p.201.

Churchill offered him a cigar from a box. He took one and Sir Stewart did as well. Bond declined.

'I don't smoke sir.'

'You don't smoke, Mr Bond? How did you manage to survive the war without smoking?' he asked cheerfully. 'Without my cigar, I would have had a nervous breakdown. The greatest injury against me that the Germans could have done would have been to deprive me of my cigars!'

'Mr Bond is not conventional, Mr Prime Minister,' Menzies replied.

'I guessed that already. His accomplishments are proof of that. However, will you have a drink? I hope you do not abstain from alcohol as well?'

'No, sir, I don't.'

'Excellent! So, some whisky?'

The Prime Minister called the butler who returned with a silver tray, three crystal glasses and a bottle of whisky.

He served them.

'Mr Bond, I read your report. However, I would like to hear it from you. The details of the mission. It's different when I hear it directly.'

While Bond related the details of the assignment, Churchill regarded him closely.

The young man reminded him of himself, about 50 years ago, when he was covering the Battle of Omdurman and the Boer War as a correspondent.[88]

He had a quality of decisiveness, bravery and a certain casualness. As long as Britain had such men, it had a future. He thought to himself that, even if the hour had come, or if it came,

---

[88] On the orders of General Sir Herbert Kitchener, the British defeated the Mahdists (jihadists) in Sudan in 1898. The Boer War (Boer, "farmers" in Afrikaans) took place in 1899-1902.

to lose first place on the world stage to the new powers, to the USA and the Soviet Union, Great Britain would do so with a deep, triumphant bow. The country would go to the side-lines as victors in a just war!

Bond concluded his narration.

'Thank you, Mr Bond. Great Britain and I, personally, are obligated to you. As is Greece. The Greeks might never learn how much they owe to you. However, you will have the satisfaction that you did your duty. I will recommend you for an OBE. And perhaps we should also decorate Wolf, the dog that saved you. You know, it has been done before,' the Prime Minister recalled. 'Queen Victoria herself received Bobbie at the Palace as a hero …'[89]

The Prime Minister rose, shook hands with them and said goodbye.

'How did the meeting with the Prime Minister go? What is he like as a person?' Amanda asked with curiosity and a little impatiently.

Wolf greeted Bond by rising on his hind legs, placing his front paws on his chest and licking his face. Bond scratched him behind the ears.

'He was very friendly, very affable, not at all aloof. He listened closely. And he laughed at my description of the surprise expressed by the British second lieutenant when we arrived at the first guard post in Iran. An unusual procession. In the lead was the Azerbaijani warlord with his beard and a cartridge belt over his shoulder, carrying a little girl on his back. He was followed by his

---

[89] Bobbie was a stray dog who became the mascot of the British 66th Regiment of Foot. On 3 July 1880, at the Battle of Maiwand, the regiment was decimated fighting ten times more Afghans. Bobby fought with the soldiers, was wounded and was one of the few survivors. His preserved body is on exhibit at the military Museum in Salisbury (see Th. Mastakouris, *Dogs in War*, 'History' 551, May 2014, pp.100-108.

sullen warriors, and a limping Tolmides in the centre, supported by his wife. And myself at the end of the procession, with a dog on my back wrapped in the scarf you had knitted for me and his leg in a temporary wooden splint. You can image the Briton's big surprise when I introduced myself as Commander of the Royal Navy ... what was a naval commander doing in the Caucasus? I asked him to contact headquarters in Teheran and to send us a vehicle. Oh, and by the way, Churchill has recommended me for an OBE.'[90]

Amanda smiled. One of the characteristics that she admired and liked about Bond was his irony and light self-sarcasm.

'You're making me jealous,' she said. 'I'm thinking back on my days at the SOE.'

'You've done enough and your work now might not be as exciting but it is just as essential. Anyway, the only thing about Hitler that I agree with is his position on women: "children and the kitchen".'

Of course, Amanda knew that he was joking.

'Isn't it strange,' Bond added thoughtfully. 'That the fate of a country can depend on the devotion of a dog ... what a strange sequence of events.'

'Perhaps it's fortunate that a solution can appear when least expected,' Amanda said thoughtfully.

'Perhaps.' Bond replied. 'But enough philosophising. We have to celebrate. And one day, I want to introduce you to Tolmides and his family. An extremely brave family ...'

'I'd like to. But now something else has precedence.'

Bond did not have a chance to answer because Amanda had embraced him and was searching for his lips.

---

[90] Order of the British Empire, a high British distinction.

London, 5 December 1944

'Mr Prime Minister, an urgent message from General Scobie[91] in Greece, sent by Hastings Ismay,' Eden said to Churchill.

Churchill took the message and read it.

An uprising in Greece. ELAS,[92] was trying to seize the city.

Eden was surprised to see the Prime Minister's reaction.

He didn't appear worried, and his eyes shone with what looked like a hidden enthusiasm.

'Excellent news, Anthony! They've thrown down the glove and we'll pick it up. It's an opportunity to clarify the situation. It's an opportunity to fight in a region where we have an advantage. In a city, where our tanks and aircraft have superiority Instead of up in the mountains. But are their leaders so stupid? To invite us in our arena!

'Perhaps they think that we won't get involved. Perhaps they think that the Soviets will support them. Scobie is worried about this also.

'They are deceived on both counts, a pitiful misconception. We're not going to let Athens fall into the hands of the communists. Reassure Scobie that he can act without fear of foreign intervention. Let's notify Ismay to send as many reinforcements as necessary to Greece, from Italy. Fortunately, because it's winter, it's quiet on the Italian front.'[93]

---

[91] General Scobie was the director of the British forces in Greece after the Germans had retreated. General Hastings Ismay was the British Chief of Staff.

[92] The Greek People's Liberation Army commonly known by its acronym ELAS. It was the military arm of the left-wing National Liberation Front (EAM) during the period of the Greek Resistance until February 1945 when it was disarmed and disbanded.

[93] At the beginning, Scobie's forces in Athens consisted of the 2nd Regiment of Paratroopers, the 23rd Armoured Brigade, the Greek Mountain Brigade

Eden was impressed once more by the Prime Minister's foresight. Hadn't he warned of the dangers of Hitler's Nazism, although at the beginning it was in vain? He had already sent a telegram to Scobie at 3 o'clock on the morning of 3 December when a bloody protest had taken place in Athens.

'You are responsible for maintaining order in Athens and for neutralizing or destroying all EAM-ELAS bands approaching the city … Do not, however, hesitate to act as if you were in a conquered city where a local rebellion is in progress.…

'With regard to ELAS bands approaching from the outside, you should surely be able with your armour to give some of these a lesson which will make others unlikely to try. You may count on my support in all reasonable and sensible action taken on this basis. We have to hold and dominate in Athens. It would be a great thing for you to succeed in this without bloodshed if possible, but also with bloodshed if necessary.'[94]

* * * * *

'Anthony, isn't it strange,' the Prime Minister asked Eden, 'to be criticised by our own people, by our friends, regarding Athens … Don't they see that it can't be otherwise? What choice was there? Should we have allowed ELAS to seize Athens violently? In the same way that the Bolsheviks stormed the winter palace of St.

(under Thrasyvoulos Tsakalotos). They were reinforced with police units, also from Italy, such as the 4th British Infantry Division as well as two units of the 46th Infantry Division. Air support comprised four British and three Greek squadrons, with Spitfires and two-engine Beaufighters of the 46th Division (see Menelaos Haralambides, *Dekemvriana*, Alexandreia Publications, 2014.

[94] The telegram was sent on 5 December 1944 at 4.50 am (see Churchill, vol. VI, p. 252).

Petersburg? Is that what they, the State Department and Edward Stettinius, wanted?[95]

'And even at home, what a turmoil there has been! The *Times* and *The Manchester Guardian* pronounced their censures upon what they considered our reactionary policy …'[96]

'Obviously, they don't have a complete picture or even accurate information,' Eden replied.

'Anthony, prepare a reply to Stettinius. And make sure it's leaked to the press. Explain what ELAS is, what they did during the Occupation, how they fought against other Greeks, about the murders they committed … I remember something from the reports made by our people, about a colonel, a member of another resistance group, that they murdered. Have your services find out more.[97]

'But the main thing is that Stalin adhered strictly and faithfully to our agreement … and not one word of reproach came from *Pravda* or *Isvestia*.[98]

'What an irony, that *Pravda* and *Izvestia* should serve as our pro-government newspapers! Of course, there are many that are wondering about this. Let them wonder. The secret will remain a secret.'[99]

'We also have the amendment that Sir Richard Acland has recommended to the House of Commons,' Eden added.

---

[95] Secretary of State of the United States.

[96] Churchill, vol. VI, p. 255.

[97] He was clearly referring to the murder of Colonel Psarros by ELAS under mysterious conditions that the KKE, the Greek Communist party, later recognised as a mistake.

[98] Churchill, vol. VI, p. 255.

[99] Throughout the incidents of December 1944 in Athens, the two newspapers closely followed the same line of not criticising the British nor emboldening ELAS.

'The president and at the same time the only member of the British Common Wealth Party. He's supported by Mr Nye Bevan and Mr Emmanuel Shinwell ... Leave it to me, Anthony. My government is a national coalition government. It will not topple, will not fall because of Greece, no matter how much longer the war lasts. I'll prepare my speech for Parliament. I'll ask for and will receive a vote of confidence.'

* * * * *

'My dear, I'd like to read to you some parts of the speech before giving it,' the Prime Minister said to his wife, Lady Clementine.

'You're my best adviser and you know why?' he asked, taking a sip of whisky.

'Of course, I know. Because I've lived with you for many decades, during the best and the worst of times. I am, perhaps, the only one who does not look upon you as the sacred monster of politics that everyone hates but that most politicians respect, while many others fear. And the great majority of British see you as the father of victory, their symbol, the one who promised them blood, toil, tears and sweat, war on the beaches, in the cities, in the fields, until the final victory. You kept your promise. Victory is now in sight.'[100]

'Is that how they see me? As a sacred monster?'

'Come on, Winnie, you know that. Don't pretend to be surprised. I'm listening.'

Lady Clementine made herself comfortable in an armchair and Churchill began to read.

---

[100] These words refer to Churchill's famous speech just before the fall of France, with the completion of the evacuation of Dunkirk on 4 June 1940.

'Her Majesty's government would of course be unworthy of your trust if it had used British forces to disarm the friends of democracy

'But a question arises, on which we can remain: Who are the friends of democracy and how is that word "democracy" to be interpreted? My idea of it is that the plain, humble, common man, just the ordinary man who keeps a wife and family, who goes off to fight for his country when it is in trouble, goes to the poll at the appropriate time, and puts his cross on the ballot paper showing the candidate he wishes to be elected to Parliament – that he is the foundation of democracy. And it is also essential to this foundation that this man or woman should do this without fear, and without any form of intimidation or victimization. He marks his ballot paper in strict secrecy, and then elected representatives meet and together decide what government, or even in times of stress, what form of government they wish to have in their country. If that is democracy, I salute it, I espouse it, I would work for it …

'I do not expect a party or a body to call themselves democrats because they are stretching further and further into the most extreme forms of revolution. I do not accept a party as necessarily representing democracy because it becomes more violent as it becomes less numerous …

'The last thing that represents democracy is mob law and the attempt to introduce a totalitarian regime and clamours to shoot everyone - there are lots of opportunities at the present time - who is politically inconvenient as part of a purge of those who are said to have - and very often have not - sought to collaborate with the Germans during the occupation. Do not let us rate democracy so low, do not let us rate democracy as if it were merely grabbing power and shooting those who do not agree with you. That is the antithesis of democracy; this is not what democracy is based on.

'Democracy, I say, is not based on violence or terrorism, but on reason, on fair play, on freedom, on respecting other people's rights as well as their ambitions. Democracy is no harlot to be picked up in the street by a man with a tommy gun. I trust the people, the mass of the people, in almost any country, but I like to make sure that it is the people and not a gang of bandits from the mountains or from the countryside who think that by violence they can overturn constituted authority, in some cases ancient Parliaments, Governments and States.'[101]

Churchill completed his speech and looked at Lady Clementine, waiting for her reaction.

'You have enlisted the English language again in order to convince. I think it will endure as a rhetorical monument to democracy. Perhaps together with Demosthenes[102] and Lincoln … I think you deserve the Nobel Prize for Literature,' she said, particularly moved.

* * * * *

After the delivery of his speech, the results of the vote were a triumph for Churchill: 30 were against but almost 300 MPs gave him a vote of confidence on 8 December. The next day, 9 December, he sent a telegram to Sir Reginald Leeper, the British ambassador in Athens saying, 'I do not yield to passing clamour

---

[101] Speech made by Churchill during a debate in the House of Commons on 8 December 1944 (see Churchill, vol. VI, p. 256)

[102] She was referring to Demosthenes' speech "On the Crown", which, together with Pericles' "Funeral Oration", is a masterpiece of ancient Greek rhetoric. The Gettysburg Address of Abraham Lincoln, inspired by Pericles, is the eulogy he delivered for the dead at the Battle of Gettysburg, July 1863, the turning point of the American Civil War. It defines democracy as "government of the people, by the people, for the people." Churchill received the Nobel Prize for Literature in 1953 for his mastery of historical and biographical description as well as for his brilliant oratory in defending exalted values.

and will always stand with those execute their instructions with courage and precision. In Athens, as everywhere else, our maxim is "no peace without victory."'[103]

Kaza, Attica, Greece, 4 January 1945

With gritted teeth, motionless, trying not to show his feelings, Aris Velouchiotis and his fighters met the ELAS units that were retreating from Athens.

What he saw did not resemble an army.

It was the remnants of an army, the debris. He saw men and women fighters dragging their feet in the mud, as if it were an effort for them to lift their boots, many of which were full of holes and lacked soles. Heads lowered, empty, fixed stares. Eyes deep in their sockets, black circles from lack of sleep and fatigue. Some looked at him, seeing but not seeing him, as if he were invisible, and continued on their way. But even worse were those who saw him and recognised him. He read something like complaint in their eyes, like a smarting blow, which someone put into words by crying out:

'Where were you? Why did you abandon us?'

Aris didn't know how to answer.

How was it that, while they were fighting in Athens, he was fighting Zervas and EDES in Epirus with three battalions?[104]

---

[103] Churchill, vol. VI, p. 258.

[104] Napoleon Zervas was a Greek general and resistance leader during World War II. He organized and led the National Republican Greek League (EDES), the second most significant (after EAM) resistance organization that fought against the German occupation of Greece. This is another major unanswered question regarding the December 1944 clashes in Athens between the communists and the Greek government together with British forces. Why didn't the leaders of EAM-ELAS, Siantos and Partsalidis, use

'They slaughtered us,' another fighter, Captain Tramoundanas, added. 'The damned British! Tanks, armoured vehicles, machine guns, aircraft, while we only had light guns, a few mortars and very few cannons … how can you fight like that?'

He watched as the fighters retreated, hungry, exhausted, some having thrown away their guns, others supporting wounded comrades. Heavily injured people with bloody bandages were carried on stretchers, others groaned whenever they tripped on the uneven ground that was full of potholes.

A light rain was falling, which slowly turned into sleet. Although the fighters were freezing from the cold, their souls and spirits were even more frozen …

They resembled a procession of caterpillars, one attached to the other, that stretched for many kilometres.

They left behind the debris of their defeat: abandoned guns thrown on the road because no one had the courage nor the strength to carry them, empty boxes and others that were full of ammunition, empty tins (whatever had been left over), torn clothing, boots with holes, dead mules and donkeys. Some animals that were still alive carried supplies but the fighters no longer had the strength nor the patience to lead them. Boxes with used medicines, empty phials, syringes, bloodied gauzes were strewn on the ground. Those among the heavily wounded were fortunate if they could lessen their pain with an injection of morphine.

Men and women. The dead, who they had neither the time nor the energy to bury. The heavily wounded, who had been left at villagers' house because there were not enough stretchers to carry them or else had been left by the wayside with the hope that the British would find them and take care of them.

---

their best captain in the battle and instead of sending three battalions to a secondary battle? Obviously, if they had prevailed in Athens, the defeat of EDES would have been unavoidable.

And those without injuries, exhausted, who could make no further effort, who had lost their moral strength, their spirit, their morale.

These people had simply abandoned the struggle. They fell on the side of the road or found refuge in abandoned houses or villagers' homes, asking for some food, a roof over their heads and a corner to sleep in, a sleep that was almost like death. And those who waited for the British so that they could surrender. At least the British would give them some food.

Aris felt an icy hold tightening in his gut. How had this catastrophe occurred? Who was to blame?

Without being aware of it, he murmured, 'Stalin betrayed us, Stalin betrayed us!'[105]

---

[105] This marked the estrangement of Aris Velouchiotis and his denouncement by the Greek Communist Party, which led to his death in 1946. Regarding the retreat of ELAS, see M. Haralambidis, pp. 261-271. ELAS suffered 222 dead, 55 wounded and 416 people were made prisoners (p.264). The descriptions of the events of the Dekemvriana can be found in Churchill, vol. VI, pp. 251 ff.

BIBLIOGRAPHY

In Greek

- Ahtzidis

- Haralambidis, Menelaos, "Dekemvriana", Alexandria Publications, 2014.

- Kyriazis, Nikos "Stalin and the assassination of a Greek ambassador", *Istoria*, April 2018.

- Kyriazis, Nikos, "Stalin and the assassination of an ambassador in the Soviet Union in 1938", *To Vima*, 24 September 2017, pp. 16-17.

- Mastakouris, Th., "Dogs in War", '*Istoria*', May 2014, pp. 100-108.

- Weinberg, Gerhard, *Visions of Victory*, (in Greek translation), Enalios, Athens 2008.

Other languages

- Carell, Paul, *Barbarossa,* Verlag Ullstein, 1963.

- Churchill, Winston, *The Second World War: Closing of the Ring,* vol. V, Houghton Mifflin Company, Boston, 1953.

- Churchill, Winston, *The Second World War: Triumph and Tragedy,* vol. VI, Cassell & Co. Ltd, London, 1948.

- Eisenhower, Dwight D., *Crusade in Europe*, Doubleday, 1948.

- Green, William,

- Kirchubel, Robert, "Operation Barbarossa 1941 Army Group South". Osprey Campaign 129, 2003.

- Mustafayev, Rahman, *Azerbaijan Between the Great Powers 1918-1920*, Enalios, 2016.

- Musial, 2010

- Perratt, Bryan, "The Panzerkampfwagen III" Osprey Vanguard 16, 1980.

- Resis, Albert (1978), "The Churchill-Stalin Secret Percentages Agreement, Agreement on the Balkans, Moscow, October 1944", *American Historical Review*, 1978, 83: 368-387.

- Taylor, Philip, "Azerbaijan", Heydar Aliyef Foundation, 2004.

- Weal, John, "Bf 109 Aces of the Russian Front" Osprey Aircraft of the Aces 37, 2001.

- Zaloga, Steven, "Bagration 1944" Osprey Campaign 42, 1996.

- Zaloga, Steven, "T-34176 medium tank" Osprey New Vanguard 16, 1994.

www.ingramcontent.com/pod-product-compliance
Lightning Source LLC
Chambersburg PA
CBHW030136010826
48973CB00002B/584